Run For Your Life

He turned on his torch again, and the beam fell on the stair. It made a bright ring in a dim, dusky circle. The edge of the circle touched something which had not been there before. The stair had been empty. It wasn't empty now. He swung the bright ring sideways and saw it dazzle on a girl's white face—just a ghost of a face, which seemed to float on the darkness, eyes wide in a stare of terror, mouth open as if to scream.

But she didn't scream. She came running. There wasn't any sound at all. Her face slipped out of the circle of light, and she came running like the wind. She really did run like the wind, because he lost sight of her and could hear nothing, and then she had him by the arm, and she said, "Run!"...

James stood his ground and said, "Why?" And then, before there was time for anything else, someone fired at them.

Also by Patricia Wentworth

THE CASE IS CLOSED
THE CLOCK STRIKES TWELVE
THE FINGERPRINT
GREY MASK
LONESOME ROAD
PILGRIM'S REST
THE WATERSPLASH
WICKED UNCLE
DEAD OR ALIVE
NOTHING VENTURE
BEGGAR'S CHOICE
OUTRAGEOUS FORTUNE
MR. ZERO
THE LISTENING EYE

Published by
WARNER BOOKS

PATRICIA WENTWORTH

RUN!

WARNER BOOKS

A Warner Communications Company

I

THE FOG WAS GETTING WORSE EVERY MOMENT. THERE was not much daylight left, and in another half hour darkness would be there to give the fog a solid backing. James Elliot drove forward through it, keeping the Rolls at a cautious ten miles an hour. His face was as expressionless as the indeterminate grey eyes set about with very thick fair lashes. Very thick fair hair stood up in a thatch all over his head. It was too thick to curl, too thick to lie down, too thick for any sort of control. He kept it short, and brushed it more as a rite than because brushing produced any effect upon it. His large square hands held the wheel.

Anyone looking at him might have supposed his mind to be a complete blank, yet this was very far from being the case. To start with, he was feeling both pleased and elated, since he had almost certainly sold the Rolls to Colonel Pomeroy. That would give him a leg-up with the firm, and it would also annoy Jackson, whose idea of selling a car was to talk the customer's head off. Jackson thought no one could sell cars but himself. All right, Jackson would see. All that gas might go down with women, but when it came to a man who knew something about cars, well, it put him off. Talking wasn't James's line, but he had sold the Rolls, and he felt elated and pleased.

He also felt rather anxious. He didn't want to bring the car in with a dented wing or a scratch on her paint.

Extraordinarily easy to get dented and scratched in a fog like this. James's face showed neither elation nor anxiety. It was just a face.

Driving became steadily more difficult. If it had been like this when he came through Warnley, he would have stopped there and not risked the car, but at Warnley there had been no more than a light general haze. There was nothing for it but to go on. Staling should be within a mile or two if he hadn't got off the road. A gloomy conviction that he was no longer on the Staling road had, however, begun to gain ground. He had come that way before, and there should have been a steepish hill and a hump-backed bridge. You can miss a lot of things in a fog, but you are bound to know when you are on a hill, and you can't miss that kind of bridge.

It became borne in upon James that he had missed it, and that meant he was on some other road. He stopped the car, got out, and prospected. . . . He was certainly on the wrong road. He couldn't see a yard, but this was an enclosed place, overhung with trees by the feel of it. Moisture dripped from them. He had the sense of being shut in. There was a smell of wet woods. But the road from Warnley to Staling ran over a bare open heath. . . .

He tried to think where he had got wrong, but could make no hand of it. It might have been anywhere after he had run into the fog. He remembered a place where four roads met. He had glanced at the signpost on his way down, but having seen the name he was looking for, he hadn't bothered about the others. And there had been other cross roads. He couldn't remember. He was, in fact, lost.

He got into the car again and went on driving at ten miles an hour, because any road is bound to arrive somewhere if you follow it far enough. There was hardly any daylight now. The feeling of being hemmed in by trees grew stronger. The off wing touched something. James braked and got out again, to find his feet on grass and the wing pressed against some smooth-barked tree. He had run right off the road on to a grass verge. This was his first thought. Then he wasn't so sure. The off wheels were on grass all right, but it didn't feel like the rough grass of the roadside. It was too smooth, too even under foot for that. He stooped and felt it with his hand.

Tame grass, mown grass, rolled grass, with a neat clipped edge—that's what he'd run on to. And the road under his feet now wasn't a road at all. It was somebody's gravelled drive.

He backed the car gently and stopped to consider the position. A gravelled drive meant a house, and a house meant people. If he went up to the house, he could at least find out where he was, and how far from the nearest garage. He wasn't going to run the Rolls a yard farther than he could help. She was off the drive on the grass and as safe as she would be anywhere else for the moment. He took an electric torch and set out in what he supposed to be the direction of the house.

The torch wasn't any good. The beam struck the fog and dazzled back at him. He switched it off, and felt with his foot for the edge of the drive at every step—a very tedious business.

He hadn't gone a dozen yards before he had completely lost his sense of direction. Any fog is baffling, but this was the worst he had ever encountered. It produced the feeling, which comes with you from a bad dream, of being in some unknown dimension without the sight or sense which it demands. It occurred to James that he might not be able to find his way back to the car.

He put that away. The immediate need was to find the house. He meant to find it. He went on feeling with his foot and hoping that the drive wasn't going to be one of the mile-long kind. He might, of course, have been driving up it for some time. He couldn't remember taking anything like a turn, but a lot of these drives emerge upon a bend, so that what had probably happened was that the road had turned and he hadn't. He had driven straight on through somebody's gates, and it was a bit of luck that they hadn't been shut.

The edge along which he was feeling with his foot stopped suddenly and was no more to be found. He was still on gravel, and guessed that he had come out upon a sweep before the house. There was a more open feeling, and no more drip from the trees. If the house was near, it was showing no light. It would be a big house. There ought to be some light showing. The fog was like a blanket, but you would expect some faint seeping through of light. There wasn't any.

He walked with his hands stretched out before him and every sense straining—eyes for anything to break the dark, ears to catch the faintest sound. Some people have another sense. It tells them, without sight or touch, when they are approaching an obstacle. They will stop short for a wall, a tree, or a bank with as much certainty as if they could see it. James possessed this sense. He became suddenly aware that the house was on his left. He could see nothing, but he could feel it there, very large and not very far away.

He turned and went towards this invisible house, walking more quickly than he had done yet. The space in front of him was a large one. He seemed to have been crossing it for a long time, when he stubbed his toe against a step. But time is one of the things which behave oddly in a fog. He had no certainty as to how far he had come, but was gratefully sure that he had arrived.

The step was the bottom one of six. He guessed at a portico overhead. Arrived at the top, he put on his torch and looked for the bell. At such close quarters the beam came into action again. It showed glimpses of stone, glimpses of a close-growing creeper, all sodden and sunken in the fog. It was like looking at drowned things under water. The bell hung to his right, a stirrup handle on a long iron rod. He put his hand to it and pulled, and immediately became aware that the thing was broken. It swung loose as he pulled, while from overhead came a rattle of wire.

He went down the steps again, and very nearly fell over a bicycle which was leaning against them. He had gone up on the left and missed it, but crossing to find the bell, he had come down on the opposite side. The balustrade which guarded the steps ended in a stone pillar. The bicycle had been propped against it. It now lay sprawling on the gravel. James, picking it up, discovered it to be a woman's bicycle. He leaned it against the pillar again and went back up the steps. If this woman had got into the house, he supposed he could get in too. There would be a knocker.

There was a knocker, a plain solid ring. The light of the torch showed it weather-stained and dark. Whoever kept this house had very little pride in it. A dirty doorstep and uncleaned brass are an advertisement of neglect. James gave the house a bad mark. He didn't like brass very much, but if you had it, it ought to be shiny. In the moment that it took him to think about this he became aware of something odd about the angle of the knocker. It didn't look at him straight, it slanted at him. He ran the beam of his torch across to the left-hand jamb and found out why. The door stood a black hand's-breath open.

James looked at it. It seemed odd. Of course if the bicycle woman had just gone in and banged the door behind her, it might have started open again. Their last house but three had had a door like that, and his father blew up every time it did it because the dogs got out. Or was it the last house but four? He wasn't sure. They had been moving ever since he could remember, because life in the army is like that. You came home from Egypt and settled into a house at Aldershot, and then you got orders to go to China, and presently you came back to Aldershot again by way of India. But it wouldn't be the same house.

He went on looking at the door. It might be that, or it mightn't. There wasn't any light in the hall. James loathed people who kept their halls dark. It was one of his Aunt Lucy's pet economies, and he loathed his Aunt Lucy, at whose house he had spent some of his dreariest holidays.

He considered the lightless condition of the hall with Scottish deliberation. It was all very well for a thrifty spinster aunt to switch off the lights of an Ealing villa, but a house as big as this ought to have a light in the hall. Would have a light in the hall. Unless something was wrong.

James shifted the beam of his torch again and found the knocker. He put up his hand to it, but instead of knocking he pushed the door a little wider and took a step forward. The air of the house came out to meet him, mingling with the fog. James snuffed at it rather like a dog. Then he pushed the door with the flat of his hand and stepped in over the threshold. There was a sense of space, a sense of cold, a most clammy, damp, uninhabited smell.

James sent the ray of his torch into the space and found it very large and dusty, with a stair going up at the far end. He was in some kind of lobby, but the inner door stood open to the hall and he could see through it to where the beam shifted and slid from floor to panelling, from panelling to the grey stone of a huge, empty fireplace. He came through the inner door and stopped. The travelling beam just grazed the back of a gaunt archaic chair. The place was not unfurnished. It was certainly very bare. His feet were on stone. The stair gloomed in the darkness.

He switched off the torch and waited to see if there was any glow of light from the upper floor. Everything immediately disappeared in a complete black-out. The place might not be there at all for all he could see of it. He thought it was very odd. He thought it was none of his business, and that he had better be getting back to the car. On the other hand, the bicycle obviously belonged to someone, and that someone had probably left the door open. He, James, had set out to discover where he was, and he had a constitutional objection to giving up half way. He thought it might be a good plan to go back to the front door and do something rousing with the knocker.

He turned on his torch again, and the beam fell on the stair. It made a bright ring in a dim, dusky circle. The edge of the circle touched something which had not been there before. The stair had been empty. It wasn't empty now. He swung the bright ring sideways, and saw it dazzle on a girl's white face—just a ghost of a face which seemed to float on the darkness, eyes wide in a stare of terror, mouth open as if to scream.

But she didn't scream. She came running. There wasn't any sound at all. Her face slipped out of the circle of light, and she came running like the wind. She really did run like the wind, because he lost sight of her and could hear nothing, and then she had him by the arm, and she said "Run!" in a breath which came warm against his cheek.

II

JAMES STOOD HIS GROUND AND SAID "WHY?" HE SAID IT IN his normal voice. The torch made a spot of light on the floor at his feet. It was a very dusty floor. And then, before there was time for anything else, someone fired at them.

It was completely incredible, but it was true. The stair ran up to a gallery, and someone had taken a pot shot at them from this gallery. It wasn't such a bad shot either, for James felt the wind of the bullet as it went past, and heard the plop with which it buried itself in the panelling.

The girl dragged at his arm. He thought more favourably of her original suggestion. There seemed to be no point about being shot down by a homicidal maniac. They ran down the steps and into the fog, and a second shot followed them. James barked a shin on the bicycle. It clattered down upon stone, and above the noise of its fall he could hear the sound of running steps behind them. The girl pushed him hard to the left. The hand on his arm pinched fiercely. The voice that had said "Run!" said, "Idiot! This way—quick!" all on one soundless breath.

And then they were running again, flagstones under their feet, and the fog in eyes, and nose, and throat. He guessed that they were on a paved terrace which ran the length of the house. He couldn't see a yard. A yard? He couldn't see an inch. But the girl seemed to know where she was going. She turned left-handed again. Then she stopped running and went slow, and once they stood listening, and heard what might have been a step on the gravel a long way off. She pulled him on. He made as little noise with his feet as he could, but she made none that he could hear. She might have been bare-foot, or she might not have been touching the ground at all.

She stopped and felt in the dark with her free hand. She said "Steps" in his ear, and they went down six of them and through a gateway into another paved place. James knew that it was a gateway because he scraped his shoulder against the left-hand pillar. He stopped there, and said,

"What's all this about? I want to get back to my car."

She leaned so close to answer him that her lips just touched his ear, a little fugitive touch that was instantly withdrawn. Her fingers nipped his arm—small fingers, extraordinarily hard and strong. The pinch hurt sharply. She said in a mere thread of a savage whisper,

"You can't! Do you want to be shot? I don't."

James said, "Nor do I." He whispered too, but even in a whisper he managed to make it quite plain that he didn't like being pinched. He considered it a liberty.

The nip was repeated, harder.

"You will be—we both shall! I suppose you can climb a ladder? There ought to be one just about here. No—about ten steps on and a yard or two to the left. Feel about for it."

It was a little farther than she had said, but they found it. There was no more sound behind them. She let go of his arm and went away up into the dark. A faint rustling came to him from above. He climbed towards it and stepped off the ladder into a foot or so of hay. His arm was caught again. He was first pulled forward and then released. A shutter closed behind him. He heard a long breath taken, and a whispering laugh.

He said again, "What's all this?" And then, "What's this place?"

"Stable loft." Her voice sounded a little farther off. "They won't find us here. Brr! Nice to be out of the fog! I do *hope* they won't pinch my bicycle."

"Why should they?"

"They might."

Well, they couldn't pinch the Rolls, because he had locked the doors and the switch key was in his pocket. All the same—

"You haven't told me what it's all about. And I'm not

staying here—I'm going back to my car. And what we both ought to do is to find the nearest police-station and put them on to the lunatic who was shooting at us. Unless—" A sudden thought struck him. "I suppose he might have thought we were burglars, but it was a bit drastic shooting like that. He might have hit one of us quite easily."

There was a faint laugh.

"He meant to. And you can't be a burglar in the afternoon. It has to be half-past eight or something like that. And anyhow it isn't their house."

"Whose house?"

"Theirs."

"Whose house is it?"

"How should I know?" enquired a very small, innocent voice.

James felt properly angry.

"What's the good of trying to put that sort of stuff across when you've just been leading me round blind? You've got to know a place like the back of your hand before you can do that!"

She laughed again, a little nearer.

"Perhaps it's the cradle of my infancy."

"I'm going back to my car," said James.

His wrist was caught.

"I should hate you to. If you got shot, they might think I'd done it. Let's stay here and tell each other the stories of our lives. I'll begin. I'm sure you'd love to hear the story of my life."

"Not particularly. I want to make sure my car's all right."

"Are you going to leave me here?" He wasn't sure if the voice was quite steady. There was very little of it. He said,

"I could drop you if you'll tell me where you want to go."

She seemed to consider this.

"I shouldn't think we'd get farther than the nearest ditch—not in a fog like this. The lanes round here are exactly like corkscrews. And then there's my bicycle, and my shoes."

"Your *what*?" said James in an exasperated voice.

"Shoes. Things you wear on your feet, you know. Rather a nice pair—crocodiles—quite new. I don't think I ought to abandon them."

James became a good deal more exasperated. It wasn't the slightest use her doing that sort of mournful tone at him. If it had been light, she would probably have been flickering her eyelashes. He hadn't got a sister, but he had fourteen girl cousins, and he flattered himself he knew all their ways of trying it on. He couldn't imagine what sort of game this was, and that naturally put his back up, but he did know when a girl was trying it on. He said,

"What have you got on now?"

There was a little sigh in the darkness.

"A felt hat, a jumper suit, a tweed coat. They're all brown, if you want the colours."

"I don't. I want to know what you've got on your feet."

"Stockings," said the voice very mournfully in the dark.

So that was why she had made no sound as she ran. If she thought he was going to say "Your feet must be soaked," she was going to be disappointed.

He said, "Why?"

"Well, you see, those stairs make such a noise. There isn't any stair carpet, and the fourth one from the bottom creaks, so I took them off—the shoes, you know, my beautiful new crocodiles—and left them in the hall just round the corner from the bottom step, because I thought if I carried them I'd be almost sure to drop them at some frightfully critical moment."

James frowned. Of all the silly idiotic things to do—

"You mean they're still in the hall?"

"Yes, kind Preserver."

James considered the shoe question. If she had walked to the hayloft, she could walk to the car. He said so in a firm, dogmatic voice.

There was another of those mournful sighs.

"And leave my crocodiles—and my bicycle? I've got a much better plan than that."

"Well?" He wasn't going to commit himself, but you don't commit yourself very far by saying "Well?"

She echoed the word brightly. Girls always thought themselves whales at making plans.

"Well, suppose you were in a house doing something that you oughtn't to be doing, and someone came along and found you doing it, and you shot at them, and they got away—how long do you think you would stay in the house?''

''I wouldn't,'' said James.

''Nor should I. *Nor would they.* They'll hunt round for us, and then they'll go away. And then we'll rescue the crocodiles and my bicycle. And then *we'll* go away. It's a much better plan.''

It was. But that wasn't to say that it offered no grounds for criticism. James proceeded to criticize.

''Suppose they don't go away.''

''They will.''

''If the fellow who did the shooting is a lunatic—''

''He isn't.''

''Who is he?'' said James in a rage.

He heard her sigh again.

''I don't know.''

He thought she did. He very nearly said so. He went on criticizing instead.

''If they've gone, they'll have shut the door. You don't imagine they'll leave it open, do you? And then how do we get in?''

''Kind sir, I've got a key.

James had a sense of being played with and laughed at. There is nothing more calculated to set a match to the temper, and his was alight already. Yet, strangely and unaccountably, instead of flaring now it sobered down. He said seriously and without heat,

''So you've got a key. Very well, we'll wait. I suppose you know what it's all about. I don't, and I don't want to. We'll give them half an hour.''

He shot his wrist-watch out of his cuff and took a look at the luminous dial. The hands stood at six o'clock. There was just a chance that the fog might clear as the temperature fell. These afternoon fogs did clear off sometimes after sunset. They either did that or they got worse. If it was going to get any worse, he was stuck anyhow.

The girl leaned over to see the time. He felt her quite near for a moment. Then the hay rustled as she settled herself again.

''Half an hour—that's a long time in the dark. Shall we say the multiplication table, or the Kings of England? You wouldn't have the story of my life. I did offer it to you. What about yours? Are you just 'Hi, you there!' or have you got a name?''

"My name's Elliot—James Elliot.''

"How nice and ordinary. Mine is Aspidistra Aspinall.''

If she had been one of his cousins, James would have said "Liar!" He very nearly said it anyhow. She needn't suppose he had the slightest desire to know her name. He said nothing.

The hay rustled.

"It's not my fault, it's my misfortune.'' The voice wobbled for a moment, and then went on in a bright, sweet monotone. "I was born an orphan, and my ruthless relations—''

"You can't be born an orphan!'' said James.

"Oh, but I *was*. Truly. Absolutely. Because my father was killed in the war and my mother died when I was born. If that isn't being born an orphan, I don't know what is.'' This with some earnestness. Then, resuming the monotone, "Ruthless relations brought me up. The Society for the Prevention of Cruelty to Children prosecuted the god-mother who had had me christened Aspidistra. But what was the good of sending her to penal servitude for seven years—I'd got the name for life. It isn't even as if you could shorten it. Assy! Dissy! I'd rather be a whole Aspidistra any day!''

James supposed it amused her to talk nonsense. It didn't amuse him. He listened because he thought she was talking nonsense to cover things up—things which might make sense if he were to get a chance of putting them together. He thought she didn't want to give him that chance, but he thought the more she talked the better, because it is very difficult to talk a lot without giving something away. If the person who had shot at them was neither an enraged householder nor a lunatic, he was a dangerous criminal and a matter of concern for the police. He added his annoyance at being shot at to his annoyance at having run away, and he set them both down to the account of this person or persons unknown. He said,

"How do you come to have a key of this house?''

There was a faint, light laugh.

"Oh, sir—this is so sudden! I haven't got nearly as far as

that. Birth and Christening, that's where we were—Ruthless Relations and Unchristian Names. Upbringing comes next." She seemed to hesitate, and then said quickly, "It's your turn really. I suppose there are about a million James Elliots—the Scotch are so economical about names. But were you at Wellington?"

"I was. Why?"

"Oh, because—" said Aspidistra Aspinall. "I just wondered. Quite a lot of people do go to school there. I didn't of course. I think Co-education might be rather fun—don't you? I had governesses, and after they buried the third they sent me to a fierce games-playing school where they broke my spirit with lacrosse and net-ball."

"I want to know why you've got a key to this house," said James.

She said, "Oh, Mr Elliot!" in a shocked voice. And then, "All my relations would think it most improper for me to tell a total stranger a thing like that—in the pitch dark too!"

"I think I'll be getting back to my car," said James.

"You can't. You agreed to give it half an hour—you know you did. Scotchmen always keep their words—at least high-minded Scotchmen. Your voice sounds devastatingly high-minded."

"I do wish you wouldn't talk such frightful nonsense!" said James, but he stayed where he was.

He heard a funny little sigh with a catch in it.

"Would you rather I burst into tears? On your shoulder? I can quite easily—if you want me to. If I stop talking nonsense for more than half a second, I probably shall whether you want me to or not."

"I certainly don't want you to."

"Well, there you are. *You have been warned.* I'd better go on. Before my Aunt Clementa died she said I was to have her diamond necklace. She kept on saying so, and every time the nurse went out of the room she clutched my wrist and said—"

"Who clutched your wrist?"

"You're not listening. My Aunt Clementa did."

"It might have been the nurse."

"Well, it wasn't—it was my Aunt Clementa."

"Why?"

"There isn't any why about it. She just clutched me, and she said, 'It's worth a lot of money. You'll find it when I'm gone. It's somewhere in this room. Don't let them get their hands on it.'"

"Who is *them*?"

The hay rustled vaguely.

"Oh, just Ruthless Relations—the assorted kind. So when I got the chance I thought I'd come along and do a little quiet treasure-hunting. There isn't an awful lot you can do in a fog like this, so I put on my crocodiles to give me courage, and I pinched somebody's torch and the housemaid's bicycle and happened along."

"Yes?" said James in a nasty unbelieving tone of voice.

"Well, it didn't come off. Things don't. You plan them beautifully, and they walk out on you in the middle of the plan. There was someone else with a torch there first, all very hush-hush, so I ran away, and then the shooting began. And I've simply got to go back, because the person the torch belongs to will have my blood if I've lost it, and it may be anywhere by now, but I dropped it about a yard from the door of Aunt Clementa's room, and I'm simply bound to collect it if it's still there. And I cannot desert my crocodiles."

III

THEY WAITED THE FULL HALF HOUR BY JAMES'S WATCH. It seemed longer. At least it seemed longer to him. He had no means of knowing what the girl felt about it. After letting off what he firmly believed to be the cock-and-bull story about her Aunt Clementa's diamond necklace, she had bombarded him with questions until it was less trouble to answer them than to sit there in the hay and say nothing—"How old are you?" "Have you got any people?" "Is your father alive?" "What does he do?" "What do you do?"

To this questionnaire James replied in due order, "Twenty-five." "Yes." "Very much so." "Commands a regiment, and his family." "I demonstrate cars. I hope I've just sold one."

He heard her laugh. He thought she tried not to, but it got away.

"Why didn't you go into the Army? If your father's that sort, he wanted you to, didn't he?"

James remembered the Great War, not the paltry European *fracas* of 1914–18, but the long, stubbornly contested struggle over the question of whether he went to Sandhurst or not. If Colonel Elliot had put his foot down a little less firmly, or had occasionally stopped bellowing when the subject came up, James might conceivably have wanted to go into the Army, but every time his father roared at him he reacted vigorously in the direction of civil life. James made much less noise, but he was more really obstinate, and in the end he got his way and a mechanical training which he hankered after. His mother, the sweetest of women, maintained a surprising calm. She had a talent for tête-a-têtes, and whether she was talking to an infuriated husband or to an exasperated son, her response hardly ever varied from a simple but effective "Oh, yes, darling—I do see what you mean."

James did not, naturally, explain all this to a total stranger in a hay loft. He said moderately, yes, his father had wanted him to go into the Army, and no, he, James, hadn't wanted to. He had had a small legacy from a great aunt, and had used it for a premium. It was very important to get into a good firm. He was with Atwells. They were very good people.

He looked at his watch and said abruptly,

"We'd better be getting along. Anyone who was going to clear off must have done it by now. If there is still anyone there, we shall probably get shot at again. A nice crew you keep in these parts, I must say! What we ought to do is to go straight to the police."

"You said that before. I'm not going to."

"That's because you know who the fellow is."

She must have got up, because he heard her stamp her

foot in the hay. He heard her stamp, and he heard her wince. Then he heard her catch her breath.

"I say, have you got a handkerchief?" she said.

"It's got petrol on it. What do you want it for?"

"My foot's cut. If I go dripping blood all over everything, it'll be a give-away."

"How did you cut it?"

"How on earth do I know? That blighted bicycle, I shouldn't wonder. You don't mind if I tear the rag, do you? Because I must hitch it on to my ankle somehow."

She hitched it, and they came down the ladder and back to the house. The bicycle lay sprawling where it had fallen. The door was shut and fastened. The fog brooded over all. Miss Aspidistra Aspinall produced a key, opened the front door, and was gone. It was exactly like a disappearing trick on the stage. One minute she was there with her shoulder practically touching his, making little clinking sounds with a key-ring, and keys, and the lock which one of the keys was supposed to fit, and the next there was neither sound nor feel of her.

He listened, and got nothing at all from the silence. He called to her under his breath, using a slightly conventionalized variant of the "Hi, you there!" type of address, and still he got nothing. He raked out his torch and switched it on. She said she had left her shoes just to one side of the stair foot. Well, she might have been telling the truth, or she mightn't, but it was a bed-rock cert that there were no shoes there now.

He slid the beam to and fro and looked most carefully. He found a little smudged space on the dusty floor behind the right-hand newel-post. The shoes might have stood there, but they certainly weren't standing there now.

He went to the top of the stair and flicked about with his torch. The main flight divided half way up, and led on either side to dark, empty-feeling corridors which ran away to the right and to the left.

James called into the empty-feeling space, "Are you there?" but nobody answered him. He began to experience symptoms of the parental temper. If this dashed girl thought he was going to search this dashed house for her, she could just start thinking again. It probably had twenty bedrooms, to say nothing of garrets, and cellars, and what house-agents call offices. He was prepared to let her collect her shoes and then give her a lift to wherever she might be staying, but he was hanged if he was going to play hide-and-seek with her in this mouldy house.

He scowled at the left-hand passage. And then, from the hall below, he heard a sound. He leaned over the gallery, and an uprush of cold air came to him. He had left the hall door shut, but it was certainly open now. The sound he had heard was the sound of shod feet treading lightly. Miss Aspidistra Aspinall was evidently no longer shoe-less. The crocodiles had been recovered. Her voice came up to him in a faint, floating "Coo-ee!" He stared down, and could see nothing. The smell of the fog came drifting up. The girl's voice came with it.

"Good-night, James Elliot."

IV

IT TOOK JAMES ONE SOLID HOUR TO FEEL AND GROPE HIS way as far as Staling. He got there in the end more by luck than good management, having first crawled down the drive into what proved to be a widish lane, and then continued along the lane at a snail's pace until it brought him out upon the road. The road ultimately brought him to Staling, and just as he came to the first house of the village, he ran out of the worst of the fog.

He knew where he was now, and the road was drivable. The local pub would certainly not have any accommodation for a Rolls. He decided to go on, and in half an hour was clear of the fog and making up for lost time on the long straight stretch over Wilder's Heath.

His mind was now free to consider the whole adventure. The Aspidistra girl was certainly a most unblushing liar. Only impudence of the first water would have produced a name like that. It was, of course, arguable that it could hardly have been intended to deceive, but this only added to his just annoyance, to be offered a completely unbelievable lie being a gross insult to one's intelligence.

He wondered a good deal about the shooting. There was something very odd about it. The shot might have been a random one intended to scare an intruder off the premises, but not meant to hit. This theory would have made everything much easier. James felt obliged to reject it. The shot had passed too close to him at a moment when his torch was affording a mark. It would have been perfectly easy for the person unknown to fire wide, and he hadn't fired wide, he had had a jolly good shot at either James or the girl. The torch had spilled a little pool of light between them. It must have been quite obvious that there were two people in the hall. James had an unpleasant conviction that the person unknown had aimed at one of them. He couldn't possibly have wanted to kill James, who was a total stranger. Then he must have been aiming at the girl.

One fact emerged quite plainly from the confusion, and that was that the girl could make a pretty good guess at who had fired the shot. She had rushed out with "He's not a homicidal maniac," and how could she possibly say that if she didn't know who he was? No, she knew—she knew jolly well.

But she wouldn't go to the police. Why wouldn't she?

Two reasons suggested themselves. She might be mixed up in whatever it was that he had butted into, in which case she wasn't in a position to denounce a fellow-criminal. Or—she might be afraid—

James thought about this.

He gave her marks for courage. Most girls would have screamed if they had been shot at in the dark, and most girls would have cried in the hayloft. Girls could be extraordinarily brave, but they nearly always cried afterwards. This girl hadn't—at least not as far as he knew. And she had cut her foot pretty badly too. He found himself admiring the presence of mind with which she had grabbed him and said "Run!"

He only just stopped himself on the edge of reflecting that she had a very pretty voice. On the other hand, she was the most infernal little liar. And that bunk about her Aunt Clementa and a diamond necklace—whoever heard of a name like Clementa? The girl just couldn't speak the truth. She couldn't even produce a reasonable, plausible lie. If the aunt had had any of the names which aunts do have, he might—no, not he, but some more gullible man might have believed her. James was not gullible. His fourteen cousins had taught him a lot about the general untruthfulness of girls. His cousin Daphne, with whom he had once been in love, had considerably undermined his faith in women by getting engaged to three separate men during three successive dances at her coming-out ball. James was one of the three, and though he now regarded Daphne as a Lucky Escape, the incident had added considerably to his native caution. His native caution told him not to believe a single word the girl had said. It added with no uncertain voice that he had better put the whole thing out of his mind and keep it out.

He had a good quick run back to town, with only one more belt of fog, and that not very thick. He bought a paper in the Fullham Road whilst he was held up in a traffic block. He thought the names of the Scottish Rugger team might be out. He hoped they were going to play Lind. Just as he was going to look and see, the block broke and a woman in a baby Austin behind him hooted in the most annoying manner. After that there wouldn't be any chance of opening the paper until he got back to his rooms. He put away the Rolls, and was glad to have a walk to stretch his legs.

He was, for the moment, occupying his cousin Gertrude Lushington's studio in Simpson's Mews, Gertrude being on a walking tour somewhere in Eastern Europe. She might turn up at any time, preferably in the middle of the night, or she might stay away for a year, strolling in in a casual manner just when the family had decided that she had definitely got herself murdered this time and they had better see about going into mourning. She refused to take any rent, but James determined to contest this point when she returned. Meanwhile he cooked his own breakfast and supper on her gas stove, and paid the rates when the demands came in. As Gertrude was considerably in arrears, he did not feel under too much of an obligation.

There were two rooms, and a place which had been a loose-box and now contained a gas stove, a sink, and a bath. The bath was served by a geyser. James turned it on, and went up a steep stair into the studio, where he switched on an overhead light and took a look at the football news. The names weren't out yet.

The geyser took twenty minutes to produce a decent bath. He stood there skimming through the paper. Mussolini had made a speech. Monsieur Laval had made a speech. Mr. Eden had made a speech. James thanked heaven that he did not have to make speeches. He supposed some people liked doing it. There was no accounting for tastes.

He turned to another column and cocked an eyebrow at a highly decorative picture of Ambrose Sylvester. The famous novelist's famous profile was displayed. James, who had stuck in the middle of *Links in the Chain*, wondered why some novelists were famous and some were not. Everyone raved about Ambrose Sylvester—that is to say, all the women did. Daphne, Kitty, Chloe, Linda, and Susan all declared that his profile was simply divine. He supposed they also read his books. He didn't seem to have written very much—three novels—nothing for the last five years or so. The legend under the photograph said, "When are we to have another link in the Chain?"

He left Ambrose Sylvester, and read without interest the odds that were being offered at Hollywood on a popular film-star's matrimonial chances. He was just going to turn over the page, when his eye was caught by a small paragraph tucked away in the right-hand corner. It was headed *Windfall for our Dumb Friends*. But that wasn't what had caught his eye, it was the name immediately below it—Lady Clementa Tolhache.

James stared at it as he might have stared at a fiery disc, or a blue dragon, or a luminous snake, or any other product of a disordered imagination. Not much more than an hour ago he had decided that there was no such name as Clementa. He did not find it at all easy to reverse this decision. He preferred to disbelieve the evidence of his senses. After all, if you see fiery spots floating in the air, you don't believe they are really there—not unless you are very far gone.

He looked away from the paragraph and gazed fixedly at one of Gertrude's pictures which hung on the farther wall. It depicted a greyish female with an enormous body and a very small head in the act of eating a bright green apple with red spots on it. There was a huge lobster in the foreground, and a thing like a bright blue tadpole in the right-hand top corner. This work was called Eve, and James thought it was the most frightful thing he had ever seen. The fact that he now remained looking at it for some moments showed how much he had been thrown off his balance. As a matter of fact, he was not seeing it at all, he was seeing that ridiculous name, and when after blinking rapidly several times he looked back at the paragraph he saw it still—Clementa—Lady Clementa Tolhache. There it was, in print. He read it three times, and then finished the paragraph: "Lady Clementa Tolhache has made a generous bequest to the Society for Prevention of Cruelty to Animals. There are a number of other legacies, but the bulk of her estate passes to her great-nephew Mr. John Jernyngham West, at present with his regiment in India."

James felt exasperated to the last degree. Without the slightest warning life had become completely mad. He had had an unbelievable adventure with an impossibly named girl who pitched him an incredible tale about her Aunt Clementa, and here was a paragraph featuring Aunt Clementa's will. And as if that wasn't enough, it also featured Jack West—old J.J. It couldn't be anyone else. There weren't two John Jernyngham Wests in the Army, he'd take his oath on that. No, it was J.J. who had fagged for him at Wellington, and he was Lady Clementa Tolhache's great-nephew and heir. The paragraph said so. He was surprised at its moderation in the matter of the diamond necklace. It might have insisted on his believing in that too.

He went down to his bath obstinately determined to go on regarding the necklace as a myth.

V

IT WAS NEXT DAY THAT HIS COUSIN DAPHNE RANG UP. HE heard the telephone as he put his key in the lock. It herded with the sink, and the gas-cooker, and the bath in a manner which everyone except Gertrude Lushington found extremely inconvenient. Gertrude herself merely observed vaguely that it was so nice not to have to get out of your bath when people rang you up.

James said, "Be quiet, you brute!" switched on the light, tripped over a hot-water can, and unhooked the receiver. The voice of his cousin Daphne came fluting sweetly to his ear. She had not married any of the three men to whom she had become engaged at her first ball, and was now the wife of Bonzo Strickland, the oil magnate.

"Darling, I've been trying to get you for hours. Where *have* you been?"

"Working," said James. "Some of us have to, you know."

Daphne managed to transmit a shudder.

"Too horrid! My poor angel!"

"Cut it out!" said James austerely. "What do you want, Daph?"

"Darling—how unkind! Couldn't I just want to hear your voice?"

"You could, I suppose, but you don't. What is it?"

"Darling, I really do think you've got the most foully suspicious mind."

"Oh, come off it!" said James. He spoke loudly and fiercely in the telephone. "What—do—you—want?"

"Well, Bonzo's gone to see his mother. He does, you

know—too filial. And I'm throwing a party here—just a few bright spirits. I thought we'd dance. You'll come, won't you?''

"I don't dance," said James.

"Darling—what a *lie*! Why, you proposed to me in the middle of a waltz.''

James grinned at his end of the telephone.

"That's why—too dangerous—I mightn't get off the next time.''

"Darling, you must come. I won't let anyone propose to you—I really won't. And I'm a man short. You wouldn't like to spoil my party—would you? And I've really got a secret, particular reason why I want you to come. I can't tell you about it, because I promised.''

"And you've never been known to break a promise—have you?'' said James in a nasty sarcastic voice.

"Darling, what a bad temper you're in. How's chauffing?''

"Not too bad. I sold a Rolls yesterday.''

"Well, I don't say for certain, but I think you might sell another, perhaps day after tomorrow. Bonzo hasn't exactly promised, but he always comes back very fond of me, so I should think there's quite a decent chance of our blowing in one day this week. *Now* will you come to my party?''

"That's bribery and corruption.''

Daphne cooed back at him.

"I know. Shocking, isn't it? You will come, won't you, darling?''

"I suppose so," said James.

The Stricklands had an immense house, in which their opposite tastes contended without mingling. The hall contained portraits of Bonzo's grandparents, marble busts of his father and mother, a tessellated floor, and the heads and horns which he had collected on his various shooting expeditions. James counted eight tigers mounted on red cloth, two rhinoceri, and a quantity of antlers and horns. The dining-room was also pure Bonzo. It had the bright red walls of the Victorian period. His mother had had a bright red wallpaper in her dining-room when he was a little boy, and at forty he was still unable to think of a dining-room except in terms of Pompeian red. Daphne knew when she was beaten, and having to give way, she did so with the greatest charm. Bonzo was permitted, even encouraged, to go the whole hog. There was a blue and crimson carpet, red velvet curtains, and a massive mahogany suite.

But the drawing-room was Daphne's, floor, walls, and lighting all modern, daring, and bright. The room was cleared now ready for dancing. A trio occupied an alcove, and a twostep was in progress. James stood at the doorway and waited for the music to stop. Daphne's idea of a few bright spirits amused him. The floor was packed. He caught a glimpse of her and lost it again. She was looking insufferably pretty. He did not see anyone else he knew, and he thought that he had been a fool to come. He had probably still got oil on his hands. You soaped them and you scrubbed them, and they looked all right, and then next time you looked at them the oil seemed to have worked out again. He didn't mind dances when he knew the people, but he wasn't going to know a solitary soul in this crowd.

The dance ended, and Daphne emerged. She slipped her arm through his, addressed him as "Angel," and began to edge him along to the end of the room.

"I've got a partner for you. You can thank me afterwards—I hope she will. You usen't to tread on people's toes, but that was when I was taking a lot of trouble over you. Hi, Rabbit, let us through! Just one more good shove, James. That's done it! I told her to stay just here, so if she's gone—"

They came into a sort of backwater beside the fireplace. There was actually a bare square yard of space. A sheet of glass ran from ceiling to floor, moulded curiously into fantastic pillars on either side and arched above a flickering electric fire. The pillars followed and distorted the human form, but the distortion had a rhythm of its own. Against the nearer pillar a girl stood waiting for them, and the first thing that James noticed about her was that she had green eyes. And that was nonsense, because people didn't have green eyes.

"Here he is, Sally," said Daphne in her high sweet voice—"James Elliot. He sells cars. I can't swear he won't step on your feet." And with that she was gone.

James had another look at the eyes. Of course they weren't really green. They just looked green because she had on a green dress. They had very soft black lashes, as black as soot. But her hair wasn't quite black, though it was very dark. It was done up in rows of little curls across the back of her head. Frightful waste of time doing up those curls every day—he supposed they had to be done every day. He remembered his cousin Kitty having her hair brushed round and round her nurse's finger to make it curl.

The green eyes were lifted to his, and a very soft voice said,

"Have I got a smut on my nose?"

James blushed a little. It didn't really show, but he could feel himself doing it.

"I'm afraid I was staring."

She nodded.

"You're quite sure I haven't got a smut?"

"Oh, yes, quite."

She looked modestly down. Her lashes were really very black indeed. James wondered whether the colour was natural, or whether she put stuff on them. They looked natural, but then so did Kitty's, and Kitty's eyelashes had been as near as a toucher white till she came out, so you could never be sure.

He said rather suddenly, "They're just going to start again. Would you like to dance?" And she said, "No, I don't think so."

"I don't really step on people's feet."

She said without looking up,

"I love dancing, but I've hurt my foot. Do you think we could find somewhere to sit?"

This appeared to be a rhetorical question, because she was able immediately to lead the way to two very comfortable chairs on a half-way landing. She sat down, heaved a sigh of relief, and enquired,

"Why did you stare at me like that? Did you think you'd seen me before?"

James shook his head.

"I'm quite sure I haven't." And then in the most disturbing way his certainty wavered. "At least—"

"There—you're not sure!"

"Yes, I am—I'm positive."

"Why?"

"I should remember your eyes."

"Oh, my eyes?"

"I didn't think anyone had green eyes really."

She shook her head.

"Mine aren't—not really—only when I wear green. Really green-eyed people are supposed to have red hair, but I once saw a child who had pale gold hair and eyes the exact colour of jade. It wasn't pretty, you know. It gave you a sort of squirl."

James didn't want to talk about children with jade eyes. Something was bobbing up and down in his mind, and he wanted to catch hold of it. He said,

"How did you hurt your foot?"

And she said,

"That blighted bicycle, I shouldn't wonder."

VI

THERE WAS A SILENCE. JAMES GRABBED AT THE THING that had been bobbing up and down in his mind and caught it. This girl was the girl who had clutched him in the dark and said "Run!" And someone had started taking pot-shots at them, and they had run like the dickens. And she had borrowed his handkerchief to tie up a cut on her foot, and when he asked her how she had hurt it, she had said, "That blighted bicycle, I shouldn't wonder." She was that girl.

Nonsense! She couldn't be.

What do you mean by she couldn't be? How couldn't she be?

It's a coincidence.

James ran a hand violently through his hair, a thing

Daphne had always been very strict with him about—she said it made him look exactly like Strewelpeter—but in moments of emotion he still did it. He didn't know that he had done it now. He stared at the girl with the green eyes and said in an explosive voice,

"What bicycle?"

The girl looked down at her toes, which were encased in pale green slippers of the rather sketchy sort which consist chiefly of a heel, and a strap, and a diamond buckle. "Encased" is perhaps the wrong word, because a good deal of the toes showed through. They were pleasantly shaped and extremely flexible. She appeared to be twiddling them. James tried to imagine them tied up in his large and very oily handkerchief. He failed. He repeated his question rather more moderately, because if this wasn't the girl, she was probably beginning to think that he was a dangerous lunatic.

"What bicycle?"

She said without looking up,

"It was the housemaid's really, but I borrowed it. She'd have been frightfully sick if I hadn't brought it back, because she saved up for it for two whole years. She put all her tips in a savings-box. Her name is Gladys White, and she's got a young man in the motor trade. He's a mechanic—horribly oily except on Sundays, but most attached and steady. Gladys says they're all very steady in the motor trade. She ought to know. She says she tried six other trades before she settled down with Albert Wilson for her regular boy. They're thinking of getting engaged in the spring."

This was all with a gentle deliberation, a bit at a time, with some toe-twiddling in between.

James felt a just anger. If she thought she was going to put him off in that way—He gave an unwilling glance at his hands. Had she meant anything by that "horribly oily," or hadn't she? The hands were all right. He hoped she hadn't seen him look at them. He said firmly and plainly,

"That's not answering."

"You did ask me what bicycle, you know, but perhaps you've forgotten. You forget rather easily, don't you?" The words were impudent, but the tone was the merest murmur, and she never looked up.

James had never felt angrier with anyone in his life, but at the back of the anger there was the horrid niggling fear that she really might be Sally Something and a total stranger, and not yesterday's *soi-disant* Aspidistra Aspinall, in which case he was making a fool of himself, and she *was* probably thinking he was a lunatic. He hesitated on the brink of a direct question, steadied himself there, and plunged.

"Do you mind telling me your name?"

He saw the green eyes for a bright moment. The brightness might have been laughter, or devilry. There was only a flash of it and the sooty lashes were down again.

"Didn't you hear Daphne call me Sally?"

"Sally what?"

She gave a very faint laugh. He could swear that he had heard it before—in a hayloft.

"How fast you go! I've known people for months without bothering about their surnames."

"Is yours Aspinall?"

She looked up at him as innocent as a kitten.

"Oh, no."

"What is it?"

He wasn't sure that she hesitated. He thought so.

She said, "West—Sarah Elizabeth West. Only I've never been able to get them to call me anything but Sally."

"Not Aspidistra Aspinall?"

Her eyes went blank. The thin black line of eyebrow took an upward kink.

"Aspidistra Aspinall? What a peculiar name!"

"Very."

"It doesn't sound real to me."

James spoke with whole-hearted conviction.

"It isn't."

"Then—I'm afraid I don't understand."

Suddenly James was quite sure. There wasn't anything to make him sure, but all at once he stopped being afraid that he might be making a fool of himself. He also stopped being angry. He met the innocent green eyes with a friendly grin.

"All right," he said, "nobody's ever heard of Aspidistra. She's a wash-out. Done. Dead. Buried. You're Sally West.

I'm still James Elliot—and the only person who ever called me Jimmy got a thick ear. Now how do we go?''

Sally went on looking at him for about a minute and a half. The kink in her eyebrows straightened out. Her eyes stopped laughing. They considered him in a serious way. James had the odd feeling that things were happening between them. It was as if she said "I want to come in and look,'' and it was as if he opened his door and said "Here you are—you can look at anything you like,'' and back of this the hope that things were reasonably clean and tidy.

So Sally came in.

He could feel her there, moving round, looking where she wanted to, touching things gently, straightening somewhere here and there, as a woman does when she comes into a room. The oddest part of the whole odd business was that it all felt quite natural. She might have been there always. It might have been her room as well as his. The blood came up into his face. Sally went on looking at him, and said,

"Did you recognize me before I said that about the bicycle? I think it was very clever it you did, because I made my voice quite different—nice and gentle and modest. It's Sarah's voice really. I keep it for great-aunts, and traffic-cops, and the policeman when I've gone the wrong way round an island or butted in at the other end of a one-way street. But I can't keep it up—not for very long, because I'm not really Sarah or Elizabeth—I'm Sally.''

"I wasn't sure,'' said James. "Something kept bobbing up, but I couldn't get hold of it. Sally's a nicer name than Aspidistra. I can't think how you thought of a name like that in the middle of running away and being shot at.''

"Oh, but I *didn't*. I've been Aspidistra since I was about six. I thought it was the loveliest name, so I had it for all my adventures. I used to tell myself a new one every night in bed—coral islands, and pirates, and flying to the moon, and a magic horse, and hunting for treasure—so the minute I had a real adventure it came quite natural to be Aspidistra. I really couldn't be anything else.''

She had the prettiest soft colour in her cheeks. Her eyes were as bright as water. James felt a foolish strange desire to be a little boy again and go adventuring with her—on a coral island—in a pirate ship—on a flying carpet that would take them over the moon. He had always wanted to see the other side of the moon, because ever since he was about five he had had the sneaking feeling that perhaps it wasn't there at all. He nodded and said,

"I see." And then, "You said Sally West. I saw a thing in the paper the day we ran away. It said Lady Clementa Tolhache had left a lot of money to her great-nephew John Jernyngham West. I was at school with a John Jernyngham West—he was my fag for a year. J.J. we called him. You said you had an Aunt Clementa. I didn't believe you until I saw the bit in the paper—"

"You've got a very unbelieving mind."

"No, I haven't—not any more than most people. Clementa on the top of Aspidistra was a bit steep, you know. I didn't really believe it even when I saw it in the paper—Clementa Tolhache—"

"They call it Tullish. Such a pity, isn't it, but they're awfully stuck up about it."

James frowned. The name still sounded so unlikely. He said abruptly,

"I was asking you about J.J. Is he a cousin of yours?"

All at once she was grave and a little pale.

"Oh, no—he's my brother. As soon as you'd said your name and where you'd been at school, I knew all about you. Jocko used to talk about you a lot."

James grinned.

"I can guess the sort of things he said. He was the cheekiest fag I ever had."

"He's a brat," said Sally. "He always was, and I expect he always will be. He goes round asking for trouble—" Her voice tailed away. When she had said "trouble" it stopped altogether. She looked hard at James and said, "I'm awfully worried about him."

"Why?"

"Because our old nurse used to say, 'If you don't trouble trouble, trouble won't trouble you,' and, 'Let sleeping dogs lie.' I don't suppose Jocko *will*. I'm not very good at it myself."

"I know. I shouldn't think you were, or you'd have kept

out of that house. Did you know there were sleeping dogs there?''

Her eyebrows did that funny little quirk again. It was very amusing.

''Well—I thought there might be, but I didn't think they'd shoot.''

''How did you know I wasn't one of them?'' said James. ''I mean, there we were in the dark. And I saw you because my torch picked you up on the stairs, but you couldn't possibly have seen me, so how did you know it was all right to clutch me and say 'Run!'?''

Sally made a face.

''I didn't! How could I? I just chanced it. Because, you see, if you were one of *them*, I was done already, and if you weren't, there was quite a good chance of getting away. Besides, I'd just about got to the point where I had to clutch someone. You can't think how nerve-racking it was when your horrible ray came out from nowhere and hit me in the face. I don't suppose I shall ever feel safe in the dark again.''

''What were you doing in the dark?'' said James in a portentous voice. ''What were you doing in that house at all? Don't you think you had better tell me?''

''I did tell you. I told you I was looking for Aunt Clementa's diamond necklace.''

James made the sound which is written Pish, or Tush, or Tcha.

Sally gurgled.

''Don't you believe in that either? You do make it difficult, you know. You wouldn't have believed in Aunt Clementa if you hadn't come across her in a newspaper. I don't believe everything I see in a newspaper myself, but there's no accounting for tastes. And now that you've swallowed Aunt Clementa, I don't know why you should boggle at her necklace. It's frightfully valuable and completely unwearable, you know—the sort people wore when they had a nice cushiony shelf all pushed up in front with tight stays. Aunt Clementa had a lovely one. There's a photograph of her with a waist about the size of your neck, and billows and billows of white satin, and the diamonds laid out on her shelf, and feathers in her hair, and a tiara, and a fringe right down to her eyebrows like the pictures of Queen Alexandra. I could show it to you if it would make you believe in the necklace.''

''Why do you want me to believe in it?'' said James. He thought he had startled her, and he wondered why.

Her colour rose.

''I don't want you to. You can believe just what you like. It doesn't matter to me, and Aunt Clementa's dead, so it doesn't matter to her, though she would be most awfully annoyed if she could hear you not believing, poor old pet. She was most enormously proud of her necklace. It had about fifty large brilliants and a hundred middle-sized ones, besides masses and masses of little ones. She made me learn the numbers, but I've forgotten half of them.''

James felt that he was being got at. Why should he care if Lady Clementa Tolhache, pronounced Tullish, had had fifty diamond necklaces? And why should Sally West care whether he believed in one or more of them? And what in the world had all this got to do with the adventure in the dark house? He didn't know, and he wanted to know. He very much wanted to know. He looked very straight at Sally West, and he said in his most Scottish voice,

''What's the good of all this stuff about a diamond necklace? Why don't you tell me what you were really doing in that house?''

VII

NOTHING HAPPENED—NO VOICE, NO ANSWER, NO RESPONSE of any kind. James felt that he was being snubbed. And why should he be snubbed? He'd been shot at, hadn't he, and not missed by very much either? He said with deliberation,

"We ought to have gone to the police—I told you so at the time."

"People who say 'I told you so' are always fondly loved. It says so on their tombstones."

This had no soothing effect.

"Suppose I go to the police now?" said James in a stiffened voice.

"They wouldn't believe you."

"Why wouldn't they?"

Sally looked at him sweetly.

"You'd rather lost yourself, hadn't you? I mean, the scenery was mostly fog, wasn't it? I suppose you'd be able to tell the police where the house was. I shouldn't if it had happened to me, but I'm not a cocksure Scot. I suppose you do feel quite sure you could lead them straight to the spot."

James supposed nothing of the kind. He had put in some intensive study on a map without being able to arrive at any idea of (a) where he had got off the road, and (b) where he rejoined it. (A) was probably one of the four cross-roads in the middle of Warnley Common, but it might have been anywhere else, because the common rather ran to crossroads. Further, he didn't know whether he had gone off to the right or to the left. (B) was just as difficult. He had certainly reached Staling, but three roads ran in a couple of miles short of it, two on the left and one on the right, and a very meandering lane joined the road, also on the right just before you came to the village. The dark house from which he and Sally had run was somewhere within a radius of five miles of Staling, probably much less, because distances lengthen out in a fog, but further than this he could be sure of nothing. Sally had him beat, and he knew it. The bother was that she knew it too. He said with a firmness which he was far from feeling,

"I couldn't do that, but I could describe it—to some extent."

Sally said " 'M—" She said it very softly, but she managed to make it ask a question.

"I saw the hall," said James.

Sally said " 'M—" again. This time there was no question. It said, "All right, take your hall."

James became aware that his hall wasn't any earthly

good. What was the use of offering the police a hall which they had never seen, and of which he himself had only caught dusty glimpses? He gave it up. If he felt sufficiently interested, he could of course track the house down easily enough. He could do it when he delivered Colonel Pomeroy's car next week. But why should he? It didn't concern him, so why should he bother? He said,

"I could find the house all right if I wanted to, only I don't. What I *should* like to know is why you don't want me to find it."

Sally leaned back. There wasn't a great deal of light on this half-landing, and what was there was shaded. When she leaned back she slipped into a shadow. Presently she said out of the shadow,

"It might be—safer for you."

"And what do you mean by that?" said James directly.

He heard her laugh without merriment.

"Very little—not very much—nothing at all, *or*—a good deal."

"I suppose you're trying to make me lose my temper."

"No, I wasn't thinking about that. Are you going to lose it?"

"Not unless I want to. What did you mean about its being safer for me?"

She said slowly, "Well—you did—leave your car—in the drive. I bumped into it. If anyone else did—cars have numbers, don't they?"

"Mine had a trade number."

"Well, anyone who wanted to could find out—who was driving that car—couldn't they?"

"I suppose they could if they chose to take the trouble. I don't know why they should."

Sally said very softly, "They mightn't know—how much—you had seen."

"And that would bother them?"

"Yes."

It was a very grave little word. James thought about it. Then he said,

"That's all about me. What about you? You were there too, you know."

Sally laughed again.

"I'd gathered that."

"Well, what about it? They could hardly have missed your bicycle."

"Bicycles don't have numbers," said Sally.

"And you'd left your shoes in the hall—and a torch upstairs."

"Yes, that's much worse than the bicycle—much, much worse, because—" She stopped short, and said quickly, " 'The Compromising Crocodiles, or Aspidistra's Adventure. Another thrilling instalment tomorrow.' I retrieved the torch, but let's do some good strong hoping that no one tumbled to the crocodiles. They *were* round the corner, so perhaps . . . I don't really want that thrilling instalment, you know. I've got a feeling it might be too thrilling."

James said on a deep growl, "I can't help you when you don't tell me anything."

"I know," said Sally a little breathlessly. "I'm trying to make up my mind. I haven't made it up. You see, if I tell you things, I'm bringing you into it, and that doesn't seem fair to you. But then, on the other hand, I don't know that you're not in already, and if you are, it might be—safer—if you knew where you were. And then—" She stopped. It was as if the word had been cut off. A long, slow minute went by.

James said, "And then?"

Sally looked at him. She was leaning forward again. He could see her face.

"There's Jocko—"

"Yes—and what about Jocko? He's in India, isn't he?"

"Yes."

"Well?"

"He's coming home."

"When?"

"At once. I expect he's started. He's coming by air. Aunt Clementa's affairs, you know. She left him quite a lot of money."

"And that worries you?"

She gave him a strange look. He thought it was a frightened look. She didn't answer.

James persisted, frowning.

"I do wish you'd tell me what it's all about. What's the

matter with J.J. coming home? Are you afraid he's going to make an ass of himself in some way—blow the money—run amuck—something like that?''

She shook her head.

''Then you're afraid he'll butt in on this mystery business. Is that it?''

''Well, he might.''

''And you think it wouldn't be healthy for him?''

She dropped her voice and said in an almost indistinguishable murmur,

''It might be—very—dangerous.''

''For him?''

''For everyone.'' She made a quick movement with her hands. ''I tried to stop him, but it's no good. I couldn't tell him why.''

''I think you had better tell me—I do really, Sally.''

Sally jumped up.

''Not now—not here—I can't—I haven't made up my mind—I've got to think about it. I'm going home now.''

''And when you've thought about it?''

''I'll ring you up.''

She began to go down the few steps to the drawing-room floor. James followed. Of an observant habit of mind, he could hardly avoid seeing how white the nape of her neck was under the double row of little black curls. Some dark girls had napes as stubbly as a man's chin, but Sally's skin ran white and smooth all the way up to the edge of her hair.

She checked in front of him so suddenly that he could not stop himself from taking the next step and bumping into her. He had to put his arm about her to steady himself and her, but even as he touched her she twisted free and passed him, and was up the stair and round the bend before he had time to draw an astonished breath. He went after her, and found her half way up the next flight, leaning against the wall with her hand at her throat and her eyes afraid.

He said, ''What's the matter?''

She took her hand from her throat and caught at his arm, leaning close and saying under her breath.

''There's someone I don't want to see. I didn't know they

were coming—I thought they were somewhere else—Daphne didn't tell me. Why didn't she tell me?''

He could feel that she was shaking all over. He put his arm round her for the second time. It seemed quite a natural thing to do.

"It's all right. Sit down here for a minute. Where were these people—coming up the stairs? Because if they were, you've only to let them get into the drawing-room, and then you can slip past and get away. Tell me what they're like, and I'll let you know when the coast is clear.''

She had both hands locked about his arm. She said, "Thank you," and then, "Will you do just what I say?"

"I don't know," said James.

"*Please*, James Elliot—*please*."

"What do you want me to do?"

Her clasp relaxed a little.

"I want you to go straight downstairs and out of the house."

"You want me to go?"

"At once. *Please*, James Elliot."

"What about you?"

"I'll slip away like you said. Please, *please* go."

"Oh, all right."

He felt her fingers unclasp. He dropped his arm from about her. There was a curious reluctance about this parting. He waited a moment without quite knowing why, while the sound of voices came up to them from below. He heard Daphne's laugh. Then Sally drew back, and he turned from her and went slowly down the stairs.

On the drawing-room landing he paused. Sally had said, "Go straight downstairs and out of the house." That was all very well, but he couldn't just fade away without saying good-night to Daphne. He looked in through the drawing-room door and saw her not more than a couple of yards away, laughing and sparkling up at a tall man who had his back to James.

James edged into the room and advanced a step or two, not without difficulty, because the room was now a good deal fuller than it had ever been meant to be. He heard Daphne say, "So good of you both to come on," and looking over the head of a bony girl in black, he saw that

Daphne's left hand rested affectionately on the arm of a very striking lady who obviously belonged to the tall man. He also saw that the tall man was Ambrose Sylvester. Now that the famous profile was on view, it was quite impossible to mistake it. What he had not realized from the press photographs was that the tossed mass of hair which framed the profile was of the most picturesque shade of coppery gold. A hawk-like nose and eyes of a cold and brilliant blue preserved the virility of the face, but James considered with disgust that a man who didn't aim at being a popular idol would get himself a hair-cut. He had nothing against good looks, but there were decencies to be observed, and hair six inches long was a quite obvious breach of these decencies.

He supposed the lady to be Mrs. Sylvester. She was a head taller than Daphne, dark-haired, and incredibly slim in a gold dress so tight and shiny that it reminded James of a mermaid's tail. She was as ugly as her husband was handsome, but she carried her ugliness as if it were beauty—lips a miracle of scarlet paint, eyes lazily disdainful between long mascaraed lashes, teeth very white, hands and shoulders used as only a Latin uses them.

"Queer people," was James's judgment. He wondered whether it was the Sylvesters whom Sally had wished to avoid, and he wondered why. He said over the lady's shoulder,

"Goodbye, Daph—I'm just off. Thanks for asking me."

And Daphne said, "Oh, darling, must you?" And he thought she was going to say, "Where's Sally?" and he wondered if Sally would mind, because if it was the Sylvesters she wanted to avoid—But Daphne only blew him a kiss.

As he turned away, he heard Mrs. Sylvester say in a deep, husky voice,

"Jocko is coming home. Did you know? I *adore* Jocko."

VIII

Sally stayed where she was, and heard James go down the stair. She would give him time to get away before she made her escape. She found him a very disturbing person, and she couldn't do with being any more disturbed than she was. What she wanted at the moment was Somebody's Soothing Syrup, oil on the troubled waters, Daphne's light inconsequent chatter, or the ramblings of one of life's bigger bores. Not any more James Elliot, and not—oh, certainly not—any Ambrose Sylvester.

She ran up to the next floor and into Daphne's bedroom. The modern girl is provided against the ravages of emotion. Sally did her mouth again, did her eyebrows, tried Daphne's powder, thought that it must cost about a pound a box, and approved the result.

These proceedings took some time. She decided that James must have gone, and that this was the moment for her to slip away.

At the head of the stair she listened, and heard the ebb and flow of the laughter and the talk from below. It would be perfectly safe. She must walk quietly down without appearing to hurry and the minute she got downstairs just grab her cloak and be off.

She got as far as the half-landing and stopped, because there was someone there. Ambrose Sylvester rose from the chair in which James had sat and came to meet her.

A deathly panic invaded Sally. She was to rage at herself afterwards and wonder how much or how little her face had shown, but at the moment she couldn't think at all, only fight to push the panic out and bolt and bar her house against it. She heard Ambrose say in his beautiful voice,

"Daphne said you were upstairs, so I came here to wait for you."

"Why?" said Sally with her hand on the newel-post at the turn. She managed the one word very creditably, and this heartened her.

He put a hand on her arm.

"I wanted to talk to you."

Sally pushed her last bolt home.

"All right, here I am," she said.

He drew her towards the chairs, and they sat down. Sally was herself again, but she was glad enough to sit, because her knees were shaking. She managed a small laugh.

"What is it all about? You know, you said that as if you hadn't seen me for a year."

He looked at her with an air of romantic sadness.

"It is a long time since we have really talked, and tonight I felt that if we could have one of our old talks again—if we could put the clock back for an hour—"

"No one can ever put the clock back," said Sally.

"We could if we tried—together. We might for an hour forget the years, the estrangement—"

"And Hildegarde?"

Her heart was beating a little faster. Ambrose and his ridiculous heroics—But because they had once rung passionately true they could still set her heart knocking against her side, even after all that had happened since then.

He gave a kind of groan at Hildegarde's name.

"Do you think she has ever taken your place? Do you think I don't know what she has done to me? Do you think I am happy?"

"No—I don't think you are very happy, Ambrose."

He caught at her hand.

"I live on her money. She never lets me forget it. She never stops watching me. When I am starved for a word with you, I must have it here in a public place. Oh, Sally, why did I do it? Why didn't I wait? You were such an enchanting little girl! I might have known!"

Sally pulled her hand away and jumped up.

"Good gracious, Ambrose! I was seventeen, and I had a schoolgirl *schwärm* for you, but if you think I want to put back the clock to that and go all damp and miserable over you again, you'd better wake up—to say nothing of Hildegarde probably trying to poison us both."

She was watching him through her lashes, and he put his head in his hands and groaned again.

"You can laugh at me! You don't know how damned unhappy I am."

Sally hesitated. Was it all make-believe—the sound of his own fine voice, the desire for the limelight and the centre of the stage? Or was there a struggling, unhappy Ambrose behind the actor? She sat down again and said in a new, gentle voice,

"What is it?"

"Hell," said Ambrose Sylvester. "Sally, if you ever know what it's been, don't—don't think too hardly of me. You see"—he lifted his head and looked at her with bright, wild eyes—"you take the first step and you have to go on. The ground slides under you and you can't stop. Yesterday in that damned fog I thought—Hildegarde was driving—and I thought if we could have a smash now and get out of it all, it would be the best thing."

Sally looked at him steadily. The fog—why did he mention the fog? And what was it all about, this unbelievable scene? A quick, wary thought watched for a meaning behind its unreality. She said,

"I don't know what this is all about."

"Do you know what has stopped me making an end of it, not once but many times? It was the thought of you, Sally. You see, when I think of you I am different. I think of what you may be doing. You won't laugh, will you, Sally? I think, 'Now she is reading—now she is writing to Jocko—now she is walking,' and it is a sort of companionship. Now you see how lonely I am when I have to be satisfied with that kind of companionship. And yesterday in that horrible fog I was thinking, 'Sally won't be out in this. She will be at home by the fire with a book.'"

Sally's thought spoke sharply and insistently—"That's what he wants. He wants to know what you were doing yesterday afternoon. What are you going to say? Be careful!'' Her heart stood still. Had anyone seen her go, or come back, or take Gladys's bicycle? ''Be careful, be careful, be careful!''

She said in a cool little voice, ''You know, Ambrose, this is all rather embarrassing.''

''Is that all you think about?''

''Well, someone's got to think about it, and I'd rather it wasn't Hildegarde.'' She got up. ''Honestly, Ambrose, this sort of thing's no good. It won't make you any happier, and it doesn't get us anywhere.''

''Sally!''

''It's not *going* to get us anywhere,'' said Sally, and ran down the stair.

IX

JAMES USUALLY WALKED TO HIS JOB IN THE MORNING. IT was one of the things Jackson despised him for. To Jackson the human leg was an obsolete form of conveyance. To use it betokened extreme penury or a barbaric devotion to exercise. James liked a spot of exercise, and was despised accordingly. Today, however, there was no Jackson to give him a lofty good-morning. Mr. Parkinson, the manager, had not arrived and would not arrive for another half hour. James and Miss Callender had the place to themselves.

Miss Callender was a pretty girl and a most efficient clerk. She had a tendency to roll her eyes at any young man, but it did not mean very much. James had begun by being rather alarmed, but they were now firm friends. Long practice with the fourteen cousins had made him an admirable listener. He had listened right through three of Miss

Callender's love affairs, and was now in the middle of the quarrel in progress between her and Mr. Leonard Rowbotham, of Rowbotham & Sons, haberdashers, a gentlemanly young man who used very expensive habits, on the question of whether his widowed mother should be invited to make her home with them. Miss Callender said no, and Mr. Rowbotham said yes, old Mrs. Rowbotham cried, and James recommended tact coupled with firmness. There the matter had stood when the latest accounts were to hand.

When, therefore, Miss Callender approached him with the air of a girl who is simply bursting with suppressed information, James felt quite sure that there had been important developments, and that he was going to be told all about them. To his surprise, however, Miss Callender's opening remark had nothing to do with the great Rowbotham affair. She patted the little curls at the back of her neck and said with a sidelong glance,

"Mr. Jackson's not here this morning, Mr. Elliot."

"I'm early," said James.

"So am I early. So is Mr. Jackson most days, but I'm ever so glad he's not here this morning."

James was obviously intended to ask why she was glad. He obliged.

Miss Callender rolled her eyes.

"Well, of course it's always nice to get a word with you, Mr. Elliot—just ourselves, I mean. But there was something I wanted to have a chance of telling you—if I *had* a chance, if you know what I mean."

She was in the little enclosed office, and James half in and half out leaning against the jamb. He nodded. He knew exactly what she meant.

"On the other hand," said Miss Callender, polishing her nail with her pocket handkerchief, "I don't know if I really ought to, because once mischief's been made you can't undo it, can you? My mother brought me up ever so strict about that, only what I say is, if there are things going on that are what I call downright underhand and mean, well, then it's better to know about them, and we've always been friends— haven't we?"

James was puzzled. It looked like something to do with

the business. He didn't want to hear any more. He made a movement, and Miss Callender pushed her handkerchief up her sleeve.

"Well, I'm going to tell you, Mr. Elliot, and you can judge for yourself. You know that Rolls you sold to Colonel Pomeroy—well, you'd hardly gone yesterday when someone rang up about it."

"Colonel Pomeroy?"

"Oh, no. You'd hardly gone, you know, and I wouldn't have been here, only there was those accounts I wanted to finish, and Mr. Jackson he was waiting about because there had been some talk about a cinema. I hadn't said yes and I hadn't said no, if you understand, Mr. Elliot, because I was going to let it depend on what I was feeling like when it came to the point—about Lenny, you know—and I hadn't rightly made up my mind. So when this telephone bell rang I couldn't think who it was, because really it was after hours."

"And who was it?"

"Well, they began right away about the Rolls, only they didn't say it was that at first. They wanted to know about the trade plate—had we sent out a car under a number ought-ought-something-or-other? Well, I was busy, and there was Mr. Jackson doing nothing, so I called him in. 'Here, you take this,' I said. 'It's more in your line than mine,' and I went on with what I was doing.''

"Yes?" said James. He was interested, he was very much interested.

"Well, Mr. Elliot, you can see for yourself he wouldn't be very far away, Mr. Jackson wouldn't. He took the receiver, and I wasn't paying any attention at first—I just got a word here and there, from the other end, you know. But what made me take notice was hearing Mr. Jackson say, 'Have you any complaint?' so then I listened. It was a man speaking the other end, and he said, 'Oh, no, quite the reverse. Your demonstrator obliged a young lady, and she would like to thank him.''

James whistled.

"I say, are you sure you heard that? I mean, *can* you hear?"

Miss Callender nodded with energy.

"Of course I can—it's as easy as easy. And that's what

he said." She rolled her eyes. "What's she like? Is she pretty? You might tell me about her, Mr. Elliot."

"I don't know what you mean," said James, and hoped he hadn't blushed.

Miss Callender was an accommodating girl.

"You needn't if you don't want to," she said. "Well, Mr. Jackson went away as far as he could for the flex, and he said, 'Did you wish to speak to the demonstrator?' Well, the man said he did, and Mr. Jackson said, 'Speaking.' And how he had the nerve, I don't know, but of course he didn't know that I could hear what was being said at the other end."

James tried to remember exactly what had been said.

"Look here, how do you know all this was about the Rolls I sold to Colonel Pomeroy? Jackson does most of the demonstrating."

"You wait," said Miss Callender. "I haven't told you all the bits, but I'd heard enough to know it was the Rolls all right. There was something about the fog being so thick, and you know you told me it was hard to get along in the country though it wasn't so bad in town. Oh, it was the Rolls all right—and Mr. Jackson making out he'd driven it! I didn't say anything, but I was boiling. The minute he saw there was something to get out of it, it was him who was driving the car all right! Well, then he said, 'Who's speaking?' and they said Hazeby, Meredith & Hazeby, solicitors, and they were speaking for the young lady who was their client, and she very much wanted to thank the driver personally, and what would the name be? And Mr. Jackson said, 'Jackson.'"

James began to say something and swallowed it.

"Well, I won't say you're wrong," said Miss Callender. "If it hadn't been for my mother rubbing it into us all never to take notice, or to flare up, or to answer back in business hours, well, I don't know what I'd have said. Mother had been in business herself, and she always said, 'You can't afford to make enemies with your tongue—you've got to keep friendly all round no matter what your feelings are.' And you can't say it's not good advice—can you?"

James said he thought it was very good advice.

"Well, it's all that kept me from telling Mr. Jackson what

I thought about him," said Miss Callender frankly. "Mind you, Mr. Elliot, I've never been friends with him like I have with you, but we've been quite friendly. I've been to the cinema with him once and again—that time Ernie was treating me so badly—and I won't say he wasn't quite all right though a bit too pleased with himself for my taste, but I couldn't have believed he'd have done a right-down mean kind of action like taking the credit for somebody else's job."

James laughed.

"Well, he could hardly expect to pass for me—could he?"

Miss Callender rolled her eyes.

"That's where the fog came in. This Mr. Hazeby asked particularly would he know the young lady if she was to meet him somewhere, and Mr. Jackson coughed and cleared his throat, and he said he couldn't be sure, what with the fog and all. Well, then this Mr. Hazeby said that it was the same with the young lady, and what about each of them wearing a buttonhole and meeting just outside Broadcasting House. And Mr. Jackson said that would do very nicely, but he would hold his handkerchief in his hand instead of the buttonhole because he couldn't be sure of getting one so late. And I heard him look round at me to see if I was taking notice, but I'd my fingers to my ears and adding up under my breath, and he must have thought I hadn't heard. Well, I lost a bit there, but they must have fixed it up, for I heard him say—Mr. Jackson, I mean—'All right, a quarter to seven,' and he rang off. Well, then I said, 'What on earth was all that about? I don't know how you think I can do accounts with people talking all over my office.' And he came and stood where you are now, looking as pleased as Punch, and said he'd got a nibble about a car and he was off to meet the man and have a drink with him. That was in case I'd heard anything, and I don't know how I kept from telling him that he needn't think he was taking me in, because he wasn't. So then he said he was sorry about the cinema and it would have to be some other night, and I said that was all right and I couldn't have come anyhow because I was going to the Palais-de-Danse with Len. And I did. It's all fixed up, Mr. Elliot—about Mrs. Rowbotham, I mean. She's going to move in over the way with Mrs. Bertram who's a great friend of hers and's had losses and only too glad to let her two front rooms, so we're going to get the banns put up. And you'll come to my wedding, won't you? I knew you'd be ever so pleased."

X

THE MANAGER ARRIVED AT A QUARTER TO TEN. MR. Jackson did not arrive at all. James had to take over two of his jobs, and was kept busy. In the afternoon he had to drive a Wolseley 25 down to Chislehurst. Still no Jackson. Miss Callender rolled her eyes and said it looked as if he had got off with the young lady.

"If she's an heiress and he marries her—and it ought really to have been you—I suppose you'll never forgive me, Mr. Elliot."

James said that nothing would induce him to carry an heiress.

Miss Callender adjusted a curl.

"Why on earth not?" she enquired.

"Girls think quite enough of themselves without having the purse-strings."

"Well, I think it would be ever so nice. I mean, suppose Lenny was to come in for a fortune, do you think I'd say, 'Oh, no—I can't' and 'you'd better ask someone else'? Not much!"

"Girls are different," said James.

"They've more sense," said Miss Callender, and tossed her head. Then, as he turned to go, she dropped her voice. "It seems funny Mr. Jackson not turning up, all the same."

James found the words coming back to him as he threaded his way through the traffic. He was a very good driver.

He was, as a matter of fact, a better driver than Jackson—better nerve, better judgment, quicker in the uptake. He wondered what had happened to Jackson . . . Nonsense! Nothing had happened to him. There wasn't anything to happen. Daisy Callender had made a mountain out of a molehill. He didn't believe she could have heard half the things she said she had heard over the telephone. She might have got a word here and there, but she had imagined the rest. He knew what girls were. He didn't believe the conversation had anything to do with the Rolls which he had sold to Colonel Pomeroy. The whole story sounded most awfully far-fetched. Daisy Callender had probably mixed up two conversations, one with some Mr. Hazeby who had rung up about a car, and another quite different conversation in which Jackson was making a date with a girl. Daisy said she had lost a bit in the middle. She had probably left Jackson talking to Hazeby and come back to Jackson talking to his girl.

James felt extraordinarily pleased with this explanation. It put him in excellent spirits for about half an hour, after which something looked out of a dark corner of his mind and said quite loud, "Where is Jackson?"

Well, it wasn't really James's business. He said so firmly as he drew up at the rustic abode of the Misses Palmer. It was very rustic. There was no drive in. A rustic arch led by way of a pergola to a rustic porch. There was a great deal of crazy paving. There was so many gables in the roof that it worried James to think what shape the rooms inside must be.

There were two Misses Palmer, a large authoritative one, and a little dried-up one with a bright beady eye and a twittering voice. They both drove a little, and they both wanted to drive the car. James's attention was fully occupied. The large Miss Palmer just missed a lamp-post and wrecked a bicycle. The little one would suddenly twitter "Oh, Mr. Elliot!" and abandon the wheel.

When he landed them again at their rustic arch they were almost effusive in their thanks.

"A beautiful car—a really beautiful car. But my sister and I will have to talk it over. I am not sure whether something smaller—"

And the massive Miss Palmer:

"We will let you know what we have decided."

"And we should have to consider the question of a garage—"

"It's not the slightest use considering the garage until we have decided about the car. Good afternoon, Mr. Elliot."

James drove away. The Misses Palmer would certainly be a menace on the road. He hoped he would never have to watch either of them drive again. Why couldn't they stick to gardening? There was still room for another two or three rockeries and a whole lot of crazy paving. It would be harmless, virtuous, healthful work. But no, they must urge powerful engines over which they had practically no control along the public highways until they killed some unoffending pedestrian and got sent to jug. All of which would be avoided if they would stick to gardening.

And right in the midst of these pious reflections up bobbed the question of Jackson again. The satisfying explanation seemed to have died quietly while he was engaged with the Misses Palmer. It was quite, quite dead. All his efforts at resuscitation were a complete failure. Suppose Mr. Hazeby's client was not a girl at all. Suppose Mr. Hazeby was the person who had fired at him and Sally in the empty house, or suppose it was Mr. Hazeby's client who had fired at them.

Suppose it wasn't anything at all.

Suppose it was.

He heard Sally's voice saying slowly and distinctly, "Anyone who wanted to—could find out—who was driving that car—couldn't they?"

She had said that. And he had said,

"I suppose they could if they chose to take the trouble, but I don't know why they should."

And Sally had said softly, "They mightn't know—how much—you had seen."

James shook himself. Hang it all, what on earth had all this got to do with Jackson going off on a binge? The thing that talked in the dark corner of his mind said, "Hazeby wanted to know who had been driving the car, and Jackson butted in and said that he had." So someone did want to find out who had been driving the Rolls. And they thought they had found Jackson. They thought they had found Jackson. And where is Jackson now?

"Sleeping off his binge, I should think," said James with furious common sense.

He got back just before six. There was no word about Jackson. Mr. Parkinson, the manager, was being stuffy about it in a superior, high-hat sort of way. He really could not imagine—he could not conceive—he was at a loss to understand—he had been obliged to send Smiles out with an American client, a thing that should really never have been allowed to happen. "I really am entirely at a loss to understand what has become of Jackson."

Next day there was still no Jackson. James had to go down to Chislehurst again. The Misses Palmer wished to see a smaller car. They had both rung up about it, one at nine o'clock, and the other at five minutes past. Each hoped separately that it would be Mr. Elliot who would bring the car down—such a good driver and so reliable.

Miss Callender, rather paler than usual, attempted a rallying smile.

"Looks as if you'd got off too, Mr. Elliot—doesn't it?" James made a face.

"Too?" he enquired.

"Mr. Jackson," said Miss Callender, and the smile faded out. "You don't think anything's happened to him, do you?"

"Rubbish! What is there to happen?" said James, and went to pick a mild, well-mannered car for the Misses Palmer.

He found the large Miss Palmer waiting for him at the corner of their road. When he drew up she came up to the window and told him in a brisk, domineering manner that he was to discourage her sister from attempting to drive.

"She is very highly strung, Mr. Elliot, and not at all fitted to handle machinery. I shall be obliged if you will tell her so. It will be more acceptable from a stranger and an expert. I do not wish to have to tell her that nothing will induce me to enter the car if she insists upon driving it."

James felt a certain amount of sympathy for the large Miss Palmer.

"Well," he said, "she would have to pass a driving test."

"I believe not. Unfortunately she took some driving

lessons a few years ago. I am informed that anyone possessing a licence before the new regulations came in is not obliged to pass the test.''

James said, ''I see.'' And then, ''Well, I'll do my best, Miss Palmer. I don't think she would be very safe on the road.''

She shook her head gloomily.

''I shall refuse to enter the car. Drive on to the house, Mr. Elliot. I do not wish her to know that I have spoken to you.''

James drew up at the rustic gate. Half way down the pergola which led to the front door he encountered the little Miss Palmer in a state of considerable agitation.

''Oh, Mr. Elliot—good morning! You haven't seen my sister? I did want if possible to have a word with you, but I shouldn't like her to think—I don't know if you are a gardener, but perhaps I might be showing you the new rockery.''

She took him round the house and down another pergola. The new rockery was very new indeed. It appeared to consist entirely of rocks and labels.

''We are devoted to rock-gardening,'' said the little Miss Palmer in a twittering whisper. ''We have the only monifera semper-florens in Chislehurst. Oh, Mr. Elliot, I do implore you to use all your influence with my sister to dissuade her from attempting to drive the car. It is quite useless for me to say anything, but the idea terrifies me. She is so abrupt in her movements, and she does not like to be thwarted. I do hope you will do your best. My nerves are still upset after yesterday.''

''Why don't you have a driver?'' said James.

The little Miss Palmer drew herself up.

''Thank you, Mr. Elliot, that will not be necessary. I have driven for some years. I may be a little out of practice, but I feel sure—''

''Will Miss Palmer have to pass the driving test?'' said James.

''Miss *Ethel* Palmer. I am Miss Palmer, though everyone takes my sister for the elder. Oh no—she has had a licence for years, because we used occasionally to drive our brother's car. Not very often—gentlemen are so fidgety about their cars—but it was a great pleasure, so we always had our licences. Hush! There is my sister! Yes, we intend to continue the crazy paving as far as it will go. It should look very well, I think. Ethel, here is Mr. Elliot. So kind of him—I'm sure all these cars are so delightful that it is very difficult to decide—but we must not take up too much of his time—we had better start at once.''

"Mr. Elliot will drive," said the large Miss Palmer.

"Mr. Elliot first—oh, yes—oh, of course. And then I thought I would take the wheel—"

"No, Emily!"

"Really, Ethel!"

"No, Emily!"

"Really Ethel—as the elder—"

The large Miss Palmer snorted.

"What has that got to do with driving a car? You haven't got the hands for it!"

"I have extremely light hands, Ethel."

"Emily, if you insist on driving that car, you drive it alone!"

"Really, Ethel!"

"Mr. Elliot, I beg of you—"

James looked from the large, flushed Miss Palmer to the little, pale one, who seemed to be on the verge of tears.

"I think you had better let me drive. There's such a lot on the road now, and you haven't had much practice, have you? I should really advise you to think about having a driver, for a time at any rate."

"He could give Emily lessons," said Miss Ethel, breathing heavily.

Emily gave a little gasp of pure rage.

"You needn't decide about it now," said James hastily. "See how you like the car first. It's really awfully good value for the money. A cousin of mine's got one, and she's never been stuck on the road yet. That's what you want, you know, a car that will never let you down—six cylinders, hydraulic brakes, synchro-mesh gears, S.U. carburettor—"

It was hard work, but he got them into the car and through half an hour of driving without an open outbreak of hostilities. The large Miss Palmer sat beside him on the way out, and the little Miss Palmer on the way home. They talked a good deal to James and at one another, and when he set them down at their garden gate they told him that they would ring up in the morning.

He drove away feeling rather sorry for them. Horrible to handle anything as badly as they handled a car. He felt pleased with his own easy mastery, and then sorry for them again. They ought to get a driver—they seemed quite comfortably off.

He came back to tragedy and a tearful Miss Callender. The police had called up. Mr. Jackson's absence was explained. He had been found dead in a Surrey lane—run over.

"They found him yesterday, but they didn't know who he was, not at first. Mr. Parkinson's been sent for to identify him. They traced him by the laundry-marks on his clothes, poor fellow, and his landlady told them he worked here. It's only a form Mr. Parkinson going. Poor Mr. Jackson—it's him all right. I wish I hadn't said the things I did about him. Mr. Elliot, you won't say anything, will you? I don't want to get drawn into any inquests or things like that. You *won't* say anything—will you?"

James had an odd feeling of shock. He hadn't liked Jackson very much. That seemed to make it worse. He said,

"I don't know, Daisy. I won't say anything, but I think perhaps you ought to."

"Well, I'm not going to," said Miss Callender with decision. "It won't bring him back—will it? And what's it going to look like me standing up in court and saying I listened in like that? And my picture in the *Mail*, and Lenny going off the deep end as likely as not! He's always had a sort of jealous feeling about Mr. Jackson and you—as if a girl couldn't be friendly without its meaning anything! And as sure as I got into a Court they'd have it out of me that what Mr. Jackson was waiting about for was the chance of taking me to the pictures. No, thank you, Mr. Elliot!"

XI

THE ODD FEELING OF SHOCK PERSISTED. MR. PARKINSON came back a good deal upset in a pompous sort of way. The dead man was poor Jackson all right. He had been found yesterday morning as Miss Callender had said, but he had been dead some hours then—eight or nine at least, the police surgeon opined. There had been a heavy shower round about eleven that night, but the ground beneath the body was dry.

"There is some satisfaction in thinking that the poor fellow was killed instantly. Probably never knew he'd been hit," said Mr. Parkinson. "Only what took him down into the country like that is what I don't understand. Walking too—must have been to be run down in that way. I should never have put Jackson down as a walker myself."

Mr. Parkinson continued to hold forth, but James only heard the sound of his voice. His mind was occupied with a most insistent fact.

Jackson never walked.

The idea of his leaving town for the purpose of taking exercise in the dark along a country lane was purely fantastic. Even old Parkinson was finding it difficult to swallow. Somebody else could believe it if they liked, but to James it was a sheer impossibility. He followed Miss Callender into her little office, stood with his back against the door, and said abruptly,

"What was the name of those people who telephoned—the firm of solicitors?"

Miss Callender sat down because her knees were shaking.

"Now, Mr. Elliot, you promised—"

"It was Hazeby, Meredith & Hazeby, wasn't it?"

Miss Callender's large blue eyes were frightened. Her brightly made-up lips took an obstinate line.

"I'm not saying anything—I told you I wasn't."

"That was what you did say."

He took pencil and paper off her table and wrote the names down. Then he stood back against the door again.

"Now look here—these people rang up and Jackson took the call. But are you sure he was talking to them all the time? You told me you heard him making an appointment. Oh yes, you did, and you can't get out of it now. And are you sure, absolutely dead certain sure, that he hadn't stopped talking to Hazeby and got on to someone else by the time he was making that appointment?"

"I'm not saying anything at all," said Miss Callender firmly. "I'm not going to get drawn in—I told you I wasn't."

"Well, I don't believe you heard anything. Bits and scraps in the middle of your accounts—I don't call that anything. If you heard one word, you imagined three. I didn't really believe it when you told me. For one thing, I don't believe you could possibly follow what was said at the other end of the line."

"Well then, I could!"

James made an unbelieving face. The telephone bell rang.

"All right," said Miss Callender, "you take this call. And you go away as far as the flex will let you like Mr. Jackson did, and see if I can't tell you what they're saying at the other end."

The flex took him some four feet away. He said, "Hullo!" and then, "Speaking." And then after a pause, "Yes, that's right . . . Yes, tonight if you can . . . Thank you."

He hung up the receiver, and Miss Callender tossed her head.

"That was Lucas's, and they're sending off the coil and distributor for Mr. Haydon's Lagonda. Well?"

James laughed scornfully.

"You just chanced that. You knew they were to ring up."

"Well then, I didn't! And I heard what he was saying— every word. And I heard what that Mr. Hazeby said to Mr. Jackson, all except a bit here and there like I told you."

"Look here, Daisy, will you swear Jackson made that appointment with Hazeby?"

"Well, he did. And if you're going to call me a liar, we shan't be friends any longer!" She had a bright natural colour in her cheeks and she looked very pretty.

"I'm not calling you a liar. I just thought he might have switched over to someone else without your noticing."

"Well, he didn't!"

"You're sure about that?"

"Of course I'm sure! That Mr. Hazeby said he was to be outside the B.B.C. and wear a buttonhole because the young lady wouldn't be sure of him on account of only having met him in such a fog. And he said—Mr. Jackson did—that he couldn't be sure of getting a buttonhole so late, so he'd carry his handkerchief instead, and Mr. Hazeby said that would be all right. And I'm not going into any court to swear about it, and you needn't think you'll make me, because you won't! But I could, because it's true."

James had got what he wanted. If you made a girl angry, she'd blab anything. Kitty, Hester and Lilian had taught him that. He said in a pacific voice,

"I don't want to make you do anything."

Miss Callender produced a handkerchief and dabbed at her eyes.

"I've had a most awful row with Lenny, and I just don't feel I can stand any more, Mr. Elliot."

James felt some remorse.

"I say, I'm most awfully sorry. What's it all about?"

Daisy Callender gulped.

"Sometimes I wonder if I'm doing right marrying anyone so jealous as Lenny is. I just happened to say we were all quite worried about Mr. Jackson not turning up—yesterday, you know—and there he goes off the deep end. 'You mean *you're* worried,' he said, and then a lot about my thinking more about other men than I would about him if he didn't turn up, and how I needn't think he'd break his heart if I changed my mind, because if there were other men in the world, there were other girls too, and if poor Mr. Jackson was so good-looking, he wasn't the only one—only *he* didn't say *poor* Mr. Jackson. Well, you know how they go on, Mr. Elliot. And I'm sure if I'd known what Lenny was like, I'd never have said how good-looking Mr. Jackson was, because he's got a most terribly jealous disposition, and there's no getting away from it. And when I think that poor Mr. Jackson was lying dead in that lane all the time—or I suppose he wasn't in the lane last night, but you know what I mean—well, I can't help feeling bad about it, and if Lenny sees I'm upset, there'll be another row. So I can't help wondering whether it's worth it—marrying Lenny, I mean—because there's always the chance Mrs. Rowbotham mightn't like it with her friend, and if she said she was coming to us and Lenny said she could, well, I don't see what I could do about it, Mr. Elliot—do you? Once we were married, I mean.''

"I shouldn't do anything in a hurry,'' said James.

He had always found this a very safe thing to say. It had checked his cousin Kitty on the brink of an elopement with a Levantine dancing partner, it had prevented Hester from embarking upon marriage with a completely penniless commission agent, and it had gone down well on many other occasions. It was, in fact, an old and trusted friend. It went down well now. Miss Callender dried her eyes.

"I know what you mean, and I won't. I mean it's thinking you've got to make up your mind right away and decide things that are going to tie you up for the rest of your life that gets on your nerves and makes you read the European Travel advertisements and wish you were going on the whole lot of them. When I think about sitting down with Lenny and his mother in that back parlour of theirs, and never being able to get away any more, and Mrs. Rowbotham's curtains that she bought before the war hanging in the windows—olive-green plush, Mr. Elliot—and photographic enlargements of her and Mr. Rowbotham on one side of the room, and Lenny's grandfather and grandmother on the other side, her in a widow's cap like Queen Victoria and him in side whiskers—well, I really don't feel I can do it, and that's the truth, Mr. Elliot.''

"I should think it over,'' said James. "You're quite sure it was the Rolls I took out for Colonel Pomeroy that Mr. Hazeby was asking about?''

"Well, he said so."

"He used Colonel Pomeroy's name?"

"No, of course he didn't. But he said it was a Rolls—and that foggy day—the day before yesterday it was when he telephoned, which would make it the fourteenth—and he said Sussex, so I suppose I've got enough sense to add that up, and if it doesn't come out to the Rolls you took out for Colonel Pomeroy—"

"You're quite sure he said those things, Daisy—the fog, and Sussex, and the fourteenth?"

"Yes, I'm sure," said Miss Callender crisply. "But I'm not going to say so to anyone but you, so don't you think I am, Mr. Elliot. And if you want your lunch, you'd better be going out for it, because that Mr. Hartley's coming in just after two, and I suppose he'll want to try half a dozen cars and go away and think about them like he did last time."

James went out to lunch. He had a plate of cold beef and a cup of coffee, and he did a lot of thinking. Daisy Callender kept adding bits on to the telephone conversation she said she had overheard, but he didn't think she was inventing them. Girls were like that, you never got the whole story at once. They kept thinking of new bits and tacking them on, like trimming a dress, but it didn't necessarily mean that they were making them up. It was just the way their minds worked.

He thought Daisy Callender was speaking the truth. She had rather an open nature, and she had got into the way of telling him things. No, she wasn't making it up. She had been genuinely indignant with Jackson for representing himself as the driver of the Rolls.

And this was where James had to make himself face what he had been avoiding ever since Daisy Callender had told him that the police had found Jackson dead. He had to face the suspicion that Jackson was dead because he had claimed to have driven the Rolls into Sussex under a trade number on the foggy afternoon of the fourteenth. But it wasn't Jackson who had driven the Rolls, it was James Elliot. If the suspicion was true, it amounted to this, that Jackson had died instead of James Elliot. If it had been James who had taken the call, well, then it might very easily have been James who was picked up dead.

James reacted violently. Well then, it mightn't, because he wasn't such a mug as to go meeting strange girls and then go blinding off with them into the blue.

The most frightful thought went through his mind like forked lightning—"You mightn't have thought it was going to be a strange girl. You might have thought it was going to be Sally, and you'd have gone with Sally."

For a moment after this everything crashed in confusion. Then his thoughts cleared again. That was nonsense, because when the telephone call came through he had already seen Sally. He wouldn't have needed any buttonhole to recognize her by. No, steady on—that was wrong. The call had come through just after he left work on the day before yesterday, and that was the night he had gone to Daphne's and met Sally. But if he had taken that call, would he have gone to Daphne's and met Sally there?

He thought this out. If Mr. Hazeby of Hazeby, Meredith & Hazeby—or purporting to be of Hazeby, Meredith & Hazeby—had got him on the telephone and asked him (a) had he driven a new Rolls under a trade number-plate into Sussex on the afternoon of the fourteenth, and (b) would he meet the girl he had there encountered, would he or would he not have said yes in both cases? The chances were that he would. He would probably have gone as far as the steps of the B.B.C. at any rate. It seemed a long way from there to the lane where Jackson had been found. Whether he himself would have taken that way or not he had no means of knowing. He wasn't as conceited as Jackson, and conceit always makes you gullible, but there was no knowing. You don't go about thinking that someone is trying to do you in.

He had another sharp reaction. The thing was absurd. Jackson had met with a perfectly ordinary accident. He heard Sally say, "It might be safer—for you," and "They mightn't know—how much—you had seen."

He sat quite still for ten minutes frowning at his empty plate. Then he drank his coffee, which had got cold, and went to the nearest call-box, where he looked up the number of a very well known firm of solicitors. When he got through he asked if Mr. John Poltney was in.

"No, not Sir John. I don't want Sir John. I want Mr. John Poltney. Is he in? . . . Hullo—hullo! . . . Hullo, is that you Jumbo? James speaking. I want some free information."

"You would!" said Mr. John Poltney alias Jumbo.

"Well, I do. I want to know about a firm called Hazeby, Meredith & Hazeby."

"What do you want to know about them?"

"I want to know if they're respectable."

Mr. John Poltney was heard to choke at the other end of the line.

"Oh gosh! I wish old Hazeby could hear you! No, I don't, for he'd certainly have a stroke, and he's not a bad old buffer."

"You know him?"

"Intimate friend of the guvnor's."

"Then he is respectable?"

"As the Bank of England. Firm's been going about a hundred years."

"They wouldn't handle anything shady?"

"Good lord, no! Steady, old-fashioned, highly lucrative connection. They don't touch criminal stuff."

"Thanks," said James.

"Is that all?"

James did not speak for a moment. Then he said,

"If I wanted to see Mr. Hazeby, could you arrange it?"

"How do you mean arrange it?"

"I might want to ask him something. If I did, I'd like him to know something about me first."

"All right—can do."

"Thanks," said James, and hung up.

XII

Hazeby, Meredith & Hazeby certainly did not sound the sort of firm who would ring up a young man in the motor trade and tell him to put a flower in his buttonhole and step along lively to meet a young lady friend of theirs who wanted to make his acquaintance. James put it with this vulgar baldness, but even wrapped up in the most beautiful high-toned phrases Hazeby, Meredith & Hazeby as described by Jumbo Poltney was hardly the kind of firm which would be found dealing with that kind of business. The Bank of England (Jumbo's comparison) does not unbend to arrange assignations.

He had been prepared from the first to find that Hazeby, Meredith & Hazeby were entirely bogus and nonexistent, because from the first he had been sure that the appointment made for Jackson was a bogus one. Now that he had discovered that the firm was not only real but ultra-respectable, it was clear that somebody had been taking its name in vain. He would make sure of this, but he was already convinced.

The appointment was most certainly bogus. Sally was already meeting him at Daphne's. Daphne had insisted on his coming when he hadn't wanted to come, and when she introduced him to Sally she prefaced the introduction by saying "Here he is." Sally therefore knew that she was going to meet him—had probably asked Daphne to get him there in order that she might meet him. *And Sally knew his name*. Knew his name—knew that Jocko had been his fag—knew that Daphne Strickland was his cousin—had known all these things from the moment—in the hay-loft—

when he told her he had been at Wellington. He was quite sure of this. Sally, therefore, apart from other intrinsic improbabilities, had no need to hire a firm of solicitors to find out who it was that she had been talking to in the fog.

But the person who had fired at them in the empty house—he or his associates—might have had pressing reasons for wanting to discover the driver of the car which had been parked on the grass verge. Sally herself had suggested a reason. "They mayn't be sure—how much—you had seen." He thought that they had wanted to be sure, and they had made a cast and caught Jackson. And Jackson was dead.

For the second time that day a nasty jag of forked lightning stabbed among his thoughts. Jab—stab—crash—and James left dizzy with the realization that Sally was in the most frightful danger. Was, must be, couldn't help being, because if they had found the car and taken the trouble to track it down and get hold of the driver, they would certainly have followed up Sally's bicycle too. They might have missed the car in the fog, because it was well off the drive and on the grass, but he didn't see how they could possibly have missed the bicycle. He hadn't missed it himself, he had as nearly as possible taken a header over it.

He tried to remember exactly how he had left the thing. He had picked it up. Yes, he had certainly picked it up, because that was when he had discovered that it was a woman's bicycle. And he had leaned it up against the step again. No, not against the step. There was a sort of balustrade thing, and he had leaned it up against the pillar of the balustrade. If it had been well away to one side, it was just possible that the First Murderer might have missed it. On the other hand, Sally obviously hadn't, because that was how she had cut her foot. She was running in her stocking feet and she had cut herself as she ran, probably on the pedal. He had tripped over it himself.

He frowned heavily and wondered what had happened to the bicycle. She might have sent it flying. He didn't remember a crash, but then he hadn't been bothering about crashes. There had been another shot just then. The bicycle might have fallen, and he might not have heard it. And it might have fallen in such a way as to pass unnoticed when the

First Murderer came bounding down the steps. He wouldn't have been expecting a bicycle. It was just possible that he hadn't seen it, and if so, Sally was safe, but if he had seen it, she must be in the same danger as he himself was. Bicycles are not so easy to trace as cars, but the F.M. might have put some sort of mark on it. James thought of several ways in which you could mark a bicycle for identification.

By this time his lunch hour was up and he had to go back and dance attendance on that notorious time-waster, Mr. Hartley.

The afternoon seemed interminable, because what he wanted to do was to get on to Daphne and wring Sally's address out of her, and then get on to Sally and tell her he must see her at once, and he couldn't do either of these things in business hours.

Mr. Hartley was a car-taster. He didn't like buying cars, he liked trying them. When he had worn out the patience of one firm he passed easily to another, all the time interlarding his conversation with such remarks as, "The Daimler I tried yesterday—" or, "I had one of the new Rollses out, and they're a pretty good proposition." By the time James got away he was feeling quite murderous. Mr. Hartley knew a great deal more about cars than anyone in the trade. Mr. Hartley was prepared to give driving hints to any expert alive. James reflected gloomily that Mr. Hartley was the sort that wanted his face pushed in.

All through the afternoon his mind was most dreadfully weighed down by the thought that something might be happening to Sally—now, at this very minute, whilst he was talking to that ass Hartley about automatic chassis lubrication, pre-selector gears, and down-draught carburettors. Of course he had no personal interest in the matter, but in common humanity you had to be horrified at the idea of a girl, any girl, being put out of the way. And if anyone had seen that bicycle, he thought Sally stood the same chance of being put out of the way as Jackson did when he claimed to have driven the Rolls on that foggy afternoon.

James's mental horizon brightened suddenly. The fog—he had been forgetting about the fog. The F.M. couldn't possibly have seen the bicycle, and it was most improbable that he had noticed it unless he had trodden on it or fallen over it. He'd have been in a hurry too, because he wouldn't have been sure whether the people he had fired at would go for the police. He would have been all set to get away as quickly as possible. And right there James began to wonder how he had got away—and how he had come. He probably had a car, rather craftily parked. Well, if he hadn't seen the bicycle or fallen over the bicycle, Sally was all right. But if he had . . . That was what it all came back to—suppose he had.

James's humanitarian feelings kept on getting stronger and stronger. He dashed back to the Mews as soon as he could get away and rang up his cousin Daphne. That is to say, he rang up his cousin Daphne's house. Daphne, he discovered, was at a cocktail party. Beyond the fact that she was dining out, and so, presumably, would return home to change, no one could give him any idea of what time he would be able to catch her. He rang again at a quarter to seven, at seven o'clock, and at a quarter past. He was still talking to a footman who sounded inexpressibly bored, when he heard Daphne say "Who is it?" The footman's cautious "Mr. Elliot" brought her on to the line.

"James, is that you? Darling, whatever you want, do make it snappy, because I'm going to be out all night, and there's a man waiting to do my hair, and a girl waiting to do my nails while Marthe does my face, so you see—"

James saw. He made it very snappy indeed. He said,

"I want Sally West's address and her telephone number."

Daphne laughed. It was a silvery laugh, which meant she was going to be irritating. James had once taken her by the scruff of the neck and shaken her until her eyes very nearly popped out for laughing like that, when he was fourteen and she was twelve. It still had exactly the same effect upon him, but he had to repress himself. He said in a tone of cold ferocity,

"I don't see anything to laugh at—and you're keeping your hairdresser waiting. I want Sally's address."

"*And* her telephone number. Don't forget her telephone number."

"I won't," said James. "What is it?"

Daphne laughed again. This time it was more of a giggle.

"Darling, I can't give it you. She absolutely made me *swear*."

"What nonsense!"

"I know, darling, but I don't see what I can do about it. I couldn't break a solemn vow."

"Couldn't you?" said James in his nastiest voice. "I should have thought you'd have any amount of practice. I seem to remember—"

"Darling, how unkind! I couldn't have believed you'd be so vindictive."

"Sally's telephone number," said James shortly.

"Darling, I positively can't. She made me swear—like glue."

"Well, look here," said James, "will you ring her up—now, at once? No waiting till you've had your hair done and forgetting all about it and going off to your blighted party and not coming home till the middle of tomorrow morning."

"Oh well—" said Daphne. "James, I think you get ruder and ruder."

"Are you going to do it—at once, as soon as I ring off—and then ring me up again and tell me whether you've got her?"

"All right. It's going to make me late."

"It doesn't matter how late it makes you. And, Daph—no messages—you've got to speak to Sally herself. If she's out, ask where she is and get her, get her somehow. I've got to speak to her at once. And hold your tongue about it, Daph!"

"Well, well," said Daphne. "All right, I'll do it."

James rang off.

It was about twenty minutes before Daphne's call came through. James had spent the time telling himself,

    (i)   That he was perfectly calm.

    (ii)   That Sally was perfectly safe.

    (iii)   That it didn't matter to him personally whether she was safe or not.

    (iv)   That it was necessary to preserve perfect calm.

    (v)   That the First Murderer couldn't possibly have seen the bicycle.

    (vi)   That it didn't matter whether he had seen it or not.

(vii)   That Sally was perfectly safe.

(viii)   That he was perfectly calm. . . .

The telephone bell rang, and Daphne said, "Hullo!"

"Me," said James.

She giggled.

"Gertrude doesn't keep a butler. All right, all right—don't be fractious, darling! I got her."

"Well?"

"Darling, I've worked like a black, and I shall be half an hour late for dinner, so I hope you're feeling really fervid, because of course she was out, and I had to track her to about six cocktail parties and she'd always *just* left as I got there. And she says—here's the important part—she says she'll ring you up at once."

"Then you'd better get off the line," said James.

"Darling! You overwhelm me! I never expected such gratitude!"

"Don't be an ass, Daph," said James, and rang off.

Five minutes later the bell rang again. A very faint, distant voice said "Hullo!"

James said "Hullo!" and the voice said, "Who is speaking?"

"James Elliot."

The voice said, "It's Sally. Daphne said you wanted to speak to me."

"Yes, I must. It's frightfully important. I want to see you."

Sally's voice sounded a little regretful.

"Sorry, James Elliot, it can't be done."

"Sally, I really must see you. Something's happened."

"What?"

"I can't tell you like this. I've got to see you."

There was such a long pause that he thought they had been cut off, but when he said "Hullo!" she said,

"All right—I'm here—I was just thinking. You're sure it's important?"

"Yes."

"Very well—just this once. We oughtn't to meet, you know. Or you don't know, but—we oughtn't to."

James took no notice of this.

"Where shall we meet?" he said.

"I'm supposed to be going to a dance. If I start early and arrive late, no one will be any the wiser—at least I hope not."

"Well?"

"I'd better come to you. You're in Gertrude Lushington's flat, aren't you? I'll take a taxi to the corner, and you can meet me there at a quarter to ten."

"I'll be there," said James.

XIII

CORBYN MEWS OPENS ON TO LITTLE CORBYN STREET, AND Little Corbyn Street runs into Hinton Road. The houses in Hinton Road, old-fashioned, inconvenient, and five storeys high, back on to the Mews. They have sunless basements and horrible long back yards, by courtesy gardens, which are the fighting-ground of every cat in the neighbourhood.

James walked from the corner fifty paces down Hinton Road and back to the corner and fifty paces down Little Corbyn Street. It was a bitter night with a cold wind blowing. Coming or going, the wind appeared to meet him full. The air smelt of frost. It was too early for the full chorus of the cats—too early, and perhaps too cold.

James hoped that Sally wasn't going to be late. He glanced at the luminous dial of his watch and found that it was just a quarter to ten. Before he had time to pull down his cuff a taxi drew up in front of the corner house. James was a dozen paces away. He stood still where he was in the shadow. He watched Sally get out and pay the driver. He watched the taxi move off and disappear up the road. Then he came up quickly and said,

"I was just wondering if you were going to be late."

"Brr!" said Sally. "Isn't it bitter? I was here first, James Elliot."

"No—I've been here ten minutes. Come along. I thought the taxi man had better not see me—just in case, you know."

Sally laughed under her breath.

"How discreet! Go right up to the top of the class! Where's this place of Gertrude's?"

"In here. It's only a step."

Sally said, "Brr!" again.

James felt an extraordinary sense of pride as he opened the door and ushered her up a ladder-like stair into his cousin Gertrude's studio. It was at any rate warm—an anthracite stove saw to that—and altogether it wasn't too bad if you didn't look too hard at the pictures. There was a Persian carpet on the floor, and some odd stripy curtains from Georgia, or Caucasia, or some other off-the-map sort of place where Gertrude had just missed coming to a sticky end. The stair came up through a hole in the floor, because the studio had once been a hayloft. James reflected that he and Sally seemed destined to meet in haylofts. He shut down the trap-door to keep out the draught, folded the rug back over it, and offered Sally a shapeless old red leather chair which he knew to be comfortable.

"Lovely and warm," she said. "My goodness—what's that?"

James said gloomily, "It's called Eve."

Sally gazed fixedly at the gaunt, grey female with the apple. Then she looked at the lobster in the left-hand corner and said,

"What's that?"

"A lobster."

"Why?"

"Ask Gertrude."

"Do you think she's going to eat it? It's already cooked."

"It's symbolic. The blue tadpole thing in the other corner is symbolic too. Gertrude told me so."

"I don't wonder Gertrude can't stay at home." She pulled her chair round so that she didn't have to look at Eve.

James took the other chair, the one you had to sit in carefully because the off front leg was loose.

"I oughtn't to be here," said Sally in rather an irresolute voice. "We ought never to see each other, or telephone, or anything. It's frightfully dangerous."

"For you?" said James.

"For both of us," said Sally.

She sat up straight in the leather chair and threw back her cloak. It was very long, and it was made of black velvet with a lining of white fur. Under it she had on a soft white filmy dress. There was a string of pearls round her neck. James told himself that there was no earthly reason why he should not admit that she was easy to look at—very easy—very, *very* easy.

"You're not listening," said Sally.

James blushed under the unshaded electric light. To his own horror, he heard himself say, "I was looking at you."

"Staring," said Sally.

James pulled himself together with a jerk.

"Perhaps you wouldn't mind repeating what you've said."

"I didn't say anything."

"But you said—"

"No I didn't. What was the good of saying anything when you weren't listening?"

James gave it up. Girls were like that. He said in a forbearing voice,

"All right, I'm sorry. Let's begin again. You said it was dangerous for us to meet. Why?"

Sally opened her green eyes wide.

"Can't you see that they mayn't be sure about you and they mayn't be sure about me, but if they see us together, they'll be sure about both of us."

"Why couldn't we have met at Daphne's? As a matter of fact we did. If you know Daphne, why should it be so compromising for you to know me?"

"I've known Daphne for more than a year. We met in the Tyrol. But that's not the point. Don't you see that if they saw your car the other day, and if they took the number, they could find out what firm it belonged to? Say they were rather suspicious of me, but not sure enough to do anything about it—well then, don't you think that if I'm friendly with someone employed by that firm, they'll be much, much more suspicious about both of us. They mayn't know you drove the car, but they're bound to keep an eye on anyone who might have driven it.''

"I've got to tell her about Jackson," said James to himself.

He got up and went over to the stove and rattled at the thing that let the ashes through and came back again.

"Look here," he said, "you keep on saying *they*, and I don't know who *they* are, but *they* don't think it was I who drove the car—*they* think it was Jackson."

"Jackson?" said Sally in a small startled voice.

"He was at Atwell's with me. He did most of the demonstrating."

"Did?" said Sally.

"He's dead," said James.

"Oh!" said Sally. It was more of a startled breath than a word—the sort of sound that she might have made if she had hurt herself. Only when they were running away together and she had cut her foot she hadn't made any sound at all. James remembered that.

He saw her black lashes dip for a moment and rise again. Her eyes were steady. So was her voice, though she only managed one word,

"How?"

"Someone rang up—after I'd gone, a couple of nights ago. He said he was Mr. Hazeby. Hazeby, Meredith & Hazeby are a very respectable firm of solicitors. I've made enquiries about them. I'm quite sure they hadn't anything to do with the business. I'm certain someone was just using their name."

Sally took a breath.

"Go on. What happened?"

"Jackson took the call, but the clerk, a girl called Daisy Callender, told me about it. She swears she could hear both ends of the conversation. I believe she did, because she told me what Lucas's said to me when I was talking to them this afternoon. She's got ears like a cat."

"What did she hear?" said Sally breathlessly.

"She heard this person who called himself Hazeby make

an appointment with Jackson. He began by asking about our trade plate and the Rolls, and Jackson said was there any complaint, and he said quite the reverse, and that the driver had been of service to a girl who was a client of his and she would like to thank him."

"*What*?"

"Yes. And as she'd only met him in the fog and couldn't be sure she would know him again, would he wear a buttonhole and meet her on the steps of the B.B.C."

"You're making it up."

"I'm not. Daisy Callender swears to it. And that ass Jackson fell for it, poor chap, and said he was the driver and buzzed off to meet the girl. He was like that, you know—a bit of a chaser."

"Yes," said Sally. "And?"

"He was picked up dead in a Surrey lane early next morning—run over."

Sally put a hand on either arm of her chair. Her fingers closed so tightly upon the worn red leather that the knuckles stood out white. She did not say anything at all. Her lashes went down, and the colour went out of her face. James hoped very much that she wasn't going to faint. She took a moment. Then she said quick and low,

"It might have been you."

"It may have been an accident," said James. He spoke quickly too, because quite suddenly he was most frightfully glad to be alive and it wouldn't have been decent to say so—not when they were talking about Jackson.

Sally shook her head.

"No, it wasn't an accident."

And with that James burst into speech.

"Look here, Sally, we can't go on like this. You can't just say it wasn't an accident and expect me to leave it at that, because, you see, if it wasn't an accident, it was murder, and if Jackson was murdered, he was murdered instead of me. He was a silly ass, and I've often thought he was an offensive ass, and he blobbed right into the middle of this thing because he *was* a silly ass, but the fact remains that he got murdered instead of me. I'm safe as long as they think they've wiped out the person who drove that car. I'm safe because Jackson was murdered. Don't you see, that puts it up to me to get back on them? I can't just stay safe and let them get away with it. You must see that."

Sally looked up, opened her lips to speak, shut them again, and looked down at the white stuff of her dress.

"Yes, I see," she said.

"Well, what are you going to do about it?"

She took her hands from the arms of the chair and folded them in her lap.

"If I tell you things, it's not going to be—safe—for you."

"I don't want to be safe while other people are being murdered, thank you."

Sally nodded.

"One has that feeling," she admitted.

"What about you?" said James.

She gave the faint laugh he had heard in the hayloft.

"Oh, *me*?" she said. "I shouldn't think it would make any difference. They mayn't bother about me, or they may. They haven't up till now."

"Sally, who are *they*?"

She looked down at her hands—pretty, bare hands with no rings.

Then she wasn't engaged. And what did it matter whether she was or no?

She said, "James—I'm going to tell you things. It isn't easy. It's not easy, because I've got to be fair, and it's very difficult to be fair about a thing like this. I'll tell you some things that happened, and you must draw your own conclusions. I don't want to tell you what I think about the things I'm going to tell you. I would like to know what you think about them. I'd like you to sit down."

James sat down in the uncertain chair.

"All right, Sally," he said, "go ahead."

She looked up then, but not at him. Her eyes went past him. She said,

"I told you I met Daphne in the Tyrol. Not last summer, the year before. It was at a place called Holbrunn. Jocko and I were both there—we were with a party. We got to know the Stricklands awfully well, and we did quite a lot of climbing." She stopped and looked at him. "It's awfully difficult. I don't think I've begun right. I think I ought to have begun with Aunt Clementa.''

"All right, begin again.''

She took a deep breath.

"I'm doing it very badly. You know what I told you in the hayloft about Aunt Clementa and her diamond necklace?''

"I know there was something about a diamond necklace.''

"I told you she'd hidden it and I'd gone to the house to look for it.''

"Yes,'' said James drily—''it was something like that. I thought it was a yarn.''

Sally looked away.

"Well, it was and it wasn't. She did hide something, but it wasn't the diamond necklace. At least she told me she'd hidden something. She was bedridden, you know. That's to say everyone thought she was bedridden, and she was awfully old and ill, so I didn't take much notice at the time. The nurse was in the bedroom with the door open between. She had two nurses and they took turns. One of them was always there. And when I really began to think about things I thought about that, because nurses generally go away tactfully when you come to see your bedridden relations. But these two didn't. Never. One of them was always hovering. And I didn't like either of them. One was smarmy, and the other all tight and starched—you know the kind. Well, that day it was the starched one. Aunt Clementa was supposed to be more or less unconscious—it was only a few days before she died—but all of a sudden I saw her looking at me. She was lying on her side with her back to the nurse, and she hooked a finger out of the bed-clothes and beckoned to me, so I bent down and said 'What is it?' and she began to whisper right in my ear. She said, 'I've got a letter for Annie. I want you to address it to her and post it yourself.' Well, I thought she was wandering, but she put her hand under the pillow and pulled out a crumpled envelope and pushed it into my hand. She said, 'Don't let her see. Quick—put it down the front of your dress!' So I did. And the nurse came out of the bathroom and asked if she wanted anything. I really did think Aunt Clementa was wandering, but I hated the nurse, so I said, 'I think she wants her handkerchief.' And Aunt Clementa groaned and rolled up her eyes. After a bit the nurse went back, and Aunt Clementa looked at me and winked."

"Who was Annie?" said James.

"The old maid she used to have. She'd been there twenty years, but she couldn't get on with the nurses, so she left. I thought she might have stuck it out myself, because the poor old pet missed her frightfully. All the old servants left round about then. They were supposed to be extravagant and I don't know what, but she liked them and they looked after her, and I thought it was a shame. Well, I wanted awfully to get rid of the nurse for a moment, but I didn't know how. Then I thought of a message, and she came over to the bed and took a good look at Aunt Clementa and primmed up her mouth, and I wondered if she was going to refuse, but she went. And the minute she was out of the room Aunt Clementa began to whisper again. She clutched at my hand, and she told me she had hidden the diamond necklace."

"I thought you said it wasn't a diamond necklace."

Sally threw him a fleeting glance.

"No, it wasn't a necklace, but I think we'd better go on calling it one."

"I thought you said she was bedridden."

"Well, she said she wasn't. That was one of the things she told me. She said she got up in the night and walked about, but no one knew, not even Annie. And I suppose she might have done it, because she hadn't had a night nurse very long, but of course she may just have imagined the whole thing. She hadn't time to finish telling me, and I couldn't ask any questions, because the smarmy nurse came in all hot and bothered. The other one must have sent her up whilst she went on my message, and that made me think a bit too. I didn't like any of it at all."

XIV

"WHAT DID YOU DO?" SAID JAMES IN HIS PRACTICAL WAY.

"I posted the letter to Annie. I didn't tell anyone, and I posted it. And next day we went off to the Tyrol—Jocko and I and the party I told you about."

"You didn't tell me who was in the party."

The colour ran up into Sally's cheeks.

"No—I didn't. I don't want to just now. I want to tell you what happened first. I didn't feel happy about leaving Aunt Clementa, but it had all been arranged, and by that time I was feeling quite sure that she had just been rambling. I wrote to two cousins and an aunt and told them to keep an eye on her and make sure the nurses were doing their job, and then I went off. Well, she died whilst I was on my way over. Jocko and I didn't go back for the funeral. We—we weren't encouraged to. Then when Jocko found she'd left him the house and a lot of money he felt rather bad about it. We both did. I suppose we ought to have gone, but—I told you we weren't encouraged, so we stayed at Holbrunn. My guardian went over, and when he came back he told Jocko about the will."

"You haven't told me anything about your guardian."

"No," said Sally. "But I will presently." Then she went on quickly, "This is a very difficult bit to tell. It's all difficult, but this is the worst bit."

"All right, go on."

"It's dreadfully difficult. We were all at breakfast one morning, and the post came in. There was a letter for Jocko, and when he opened it he said, 'Good Lord! What's old

Annie writing to me for?' And I tried to kick him under the table, because I knew it must be something to do with the letter I'd posted for Aunt Clementa, but I expect I kicked the wrong person, because he began to read Annie's letter out loud, and it just said Aunt Clementa had asked her to send him the enclosed, and she hoped he was very well, and kind regards from Annie. Well, 'the enclosed' was the crumpled envelope Aunt Clementa had given me. Everyone just sat, and Jocko opened it and took out the most awful scrawl and began to read that too. It began, 'Dear Jocko,' and then it went on, 'I'm going to die, and I've left you this house. I want you to find what I've hidden here. I've had to hide it because of *them*.' And when he'd got as far as that I couldn't bear it any longer, and I said, 'Jocko, you oughtn't to read that out. She didn't know what she was writing. It's not fair.' And my guardian said, 'Quite right, Sally,' and Jocko stopped. He just looked down the page, and he said, 'She must have been mad, poor old thing,' and he put it in his pocket. Well, after breakfast we all went out. We weren't doing a real climb, only scrambling about. Jocko had a very bad fall. He went over a place which ought to have killed him. There was a good wide ledge and lots of room. I was in front, so I didn't see what happened. Someone screamed, and when I turned round Jocko wasn't there. It was the most frightful time I've ever had, because it took us more than half an hour to get to a place where we could climb down, and then we had to work back to where he'd gone over, and when we did get there I thought he was dead. He wasn't, but I thought he was. I made a fool of myself. I just sat down and put my head in my hands, so I don't know what happened, but presently they said he wasn't dead—I think it was Daphne who said so—and between us we got him back to the hotel. By the time we got there I was all right again. I kept with him, and before they started to undress him I looked for Aunt Clementa's letter, but it wasn't there. I knew which pocket he'd put it in, but it wasn't there. I looked in all his pockets, and it wasn't in any of them.''

''It could easily have fallen out when he fell.''

Sally shook her head.

"No, it couldn't. It was in an inside pocket, and he had on a jerkin. It couldn't possibly have fallen out."

"Well, what did he say about it himself—about the fall and everything?"

Sally lifted one of her hands and let it fall on her knee.

"He never remembered anything. He had a very bad concussion, and he never remembered a single thing."

"Do you mean he didn't remember what was in the letter?'

"Not a thing—not then." .

"How do you mean, not then?"

Sally hesitated.

"He's remembered now—what was in the letter, I mean. At least I think he has. He hasn't told me straight out, but I think he's remembered, and I think that's why he's coming home."

"Yes?" said James.

"And I think it's very dangerous," said Sally.

James leaned forward.

"Why are you telling me all this?"

"Oh!" said Sally on a startled breath. She leaned back against her black velvet cloak and the red leather of the chair.

James looked sternly at her.

"What's the good of telling me anything if you don't mean to go the whole way? First of all you say I'm not to ask any questions, and then you give me about half the bits of a jigsaw puzzle and say 'Go on—make your own picture.' How can I make any picture if you don't give the pieces?"

"What pieces do you want?" said Sally.

"I'll tell you. If you answer my questions, I'll pick out what pieces I want."

Sally looked at him, and looked away, but she didn't speak.

"And the first thing I want to know is, did your Aunt Clementa really hide anything?"

"I don't know. She said she did."

"What did she hide?"

"I can't tell you that."

"You must."

"Papers," said Sally with a sigh. Then she straightened up. "And it's no good your putting over any more of that third-degree stuff on me, because I can't tell you what I don't know.''

"All right, all right. Now this business about Jocko. Who was there when he got your Aunt Clementa's letter?''

"All of us.''

"Who's 'all of us'?''

"It was at breakfast. We were all there.''

James gave her a raging look. He thought he knew something about how enraging girls could be, but Sally really was the limit. They generally did it to make you lose your temper, so he held on tight to his.

"You keep on saying 'all,' and 'we.' Do you mind telling me what that means? All the names please—one at a time.''

Sally's colour rose.

"Well, I was there,'' she said.

"Yes?''

"And Jocko.''

"Yes, I'd gathered that.''

"And Daphne and Bonzo,'' said Sally quickly.

"Bonzo? Was Bonzo Strickland there?''

Sally nodded.

"All the time. We were all great friends—we did everything together.''

"Well? Who else?''

There was a longish pause. The colour in Sally's cheeks burned high. Then she said all in a hurry,

"There was Hildegarde, and Henri.''

"Now we're getting there,'' said James to himself. "Bonzo and Daphne indeed! Stuff and rubbish!'' He said out loud,

"Do you mind telling me about Hildegarde and Henri? Who are they? You're not being exactly helpful, you know.''

"Oh—'' said Sally. And then, "Henri is Henri Niemeyer. He is Hildegarde's cousin.''

"Oh, he's Hildegarde's cousin? That explains everything— doesn't it? And who is Hildegarde?''

"Hildegarde is my guardian's wife.''

"And who is your guardian?''

She said in a perfectly colourless voice.

"My guardian is Ambrose Sylvester.''

XV

"*WHAT?*" SAID JAMES.

Sally said nothing. She looked down at her clasped hands.

James took her by the left wrist with his right hand and by the right wrist with his left hand and pulled her fingers apart. He kept his hold of her, a strong, hard hold, and he said,

"Are you making this up?"

Sally said nothing.

James rather shouted at her.

"Is this another Aspidistra Aspinall stunt? Because if it is, I'm not taking any!"

"No, said Sally—"it's true."

"Ambrose Sylvester is your uncle?"

"No, I never said he was my uncle. He's my guardian till I come of age. I'm not twenty-one yet."

James went on holding her wrists.

"You don't mean Ambrose Sylvester the novelist?"

"Yes, I do."

"The one with the profile?"

Sally was like all the other girls. She sighed.

"It's a lovely profile."

James shook the wrists he was holding.

"What does a man want with a profile?"

An odd look flitted over Sally's face. She didn't say anything.

"Can you read his stuff?" said James.

She nodded.

"Yes—it's beautiful."

James let go of her and sat back.

"Well, let's get on. Is that the lot? Or was there anyone else in your party?"

"No—no one else."

"Well, that's you and Jocko, and Bonzo and Daphne, Sylvester and Mrs. Sylvester and her cousin Niemeyer. How many of these people were on the ledge with Jocko when he fell?"

"All of them," said Sally.

"Do you know who was nearest to him?"

She shook her head.

"I was in front. The last time I looked back Jocko was between Bonzo and Hildegarde. It was quite a wide ledge and there was room to pass. Daphne says she stayed behind to pick gentians—she didn't see what happened. The ledge was very winding. Honestly, James, if he was pushed, anyone might have pushed him, and if the letter was taken out of his pocket, anyone might have taken it." She slid back the chair and got up. "I'm glad I've told you, because I had gone over it, and over it, and over it in my mind until I'd got it all twisted up, but now I've told you, I can see that there isn't anything in it. It was just an accident—it must have been."

"Yes? What about the letter?" said James.

She flashed into a sudden radiant smile.

"I've been stupid. Oh, how stupid I've been! Don't you see, Jocko must have torn it up himself. Why should he keep it? Of course he tore it up. What a relief!" She snatched up her cloak and pulled it round her. "I must hurry, hurry, hurry! I *want* to dance now—I didn't before! Oh, don't you wish you were coming too? Would you like to?"

Suddenly, violently, James did wish it. His eyes said so. His tongue said something that it had begun to say.

"Somebody shot at us all the same. And someone did Jackson in."

That was what his tongue said, but next moment he could have bitten it savagely, because Sally's smile went out and her eyes stopped shining at him. She said in a woeful voice,

"I'd forgotten. I was only thinking about Jocko. You mustn't come. We mustn't see each other again."

It knocked James off his balance. He minded. That was

what knocked him over—he minded frightfully. Why? He had met her three times, and of those three times he had only seen her twice. Why should it knock him over like that to be told that he couldn't see her again? He stood there staring at her and stammering her name.

"Sally—Sally—"

She was clutching the big black cloak about her. It flowed over her in dark waves and hid all the whiteness of her dress. She went back a step and tapped the floor with her foot.

"Don't! You mustn't! I must go."

"Sally!"

She was on the edge of tears. She tapped the floor again.

"Open it and let me go!"

James got hold of himself. He said in quite a steady voice,

"In a moment, Sally—you can give me a moment. We've got to straighten this out. You say we mustn't meet. Why?"

"Dangerous—I told you—" She choked a little.

"Dangerous for you, or for me?"

"For you—and for me—and for Jocko-—dangerous for us all."

"They think it was Jackson," said James doggedly.

"Suppose they find out it wasn't—and they find out we're friends. How long do you suppose it would be before one of us—had—an accident? And Jocko is coming home— he'll be here any day now—and we'd be dragging him into it. Don't you see it won't do? Let me go! I oughtn't to have come—I knew I oughtn't to!"

James stood obstinately on the trap-door which covered the stair.

"Why did you come?"

Sally looked at him.

"Because I wanted to."

"Do you want to go?"

She shook her head.

"Then must you?"

She nodded. A round, bright tear fell upon the velvet of her cloak.

James came forward, but he didn't touch her. He folded back the carpet, raised the trap-door. The steep ladder-like stair showed under the overhead light. He stood aside to let

Sally go down, and slowly, still clutching her cloak about her, she went down out of his sight. When she had reached the bottom he followed her.

The passage was very narrow. It was very dark there. He went to the outer door to open it, but at the last moment his hand dropped from the knob and he turned round again.

"Come here, Sally," he said, and Sally came. She came right into his arms and put up her face to be kissed, and he kissed her. Then she put her head down on his shoulder and cried.

James held her in a strong, angry clasp. He was feeling a strong, furious anger which made him want to smash something. Not Sally. She was his little Sally. To have and to hold. That was out of the marriage service. He had heard Bonzo say it to Daphne, and he had thought that Daphne would want some holding. Well, he meant to hold Sally against the world, and he meant to smash anyone who tried to come between them.

Sally said in a soft, crying voice, "Let me go," and his clasp tightened. He said,

"I'll never let you go. You're mine."

"I can't be," said Sally—"I mustn't."

"You are."

Sally gave a small heart-broken sob.

"It's no use. Why does it hurt like this? We don't really know each other. We've got to forget."

He tipped up her chin and kissed her. Her face was all wet with her tears. Her lips were trembling. They trembled against his. He said in an angry voice,

"Are you going to forget?"

Sally said "No" with a sob. And then, "I must. They'd kill you."

"Now we're getting down to it!" said James. "Now look here, Sally, I'm not taking any of this stuff about our not seeing each other again. It's no earthly use your trying to put it across me, because I'm not having any. I suppose I've fallen in love with you, and I suppose you've fallen in love with me. I don't know why it's happened to us, but it has. You're mine and I'm yours, and we're not going to give each other up. We're going to belong."

"We can't," said Sally.

"I do wish you wouldn't keep on saying that sort of thing! Whatever way you look at it, seems to me you want someone to look after you, and if there's any dirty work going on, well you want someone all the more—don't you?"

Sally said, "Yes." And then, "Let me go now."

James went on holding her.

"We can meet without anyone knowing if you think it's necessary. I shouldn't have said it was myself."

Sally pulled away from him with a sudden strength.

"James—please let me go. I must show up at this dance. Let me go now. I'll write to you—I promise I will."

"Swear?"

"Yes, I will. Don't you think I want to?"

He stood away from the door and opened it.

"I'll get you a taxi."

"No. It's only just round the corner—24 Hinton Road— the Naylands. You can walk round there with me if you like, but I must tidy up my face first. Is there a light down here?"

He put it on. They were back to ordinary things again, but the tears that stained her face had been shed against his shoulder. The salt taste of them was still upon his lips. He watched her with her powderpuff and lipstick, and at the end she looked at him with a shaky smile and a lift of the brows which asked,

"Am I all right?"

James said, "Yes." And then, "There's a little too much powder on the left side of your nose."

And then he took her round to No. 24 and rang the bell, and stood well back in the shadow to see her go into the brightly lighted hall. He did not kiss her again.

XVI

James rang up his cousin Winifred Lushington and asked her to lunch next day. She was Gertrude's sister, and they were a good bit older than the other cousins, being the daughters by an early and extremely improvident marriage of his mother's eldest sister, Frederica.

Winifred Lushington had pushed her way brightly into journalism at the age of seventeen. She was now the assistant editress of a woman's paper. Like her sister Gertrude she was strongly and squarely built and rather wildly dressed. Her thick iron-grey hair always looked as if she had just cut it herself with a pair of nail-scissors. She wore large tortoiseshell glasses with bright yellow rims. Behind them her hazel eyes were very intelligent and alive. She was never quite able to forget that she was fifteen years older than James and had frequently spanked him in the past. She had even, under supervision, given him his bottle. These things had induced a superiority complex which sometimes annoyed James a good deal. He was, however, prepared to put up with it today.

It was as well that he had braced himself, because Winifred's manner was distinctly tinged with the kind of solicitude which you expect from an aunt but resent in a cousin. She ordered lentil cutlets with tomato sauce, and a large cup of cocoa, a combination which made James shudder, and enquired how he was getting on at Atwells, using exactly the tone which all his aunts had used whenever they came down to see him at school. It required an effort of will to prevent himself from frowning as he replied that he was getting on all right, thank you Winifred.

The lentil cutlets having arrived, Winifred Lushington helped herself to butter, pepper, salt, mustard, and vinegar. She stirred these into the tomato sauce, and then mashed the cutlets and mixed the whole thing together, talking all the time.

"You've been with them two years now, haven't you? . . . Oh, not quite? Well, I thought it was, because it was just after Daphne's wedding, but of course you ought to know. Well now, have you decided whether you'll put Aunt Millie's money into them or not?"

James said he hadn't decided yet.

"Well, what will you do if you don't? That's what I always say when people ask my advice. The job mayn't be perfect—very few jobs are—but what's the alternative? That's what I say."

"I might set up on my own," said James, who hadn't asked her advice and didn't want it.

Miss Lushington put five lumps of sugar into her cocoa and stirred it vigorously.

"Far too risky," she announced. "One of the girls in the office had a brother who did that, and he lost every penny."

James became unable to restrain himself from frowning. His fair, thick eyebrows made an angry line across his face.

"Where is Gertrude?" he enquired brusquely.

Winifred sipped her cocoa.

"Somewhere in the Caucasus, I believe. She doesn't write, you know—not unless she wants something—but she's promised us a series of articles when she gets back. I shall have to write them of course—Gertrude's bone lazy. And we're paying her quite well too."

James's frown relaxed. Winifred was all right if he could keep her off his own affairs, but he had asked her to lunch with a purpose, and that purpose was not to talk about her sister Gertrude. He ate cold ham in silence whilst she talked shop about Gertrude's articles, and then broke in abruptly,

"Do you know Ambrose Sylvester?"

Winifred stopped with a piece of mashed cutlet half way to her mouth.

"How do you mean, do I know Ambrose Sylvester?"

"I mean do you know him?"

"Everybody knows him, don't they? I don't know him personally."

James didn't allow himself to be disappointed. There were very few people in the public eye about whom Winifred didn't know quite a lot. You couldn't vouch for the truth of everything she knew, but if you wanted the current gossip, well, Winifred would deliver the goods. He grinned affably and said,

"Well, come along—what do you know about him?"

She ate her piece of cutlet and washed it down with cocoa.

"My dear James, you must know all about him—everyone does."

"Well, I don't. And I want to. You can begin at the beginning and go right through to the end."

"Is that what you asked me to lunch for?" said Winifred with unnerving perspicacity.

"That, and the pleasure of your company," said James, who had been quite nicely brought up, though he didn't always remember it.

Miss Lushington gave her odd short laugh.

"All right, then we know where we are. This is very good cocoa. You shall have your *quid pro quo*. What do you know already?"

"That he's a famous novelist with a famous profile—that he wrote a book called *Links in the Chain*—that I tried to read it and stuck half way."

"Very stupid of you, my dear boy, because it really is a great book. Seven years ago, and it's still selling. Well, if that's all you know, I can certainly add to it." She put her elbows on the table and her chin in her hands. "*Links in the Chain* came out seven years ago when he was about thirty. He had already published a book of travel which was moderately successful, and two novels which were not. Then *Links in the Chain* came out, and it had the most colossal boom—the sort of boom there's no accounting for. Mind you, it's a great book. I read it again the other day, and it's great. But I don't know whether it would have had quite such a boom if Ambrose Sylvester had been a plain, scraggy young man instead of the very picturesque person he was and is. He photographs beautifully, and the profile took the public eye." She paused and refreshed herself with a sip of cocoa.

"Well?" said James.

"Well, his second book was very good too—*Janet Sefton*. It went very big. Not quite so big as *Links*—second books very seldom do—but quite big enough. And he wrote about a dozen absolutely first-class short stories. They are bound up under the title of *Primrose Hill*. And then he stopped. Let me see . . . *Links* was seven years ago—and *Janet Sefton* six—and *Primrose Hill* came out in nineteen-thirty-one. And that's all."

"He doesn't write now?"

"He hasn't published anything since *Primrose Hill*."

"Why?"

Winifred sat up, called a waitress, and ordered peaches and cream and a slice of fruit cake—"and another cup of cocoa please." Then she turned back to James and said as if there had been no interruption,

"He can't."

"Why can't he?"

She shrugged her square shoulders.

"Does he say he can't?" pursued James.

"Of course he doesn't. He says he's working on his *magnum opus*. And can't be hurried. Mustn't hurry genius, you know."

"That all rot!" said James. "What's behind it?"

"What I said at first—he can't write now." She paused, looked brightly through the yellow-rimmed glasses, and added, "If he ever could."

"And what do you mean by that?" said James.

"I don't want to get run in for libel," said Miss Lushington, cutting up a peach very small and putting sugar on it.

"Be a sport, Winifred!"

The fear of figuring in a libel case is no real deterrent to women. They are much braver than men.

"All right, but you mustn't quote me. Besides I don't know anything. It's only putting two and two together, and what Leslie Merrivale said."

"Well?"

"Well, Leslie always did say that—no, I really don't think I'd better."

"Don't put any names to it, but tell me what they said."

Winifred brightened.

"Yes, I might do that. Well, what they said was that Ambrose hadn't written those books at all—he'd pinched them. And Leslie said he'd pinched them from her cousin Tim Merrivale, because he was Ambrose Sylvester's friend and they shared rooms and did everything together. And she says she knows that Tim had written two novels and a lot of short stories before he died, and nothing was ever heard of them. So it looks rather like it, because *Links in the Chain* came out six months later. And I'll tell you something only a few people know," said Winifred, warming to her indiscretion. "And I only know it because Poole who reads for Ambrose Sylvester's publishers is a great friend of Fanny Rivers, and he told Fanny, and Fanny told me."

"Yes?" said James.

"Well, he said they kept pressing Ambrose for another book, and he kept putting them off. And they went on pressing, and at last he sent one in, and it was so bad *they simply couldn't publish it*. Poole told Fanny he'd never read such stuff. He said it would have smashed any reputation. So it does look rather as if Leslie was right."

"I don't know—people do dry up like that sometimes. Don't they?"

"Oh, yes, they do." Her tone was a doubtful one. She ate her peaches.

"Well, that's that," said James. "Next instalment please, Winifred. Marriage—domestic relations—money affairs—"

"Oh, he's married," said Miss Lushington. She took a deep draught of cocoa. "He's married all right. I've interviewed her."

"All right, spill the beans."

"Well, her parents were Belgian refugees, and her name was Hildegarde Niemeyer. I believe her mother was half German. I think there was some talk about them on that account, and I don't think they were exactly pressed to stay over here. They seem to have gone to South America with Hildegarde. Anyhow, that's where Ambrose Sylvester met her. The parents were dead by then, and she was said to have a large fortune, but I'm sure I don't know where it came from, because Agnes Carey knew the Niemeyers, and she says they never had a farthing. Anyhow, there must have been a good deal of money somewhere, because I happen to know that Ambrose was in fairly low water that year, and there's never been any sign of it since."

"He must have made pots of money out of his books—or didn't he?"

"Quite a lot. In fact, James, what you and I would call a fortune. But he's got fairly expensive tastes, and he bought a big place, and big places take a lot of keeping up."

"Where is it?" said James.

"In Sussex. Warnley Place it's called."

James sat up.

"Warnley?" He was remembering coming over Warnley Heath in a fog, and losing his way, and finding Sally.

"Yes. Do you know it?"

"I've been over Warnley Heath."

"Well, it would be thereabouts. I think I'll have another piece of cake just to finish my cocoa."

James ordered the cake.

"Go on," he said. "What's she like, Mrs. Sylvester? You interviewed her."

"A very vivid personality. The sort of woman who never lets anyone find out how plain she is. Very smart, very up-to-date, very fine eyes, painted like a poster. The day I interviewed her she was wearing that hideous mustard shade which French women love, and she was made up a sort of Red Indian colour, with bright orange lips and orange finger-nails."

"It sounds beastly."

"A bit dazzling, but I'm bound to say it was effective. It so to speak hit you in the eye."

"When I'm hit in the eye I want to hit back. Go on—tell me everything you know."

"Well, I don't know very much—only what she told me herself. The usual blurb, you know. There was an enormous photograph of Ambrose at her elbow, and she said she adored him, and there was a Peke in her lap, and she said she adored the Peke, and there was an enormous conservatory opening out of the drawing-room, and she said she adored her flowers and she was quite sure she would die if she had to do without them. And I said there seemed to be plenty to be going on with, and she said, 'How clever!' and told me she adored clever people.''

"Is she as stupid as that sounds.''

"Oh, I don't think so,'' said Miss Lushington. "Some people are of course, but not Mrs. Ambrose Sylvester. I thought it was make-up, like the lips and nails, and I thought she was putting it on a bit thick, and I didn't feel flattered.''

"I see,'' said James.

"There's a cousin who hangs about—a Niemeyer. There's some talk about them, but of course there's always some talk about everyone. And there's a ward of Ambrose's, a girl called Sally Something-or-other—oh, yes, West—Sally West—but I don't think there's any talk about her.''

"Thanks,'' said James.

XVII

THERE WAS A LETTER WAITING ON THE MAT WHEN JAMES got back to the Mews that evening. He hadn't ever seen the writing before, and his heart gave a jump, because he guessed at once that it was from Sally.

He ran upstairs, switched on the light, and sat down on the edge of the trap to read the letter. It *was* from Sally, and it began: "Oh, James—'' And then there was a blot, and James's heart gave another thump, but not such a pleasant one, because the blot had every appearance of having been made by a tear, and why should Sally cry if everything was all right? And what sort of letter was it that began "Oh, James''? He went past the blot and found out.

"Oh, James, we mustn't—I know we mustn't really, and then you kissed me, and everything felt different, and I thought we could"—there were three little blots here very close together—"but we can't, and we mustn't see each other again, and you mustn't write. It can't go on being so bad when we've only seen each other three times. You'll meet someone ever so much nicer than me. I ought to have told you I was practically engaged to Henri Niemeyer. Goodbye. You *mustn't* write." There was a very large blot, and the signature was smudged and ran away off the paper as if she hadn't been able to see what she was doing.

James was so angry that he would probably have shaken her if she had been there. Engaged to Henri Niemeyer, was she? The cousin who hung about after Hildegarde Sylvester. No, she didn't say she was engaged, she said she was practically engaged. How could you be practically engaged? Girls just flung words about without stopping to think what they meant. She was either going to marry the man or she wasn't.

She wasn't.

James felt perfectly sure of that. He intended to make it his business to see that she didn't marry anyone except James Elliot. It was all fixed and settled. Letters like this were just a waste of time.

He considered the position. In his present job at Atwells he couldn't very well marry. He might stay on with them on a different footing if he decided to put his Aunt Millie's legacy into the business. There might be a branch managership going. Or he might set upon his own. He wanted to discuss these things with Sally in a sensible, comfortable way instead of replying to insensate letters in which she told him that she was practically engaged to someone else.

He went downstairs and called up his cousin Daphne. The footman whom he disliked answered the telephone and said languidly that Madam was in, but Madam had given orders that she was not to be disturbed.

James grinned. That meant that Daphne was lying down and reading a novel. He said,

"That's all right—it's urgent. Put me through to her room please. Mr. Elliot speaking."

"Madam gave orders—"

"Kindly tell her that Mr. Elliot wishes to speak to her urgently."

There was a pause, and after some time a click. And then Daphne's voice, rather peeved.

"James, *is* it you? Because *really*—"

"Of course it is. Look here, Daphne—"

"Darling, I do really think I might be allowed a little rest! I was up till four last night, and—"

"Dry up, Daph, and listen! I want you to help me."

"Darling, I don't see how I can if I have a nervous breakdown."

"You won't. Look here, what I want you to do is this. If I write to Sally and send the letter to you—"

"If you *what*?"

"Daph, you're not listening. If I write a letter to Sally—"

"Sally *who*?"

"Sally West, of course."

"Why don't you ring her up? I mean, darling, *really*—I mean, why ring me if you want Sally?"

James gritted his teeth, and he hoped Daphne could hear him doing it.

"I don't want to ring her up, I want to write to her."

Daphne giggled.

"All right, why don't you? I don't mind, and I don't suppose she will. It's 18 Messenger Square, if you want the address. She's Ambrose Sylvester's ward, but I suppose you know that."

"Her brother was my fag at Wellington."

Daphne yawned.

"Yes—she said he was. Is that all, because—"

"No, it isn't. I said I wanted you to help me. If I write to Sally, can you give her the letter without anyone knowing?"

"Darling, how thrilling! Are you proposing to her? And why so hush-hush if you are? She probably won't have you—she's supposed to be engaged to Henri Niemeyer."

James said in a tone of concentrated fury,

"Daphne, will you dry up and listen! I want Sally to get this letter, but I don't want anyone to know about it. She won't let me write to her, but she's got to have this letter. I want her to have it as soon as possible. I can't tell you any more than that. The question is, can you do it?''

"Darling, of course. It sounds too romantic. She's practically sure to be at Marcella's tonight.''

"Well, mind you don't muff it,'' said James ungratefully. "I don't want anyone to know.''

"Trust your Daffy.''

"All right,'' said James, "I'll come round with the letter. I'll put it inside one addressed to you. And mind you don't give the show away.''

He went back to the studio and wrote to Sally. There was no beginning to the letter. He wrote:

"I do wish you wouldn't send me letters which don't mean anything and are simply a waste of time. And I do wish you wouldn't write letters that make you cry. I don't mind telling you that your letter made me very angry. The bit about your being practically engaged to Niemeyer doesn't seem to me to mean anything at all. You are not going to marry him, so what is the sense of saying you are practically engaged to him? It just doesn't mean anything. Daphne is going to give you this, so you needn't be afraid that anyone will know.

"Now I want to tell you about myself, because if we are thinking of getting married, I should like you to know where I stand. I told you my father was in the army. He is at present commanding his regiment, and will probably retire next year. He has about five hundred a year private means, but he won't expect to give us an allowance, as he and my mother will want it all, but I suppose it will come to me some day, though not for a very long time, I hope. I should like you to meet my mother. She is very easy to get on with. Last year my great-aunt Millicent Elliot left me two thousand pounds. I have been considering whether I would put it into Atwells' business—that is the motor firm I am working for. They might put me in as manager of a new branch. I should try to get a month's holiday, as I didn't get one at all last year and I should be putting money into the show—that is to say if I did decide to put it in. I don't know what you feel about this, but I would like you to think it over, and then we can have a talk. If you tell Daphne when and where you will meet me, she will pass it on. She's quite safe really. She talks a lot, but she doesn't give much away.

"Don't talk any more nonsense about our not seeing each other. You make me want to smash someone.

"You're not to cry any more.

"I love you very much.

"When you write your next letter tell me that you love me.

> "James."

He put this letter in an envelope and addressed it to Miss Sally West, then he put it inside a larger envelope which he addressed to Mrs. Strickland, and then he walked round to the Stricklands' house and gave the letter to the supercilious footman.

XVIII

When James arrived at Atwells next morning he was greeted by Miss Callender in a manner which immediately suggested that there had been happenings, and that she desired nothing better than to impart them. She wore an air of importance just tinged with melancholy. It was such an air as would befit a person of decorum who has suddenly been bereft of a wealthy relative and finds himself down for a substantial legacy.

James came into the little office, made some routine enquiry, and waited to see what would happen.

"No, they haven't written," said Miss Callender. "They

always take longer than anyone else. Oh, Mr. Elliot, I've broken it off with Lenny—last night.''

"Much better than going on with it if you're not sure," said James, feeling stubbornly sure that he was going to marry Sally and that Sally was going to marry him.

Miss Callender heaved a dutiful sigh.

"That's just what Mother said. And I'm sure I can't be too thankful, because really, Mr. Elliot, you've no idea how he went on—last night, I mean. And in front of his mother too part of the time, and she didn't say anything, but she sat there pursing her lips and knitting a black shawl with a purple stripe at the edge. And all at once I saw just how it was going to be for hundreds and hundreds of evenings, Mrs. Rowbotham knitting black shawls and Lenny being jealous if I didn't want to knit them too, and I said, 'That's enough, Mr. Rowbotham—there's no need to say another word, because we're not engaged any longer, and what I do and what I don't do is no concern of yours,' and I took off his ring and put it down on one of the tidies Mrs. Rowbotham made the year she was married. She's got the whole room full of tidies, and very single thing has to be put down on one of them, so I put the ring there, and I said, 'Goodbye, Lenny,' and I ran out quick, because I didn't want them to see me cry. Only when I got outside I didn't want to cry any more, and besides, it wouldn't have done, because Bert Simpson happened to come along, and he asked if he could see me home, so I said yes, but we went to the pictures instead. And oh, Mr. Elliot, you can't think what a weight off my mind it was to feel that I could go out with Bert—he's ever such a nice boy and he's always wanted to be friends—and that we could enjoy ourselves, and no business of Lenny's and no scenes afterwards. It just brought it home to me what an escape I'd had.''

As James came out of the office, he was aware of a young man in a blue serge suit and a bowler hat. The slight tilt of the hat displayed tightly crinkled hair of a flaming red which took James straight back to his school study and a fag who always burned the toast for tea. The eyes under the bowler's brim were a light, dancing hazel. James knew him at once, but before he had time to speak the young man darted at him and clapped him on the shoulder.

"Hullo, 'ullo, 'ullo! Got you in one! Daphne said I would find you here. I can't think why we haven't run into each other before. Last time you chucked a dictionary at my head."

"I expect you had burnt the toast, J.J.," said James.

"No, not that time—it was the big ink-bottle all over your best flannel bags. Well, well, I dropped out of the blue last night. Literally, you know—I've just flown from India. And I want to buy a car. And Daphne said 'Run along and do my cousin James Elliot a good turn,' and I said, 'What James Elliot?' And then she produced the family tree, and I discovered that you really were my James Elliot—old school tie and that sort of thing. So I said 'Done!' But Sally—by the way, you know my sister Sally, don't you?"

James said yes, he did know Sally.

"Well," said Mr. Jock West, "have you been having a row with her or something?"

James said no, he hadn't been having a row, and why should he?

"Well, I don't know, but she didn't seem to want me to come round. No keenness about my doing you a good turn, so to speak. She and Daphne weren't seeing eye-to-eye about it, if you know what I mean, so I left them to it and buzzed along."

"Very nice of you, J.J.," said James rather grimly.

So Sally had tried to prevent her precious Jocko from coming near him. The sooner Sally adjusted herself to the idea that he and Jocko were going to be brothers-in-law, the better. He said,

"What sort of car do you want?"

Jocko grinned. He had rather a pale face and a lot of freckles.

"Something fast and nippy. Something that will push a hole in the speed-limit and leave the cops guessing. *Quelquechose de sportif*," he added with an atrocious French accent. "And never mind the price." He smote James again. "My good man, do you realize that I'm full of money? You don't because I don't, and I don't because Aunt

Clementa's lawyers have only just coughed up, and I'd got to the point when no one would give me another ha'porth of credit—dirty dogs! So until I've landed out a good round dollop on something I shan't believe the money's real. Has Sally told you about my Aunt Clementa?''

''She said she'd left you some money.''

Jocko tipped his hat on to the back of his head and ran his fingers through his hair.

''Some money! Did she tell you how much it was? Five thousand—''

''Five thousand pounds?''

''*A year!*'' said Jocko. ''Think of it! Get it into the head—if you can! I haven't been able to yet. Fifty pounds a year and my pay—that was my form. Sally had a godmother who left her three hundred a year, but my little private income was fifty. And Aunt Clementa leaves me five thousand pounds a year and a stately home of England—also a hush-hush letter which got lost when I fell over a precipice in the Tyrol last year! By the way, Sally will be livid if she knows I've told you that. She's got the most frightful bee in her bonnet about the letter, and the accident, and all that. I suppose she hasn't said anything to you about it?''

''Why should she?'' said James. ''If you don't mind expense, and want a really first-class sports model—''

Jocko declined the red herring.

''Oh, well, she might, you know. Of course I don't know how well you know her.''

''You'd better ask her,'' said James, and began to talk about cars in a firm, professional voice.

He was assisted by the appearance of Mr. Parkinson, but presently, Jocko having demanded a trial run, he found himself heading in the direction of the Great West Road.

''I should think she'd be just what you want.''

''Well, I'm going to try 'em all,'' said Jocko. ''And we've got to get somewhere where we can let her out. Thirty miles an hour's no use to me—I'd just about as soon walk. Didn't Sally tell you about the house Aunt Clementa left me? It's called Rere Place. Aunt Clementa was a Rere—the last of the family. They've got a coat-of-arms with three rere-mice in it—bats, you know—and I think they were a pretty batty lot. There are some awfully queer tales about the house. Sally hates it, but I'm going to live there.''

''You're not going to chuck the army!''

''I don't think so. I'd rather like to do a spot of racing at Brooklands, but I haven't made up my mind. I've got six months' leave, and I thought I'd open up the house and see how I liked it. Besides, there's that letter. I expect the old girl was batty, but there's just the chance—Did I tell you about the letter, or didn't I?''

''You didn't tell me what was in it,'' said James.

''Not didn't—*couldn't*. You see, I don't suppose I ever read it, because Sally says I got it at breakfast, and she says I began to read it and shut up and put it in my pocket. And then we all went climbing, and I took a toss, and the next thing I knew was about three days later, and I couldn't remember anything about anything. I mean I couldn't have sworn that I'd had my breakfast that day, or gone climbing, or taken a toss, so naturally I didn't remember whether I'd ever finished reading the letter or not. If I did, I'd forgotten all about it, but quite likely I didn't. And the letter was gone. That's where Sally's bee comes in—she swears somebody pinched it, and I'm not at all sure she doesn't believe that somebody tried to do me in. Now I ask you—''

James gave a quick glance at him. He had an air of being innocently surprised, but then J.J. always did look innocent when he knew he had burned the toast. He thought there was a gleam in the greenish hazel eyes.

James said nothing.

Jock West laughed.

''Cautious Scot—aren't you? How much did Sally tell you?''

''You might ask her,'' said James with his eye on the road.

''Hang it all, Elliot, who could possibly want to do me in?''

''I don't know.''

''Well, there you are. All the same, I'd like to know what was in that letter. I wonder if I did read it all, because I can only remember—''

''Oh, then you do remember some of it?''

''Suppose I do?''

James glanced at him again.

"Then I think I should shut my mouth on it."

XIX

JAMES GOT NO ANSWER FROM SALLY. BY THE THIRD evening he had reached the point of ringing Daphne up to ask whether she had delivered his letter. Daphne's voice, irritatingly sweet, came fluting over the wire.

"Of course, darling. I gave it to her at once—that evening. She was at the Osbornes', and I pushed it under her cloak when she was going away and said, 'Hush—not a word!' And, darling, if it's any comfort to you, she blushed like fury. I really do feel a little bit sorry for poor Henri, because he's *very* devoted, and everybody's been saying that they're engaged, or just going to be, for simply ages."

James said something short and rude about Henri, and rang off. He then looked up Ambrose Sylvester's number and dialled it. Just what he would have done it if had been Ambrose himself, or the decorative Hildegarde, or the devoted Henri who had answered, he did not stop to think, and fool's luck favoured him. It was Sally who said "Hullo!"

James's heart gave an uncomfortable thump. He said in a voice that sounded like someone else's,

"Sally, is that you?"

There was a pause. Then Sally said,

"Yes. Who is it?"

"James. Sally, why didn't you answer my letter? Daphne says she gave it to you. Sally—*darling*—"

"You've got the wrong number," said Sally in a small cold voice. "Will you ring off, please." And with that the receiver was hung up and the line went dead.

James, quite white with anger, returned to the studio and raged up and down there, restraining himself with a good deal of difficulty from kicking holes in his cousin Gertrude's canvases. He felt a special urge to kick a hole in Eve. Several holes. It would have been extraordinarily assuaging to fling Eve down on the studio floor and stamp on her, and her symbolic lobster, and her horrible blue tadpole.

He tore himself from this thought to sit down and write a violent letter to Sally, but when he had written about five sheets he got up suddenly and crammed them into the stove, where they burned away to nothing in about half a minute. A second letter followed the first. It ran less to violence and more to passion. James found himself writing at great speed, and without stopping to think, the sort of things which it had never previously occurred to him that anyone in real life could possibly write, or think, or say. The fact that he was not only doing it, but doing it in the most unreserved manner so appalled him that he stopped in the middle of the third sheet and cremated the document.

He had just begun a third letter which was to combine poignant reproach and the sort of phrases that would go straight to Sally's heart and wring it, with perfect restraint, dignity, and a regard for the fact that he was going to be Sally's husband and must therefore begin as he meant to go on and take the upper hand. Not, it will be perceived, a notably easy task.

He was, in fact, finding it notably difficult, when he heard a faint sound of something. It was so faint that he wasn't quite sure whether it had just begun or whether he had been hearing it for some time. The trap was open, or he might not have heard it at all.

He went half way down the stair to listen, and the knocking came again. There was someone at the outer door.

James went to it, drew back the bolt, and let in a rush of cold wind, and Sally. She was bare-headed, and wrapped in her black velvet cloak. When he put his arms round her she felt as cold and stiff as a piece of wood. He kissed her, and she shivered and pulled away, and went before him up the stair, climbing slowly and as if each step were an effort. They came into the studio, and he shut the trap. They stood looking at one another, and neither of them had said a single word. Curious, primitive business of love. He had tried to hold her, and she was not to be held. His touch had said all that the burned letters could have said for him, and she would have none of him, and of his love. She stood under the light, very cold, very pale, clutching at her cloak and looking at him with bright, reproachful eyes. She was Sally who had been most dear and tender and had turned suddenly into this inaccessible stranger. Why, she could have looked at him no differently if he had insulted her in the street. This was not to be borne, and he had no intention of bearing it. He said in an abrupt, matter-of-fact tone,

"What's the matter?"

Sally's eyes were as angry as the green fire which has fed on salt. They really seemed to have flames in them, little dancing emerald flames. She said with a cutting edge to her voice,

"I told you not to write, and you wrote. I told you not to telephone, and you rang me up. Can't you get it into your head that it's dangerous?"

James said, "Drop it!" and then, "It's no good your taking that sort of tone with me. You can't drive me, and you'd better not try."

Sally glared.

"I don't want to try."

"And I won't be spoken to like that either! What's wrong with this show is that you're trying to run it and it's got out of hand. You tell me I'm to do this, and that, and the other, and I'm not to do this, and that, and the other, and all the time you're keeping me in the dark, telling me the bits you choose and keeping back the bits you don't choose. And if you ask me, you're making a damned muddle of the whole thing, and if there's any dirty work going on, you'll land yourself, and me and J.J. in some particularly nasty mess!"

"I didn't ask you," said Sally breathlessly. "I don't ask you anything except to leave me alone—and mind your own business—and not write, or telephone, or try and see me."

James looked at her with a good deal of sternness and some surprise.

"And how are we going to get married if I'm not to see

you, or write to you, or call you up? I do wish you'd be practical.''

A bright, becoming scarlet leapt into Sally's cheeks. She stamped with vigour upon Gertrude Lushington's best Persian carpet.

''We're not *going* to be married!''

''Oh, yes, we are.''

Sally stamped again.

''We're *not!*''

''Why?'' said James.

''We c-can't,'' said Sally, and burst into a flood of tears.

James experienced the most conflicting feelings of tenderness and anger. He wanted to shake Sally till her teeth chattered, and he wanted to put his arms round her and kiss away her tears and tell her not to cry any more, because everything was going to be all right. Impossible to do both these things at once, so he did neither. Instead he used an odious hectoring tone and remarked,

''Girls always cry when they've got the worst of it.''

''I *haven't* got the worst of it!'' said Sally, choking partly with sobs and partly with rage. She found a flimsy scrap of handkerchief and dabbed fiercely at her eyes.

James's mood changed suddenly. This quarrel was taking them nowhere, and they hadn't got time for it. All very well to quarrel when you have plenty of time to make it up again, but what time had he and Sally? Just this little space—to talk, to plan, to know each other's mind, to touch hands, to kiss, to say goodbye. They could quarrel another time—at leisure—

He came to Sally, pulled her up close, and kissed her.

''That's enough about all that. Done—finished—dead. Come along over here and talk. Gertrude's sofa isn't much to look at, but it's comfortable. Now, let's be rational and tell each other things. It's no use your bottling up and then telling me what an oaf I am to come butting in, because, you see, if you don't tell me things, I'm bound to try and find them out myself.''

Sally faced him on the sofa wet-eyed and scarlet-cheeked.

''Even if I ask you not to?'' she said.

James nodded.

"It's no good. I'm in it, and I'm staying in it. You can't get me out, and it's frightful waste of time to try. That's what I keep saying, only you don't seem to have taken it in. You'd better start by telling me what happened when I rang up."

"How do you know anything happened?"

"I should have thought it was obvious. I ring up, you say it's the wrong number and ring off, and immediately rush round and slang me. Naturally I want to know why. What did happen?"

"It was frightful," said Sally. "James, you *know* I asked you not to ring up or anything—and we were all in the library, and I don't know how much everyone heard."

"There wasn't anything to hear. I only said—"

Sally beat her hands together.

"I *told* you not to ring up—and you said your name, and I said it was a wrong number. And Henri said, 'He has the name of James this wrong number of yours. But how intriguing! And he makes an assignation? *Fi donc*, Sally, it is much too dangerous this assignation with a wrong number, even if he have the so respectable name of James. I do not advise you to keep it.' And Hildegarde looked at me between her eyelashes and said, 'Be wise, Sally, my dear.' And Ambrose—"

"Yes?" said James with interest. "What did Ambrose say?"

"Nothing," said Sally. She drew in her breath with a sob. "He just looked at me as if I wasn't there. And then he told Hildegarde that they'd be late if she didn't hurry, and she finished her coffee and they went off. But when we were alone Henri came over and fiddled with the telephone, and presently he said, 'The man who invented this, he is dead, *n'est ce pas*?' and I said, 'Of course.' And Henri said, 'One can be dead a long time, Sally,' and then he went out of the room. And I'm supposed to be with Daphne's party at the Luxe. She'll cover me all she can, but I mustn't stay, James—I mustn't stay—because I think Henri will try and find out whether I was really at the Luxe all the time."

"And if he finds out you weren't?"

A little shiver went over her.

"I oughtn't to have come. Henri said, 'He has the name

of James this wrong number of yours,' but if he heard that, he may have heard everything else you said.''

James grinned.

''Well, I didn't say much—you didn't give me a chance.''

Sally caught her breath.

''You said Daphne's name, and why hadn't I answered your letter, and you called me darling. And Jocko is quite liable to say something about you at any moment, and it's no good telling him not to, because he always forgets and does it. And if he begins to talk about Daphne's cousin James Elliot and says he was your fag at Wellington, and then it comes out that you're at Atwells and that it was you who drove that car, how long do you think it will be before something happens? Something—''

''What?'' said James in a practical, common-sense voice. The flame of Sally's anger was dead. Her cheeks were pale and cold. She said in a low, frightened voice,

''What happened to Jackson?''

James took her hands in his.

''Sally—you've got to tell me about all this. Someone shot at us at Rere Place.''

He felt her start.

''Who told you it was Rere Place?''

''J.J. did. Sally, do you know who it was who fired at us?''

''No, I don't. I don't know anything, James.''

''But you're guessing—you're suspecting—being afraid it's someone.''

''I don't know—I—''

She tried to get her hands away, but he held on to them.

''Oh, yes, you do—it's quite obvious. Was it Henri Niemeyer who fired at us?''

Her breath came in a choking sob.

''James—let me go—I don't know.''

''It might have been? Is that it? Or was it your guardian? Was it Ambrose Sylvester?''

She had stopped trying to get away. Her hands were cold in his.

''Or Mrs. Sylvester? Was it Mrs. Sylvester?'' He felt a shudder go over her. ''Sally, you've got to tell me. They were all on the ledge when J.J. fell, you know—Ambrose, and Mrs. Ambrose, and Henri Niemeyer. They were all there when J.J. got your Aunt Clementa's letter at breakfast, and when he fell, and when he was picked up. They were all there, but the letter wasn't.''

Sally looked at him, and looked away. She said in a hurrying voice.

''Daphne and Bonzo were there too.''

''Darling, don't be absurd! They may have been in the Tyrol, but they couldn't have been at Rere Place.''

''Oh, yes, they could,'' said Sally.

''What do you mean?''

''They were staying at Goldacre. It's only about ten miles away. They motored back to town after lunch. They could have gone to Rere Place just as easily as anyone else.''

''Why on earth should they?'' said James.

Sally jerked her hands away suddenly and sat back.

''Why should anyone try to kill Jocko? Because that's what it comes to. Someone pushed him over that ledge, and it was someone who knew he had had that letter—someone who wasn't sure how much of it he had read—someone who had to make sure that he didn't go on reading it—someone who stole it whilst we were all wondering whether he was dead.''

''Why?'' said James in a solid, matter-of-fact voice.

''Because of what was in the letter,'' said Sally, panting a little.

''Sally—what *was* in the letter?''

She beat her hands together again, an oddly effective gesture which he had never seen used by anyone else.

''I don't know—I don't know—I *don't* know—and what's the good of guessing?''

''Sally, do you know who it was—honest?''

''No, I don't. I keep telling you—and you don't believe me—and I *don't* know! It might have been Bonzo, or Daphne, or Henri, or Hildegarde, or Ambrose—or me.''

''Sally!''

She stared at him defiantly.

''I was there, wasn't I? Every one of the others has the same right to suspect me that I have to suspect them. Jocko has the same right.''

"I do wish you wouldn't talk nonsense!" said James crossly. "You're just being dramatic, and it doesn't get us anywhere. I suppose you're not going to argue that it was you who fired at us? Or are you?"

"Oh!" said Sally, on a quick angry breath. "James, I simply hate you!"

"No, you don't. Come off it! Look here—Jocko told me your Aunt Clementa had left him Rere Place and five thousand a year. Who does it go to if anything happens to him?"

"Me," said Sally.

They looked at each other for a moment without speaking. Then he said,

"And after you, Sally?"

She looked frightened and turned her head away. James put a hand on her knee.

"And after you, Sally?"

"Ambrose," said Sally in a whisper.

XX

JAMES GOT UP AND WENT OVER TO THE WINDOW. HE JERKED back the curtain and threw up the sash. A cold, damp air came in. He stood staring out into the dark. The backs of the tall houses in Hinton Street rose up like cliffs, with a twinkle of light here and there. He was thinking, Jocko first—Sally next. . . . How long for Sally when Jocko was gone? Or would Sally be done in in a different way—quite legally, morally, and religiously done in by way of marriage with Henri Niemeyer? . . . Probably. One accident might pass, but two would be rather conspicuous, especially if they left Ambrose Sylvester heir to Rere Place and five thousand a year.

His frown deepened. Was that the objective? If it was, where did Aunt Clementa's letter come in, and the shooting at Rere Place, and Jackson's death? . . . They didn't come in at all. And if they didn't come in, then there must be something more. The money and Rere Place were not sufficient motive. They were, in fact, no motive at all when it came to the shooting, and poor Jackson. He remembered something, turned round, and went back to Sally.

She had thrown back her cloak. The dress under it was black velvet too. She was all black and white—black hair, black dress, black cloak; white skin, white pearls, white face, white hands clenched in her lap; black lashes veiling her eyes.

James knelt down beside her and put his hand over hers. The cold air from the window blew upon them. Sally shivered in it, but she did not move or pull her cloak about her.

"Sally," said James, "you've got to tell me everything you know—you've *got* to."

She said, "I don't know anything," and felt James's hand very hard, and heavy, and unbelieving.

"You've got to tell me what you know. I won't go on in the dark like this. It isn't safe—for any of us. It really isn't. You've got to be sensible."

His own tone was full of common sense, but it wasn't cross any more. It was very kind, and Sally had to blink, and discourage the idea that it would be immensely comforting to put her head down on his shoulder and cry there.

James went on speaking. He said,

"Let's go back to your Aunt Clementa, and the day you went to see her and she gave you the letter for her old maid."

Sally's lashes rose. Her green eyes looked at him.

"Jocko's letter was inside it. I'm sure it was."

"Yes. We'll have to find out about that from Annie. Where does she live?"

"London—somewhere out in the Ealing direction."

"All right, I'll see her. Well, after she'd given you the letter and you'd got the nurse out of the room, you said your aunt began to whisper, and you said she told she'd hidden something, and you said it was better to go on calling it a diamond necklace. Now, Sally, I want to know what it was she had hidden.''

''I don't know. I never found it. That's what I went there for that afternoon, to try and find it.''

''You say you don't know what it was, but you know what she told you. I want to know as much as you know. I want to know just what she said.''

''James, I do really think she may have been wandering. She *was* very old and wandery.''

''Tell me what she said.''

''Yes, I'll tell you—I must—I can't go on. She began to whisper like I told you, and she said, 'All the names—I've hidden them—they don't know—wicked, wicked people. I took the book, and I hid it.' ''

''The book—you're sure she said the book?''

''I'm telling you just exactly what she said. It was all in bits, you know, and I thought she'd been dreaming, so I said, 'Don't worry, darling—it's a dream. You know you can't get out of bed.' And she squeezed my hand, and gave a funny little laugh, and said, 'They all think I can't, but I can. Even Annie—but I can. I walk about in the night and I hear things—*wicked* people. But I got the book—they don't know.' Then there was something about finding it, but I didn't get that because the smarmy nurse came in. That's all, James—it really is.''

''A book—'' said James in a puzzled voice. It all sounded quite mad. ''Have you any idea what she meant?''

Sally shook her head.

''You say you went over that day to look for this book. Why did you wait so long? She's been dead for more than a year, hasn't she?''

Sally blinked.

''I didn't think about it before. I thought she was wandering. We stayed abroad till the spring, and by then it all seemed finished and done with. Jocko was in India.''

''And what made it seem not finished and done with? Because in the end you did go to Rere Place to look for—this book.''

''I know. It was Jocko. He wrote and said he was coming home, and he said something about getting on with Aunt

Clementa's treasure-hunt, and another time something about looking for a needle in a bundle of hay, and then lots about opening the house and living there and all that sort of thing. So then I thought''—she looked at him pleadingly—"I couldn't help thinking—it might be better—for Jocko—not to stir things up—so I thought if I could find—whatever there was to find—before Jocko came—it wouldn't be so—dangerous—for him."

"I see. What made you go to Rere Place that afternoon?"

Sally threw out her hands in an odd little gesture.

"It was a beastly afternoon. I was at a loose end. It seemed a good plan. So I took Gladys's bicycle and went."

"Gladys?"

"The housemaid. She had flu. I told you."

"You told me a lot of things," said James grimly. "Most of them weren't true."

"That one was."

"Where did you go from? Where were you? You didn't ride the housemaid's bicycle down from town?"

Sally made a face at him.

"Of course I didn't! I went over from Cray's End— Ambrose's house. It's about three miles away."

"Oh, Ambrose Sylvester's got a house three miles away from Rere Place, has he? And where was he that afternoon— and Mrs. Ambrose, and Niemeyer? Were they at a loose end too?"

Sally looked down into her lap. She said in an expressionless tone,

"Not at Cray's End. Ambrose and Hildegarde were lunching in town. I don't know where Henri was."

"How do you know they were lunching in town?"

"They said so."

James laughed.

"Did they say who they were lunching with?"

She shook her head.

All this time he had been kneeling beside her. Now he got up.

"In fact you don't know where any of them were. So you took Gladys's bicycle and went over to Rere Place and let yourself in. How did you get that key?"

She looked up at him, he thought with relief. Questions about keys were easier to answer than questions about Ambrose, and Hildegarde, and Henri.

"Aunt Clementa gave it to me."

"When?"

"Just when I kissed her goodbye. She pushed it into my hand and put her finger on her lips for me not to say anything, so I didn't, but of course I guessed that she wanted me to have it so that I could get in to look for whatever it was she had hidden. You know, I didn't think she had really hidden anything, poor old pet, so I didn't bother—not then. I just put the key in my purse and forgot about it." She caught her cloak round her and jumped up. "I must go. I didn't mean to stay more than a minute."

"Yes, you must go."

They stood looking at each other. Sally's eyes dazzled.

"Oh, why can't we just be happy?" she cried.

James put his arms round her, and they kissed.

"We're going to be," he said.

XXI

SALLY HAD NO SOONER GONE, REALLY AND IRRETRIEVABLY gone in a taxi, than James remembered at least half a dozen things which he ought to have asked her. He had meant to press home a number of points and to enquire searchingly into the composition of Lady Clementa's household. Hadn't Sally said that all the servants were new? Things like that. And he ought to have got the address of Lady Clementa's old maid. Her name was Annie, and she lived at Ealing. He didn't even know her surname. They had gone off about what Lady Clementa had really hidden, and they had never got back to Annie, because when Sally said, "Why can't we just be happy?" a great drenching wave of emotion seemed to break over them both and they forgot everything except that they loved each other and never wanted to say goodbye.

James frowned and rebuked himself. He ought to have got that address. He wanted very much to interview Annie and find out more about the letters she had forwarded to Jocko. There were a lot of things he wanted to ask her. He couldn't ask any of them until he got her address, and if he wasn't to write to Sally, or see her, or ring her up, how on earth was he going to get it? And how was he going to get along without seeing Sally anyhow? He already wanted to see her again so badly that it hurt.

It was at this moment that he had the bright thought of following her to the Luxe. Ostensibly he would not, of course, be following Sally. He would merely be dropping in at the Luxe for a drink, or a spot of supper, or what not. The place is open to the public, advertizes itself to the public, solicits the presence of the public—or at least of that portion of the public which at this hour of the night is correctly attired in evening dress. James proceeded to get himself into evening dress.

Encountering him in a casual manner at the Luxe, his cousin Daphne could hardly be so oblivious to family feeling as to omit the very natural suggestion that he should join her party. It seemed to James a good idea. It even seemed a very good idea, because if he turned up like that, casually, quite a while after Sally, nobody could possibly suppose that her late arrival had anything to do with him. This may not appear to be a very convincing line of reasoning, but it was good enough for James who wished to join Daphne Strickland's party at the Luxe.

He made a very successful business of his white tie, and the night being dry, set out on foot, (a) to save taxi fare, and (b) to allow of a longer interval between Sally's arrival and his own.

Sally arrived at the Luxe, to be pounced upon by an indignant Daphne.

"Darling, I've simply lied my head off! And of course no one believes a word I've said, and Henri—"

"Is Henri here?" said Sally quickly. "You told me—"

"Darling, I didn't ask him—he simply gate-crashed. And I told him to go away, and he simply wouldn't. You'd better deal with him yourself."

Sally looked over her shoulder and found Henri there. She hadn't heard him come, but then you never did hear Henri come—he was there, or he wasn't there. Now he was there, close at her elbow, with his charming malicious smile.

"Oh, Sally—how late! But perhaps better late than never— *hein*? Do we dance?"

She slipped her arm into his and they moved out on to the floor. Henri danced like a dream, and it was much easier to dance than to talk. But it seemed that Henri meant to talk too. His dark eyes sparkled teasingly as he said,

"And where have you been, my dear?"

Sally met the look with an answering one.

"Wouldn't you like to know?"

"Yes, very much."

She laughed.

"Then want must be your master, as my old nurse used to say."

"Well, if you do not tell me, I shall make a guess. You have been meeting your wrong number—very imprudently, my dear. Wrong numbers should be rung off, and as quickly as possible—forgotten."

Sally laughed again.

"How French you are, Henri!"

"Who—I? I am not French at all—I am Belgian. And when I speak English, I am so English that no one would know that I am not a born John Bull."

Sally's laugh was quite unforced this time. Henri, with his slim height, his irregular *gamin* features, his dark eyes, and his black hair cut *en brosse*—and John Bull!

"And what have I said that is funny? No, it is not that I am so amusing. It is a little red herring that you drag in front of me, is it not? And red herrings are no use with me, Sally my dear. This James—who is he?"

"My dear Henri, do you expect me to give you a full list of all my friends?"

His smile flashed out, and was gone again.

"That would be—a little premature, shall we say? I am not yet in so fortunate a position. Shall we put it like that?"

Sally's colour rose brightly.

"You can put it any way you like, but I do wish you wouldn't spoil a perfectly good dance by talking nonsense!"

Henri laughed—a little cool sketch of a laugh.

"Ah! It is nonsense then? Well, my dear, we shall see. But I think if I were you, I should be discreet. I should not go out of the road to tell Ambrose that it is all nonsense."

"Or Hildegarde?" said Sally, looking straight up at him.

"Or Hildegarde," he agreed. "I should, in fact, keep very quiet, my dear. I should avoid assignations, and mysterious telephone calls, and the writing of letters which are so difficult to write that you tear up three, four, five sheets before you can complete one for the post."

Sally felt the colour going from her face. She knew with terror how pale she was as she said,

"What are you talking about, Henri?"

"I think you know very well, dear Sally."

Sally made a tremendous effort. If anyone had pieced those torn scraps together. . . . But they hadn't. She rallied to the thought. They hadn't. Nobody could have pieced them together, because she had burned them all, kneeling on the hearth in her bedroom and dropping the little torn shreds upon the coals. Henri had frightened her for nothing. Her colour came back, and she said,

"I didn't know reading other people's letters was one of your accomplishments. It isn't done in England, you know."

He smiled caressingly.

"Or in Belgium, my dear. Don't be frightened—I have not read your letters. I am the great detective from the crime novel. I have deduced it all from a little black ash at the bottom of your grate. I pass your door, and I hear the girl who is called Gladys say to the girl who is called Lizzie, 'Miss Sally hasn't half been burning paper—the fire's fair choked with it.' And then she says, 'If you ask me, she was up half the night writing letters and burning them, poor thing. I've done it myself.' And Lizzie asks, 'How do you know it was letters?' And Gladys says, 'Ah, it was her blue paper all right, and there was darling on a bit that wasn't quite burnt—so what do you think?' ''

Sally flashed into scarlet rage.

''I think I don't want to dance with you any more,'' she said, and pulled away from him just as the music stopped.

Henri let her go with a laugh, and she danced the next with Bonzo Strickland. Sally liked Bonzo, but she never could quite make out why Daphne had married him. He was still under forty, but he seemed a great deal more than twelve years older than Daphne—one of those smallish, dryish, greyish men. His dancing was like his conversation, correct and on the dry side. Sally and he talked about Jocko, and motor racing, and rock gardening, because oddly enough Bonzo was a passionate rock gardener, and it pleased him a good deal to know much more about it than Sally did, and to reel off the polysyllabic names of the minute rock plants which he loved. It was the great grief of his married life that Daphne adored town and could only be induced to remain at Goldacre by the presence of a large house party.

He was in the middle of telling Sally the life history of the smallest known primula, when she looked across his shoulder and saw James come in through the door at the far end of the long Gold Room. For a moment all the gold shimmered and broke before her eyes. She lost James, and the dancing couples, and Bonzo, and she almost lost herself, but when everything steadied down again, there was Daphne stopping her partner to wave to James, and James coming over to talk to her and being introduced to Gerald Crane.

Sally bit the inside of her lip very hard indeed. It was really quite impossible that James should be here, yet however hard she bit, he remained obstinately in evidence whilst she and Bonzo continued to approach the little group which consisted of Daphne, Gerald, and this impossible appearance of James.

Daphne hailed them as they came up.

''Bonzo, here's James. He never comes when I do ask him, so I didn't. He's been dining with someone who had to catch a train. Sally, you met him at my party, didn't you? James, you've met Sally.''

The group had swelled. A pretty girl called Elspeth Reid and Jocko, Lucia Crane and Henri Niemeyer, had joined it. Sally looked across at James whom she had kissed despairingly an hour ago, and said in a little cool voice,

"Oh, yes, I think we did. But we didn't dance—or did we?"

"No—you had hurt your foot," said James. "I hope it's better."

"Yes, thank you," said Sally. How much longer were they going to stand here and make polite conversation under all these eyes? Why had he come? Oh, James, did you want to see me so much—has anything happened since I left— oh, James, take care—

Daphne was introducing him to Henri, to Elspeth, to the Cranes, and then he was asking Lucia to dance. Daphne was pairing off with Henri, and Sally herself with Gerald Crane.

James prided himself on his extreme discretion. He danced with everyone else before he danced with Sally, wresting the not too willing Elspeth from a most reluctant Jocko, and having quite a success with Lucia, who had a passionate desire to own a racing car and a Flying Flea—"Only Gerald says he'll divorce me if I do, and it's much too expensive to have a divorce the same year as the wedding, so I'll have to wait."

He asked Sally in the end, and felt her shiver as his arm went round her. He talked loudly and cheerfully about Daphne and the exact degree of their cousinhood, and rehearsed the full tale of his cousins, together with their names, ages, and characteristics. And then quite suddenly he asked for Annie's address.

"Is that what you came for?" said Sally. "It's 14 West Victoria Street, Ealing, and her name is Brook—Miss Brook."

"I wanted to see you too," said James, looking stolidly practical. "I'm afraid it's growing on me. Sally, if you're going to blush, you'll give the whole show away."

"I'm not blushing," said Sally. "Go on talking about your cousins—it's safer. Oh, James, why did you come?"

"To see my cousin Daphne. I'm very fond of her. We were once engaged for about half an hour. I'm very fond of all my cousins. You'll find me very domestic."

Sally smiled, a sweet, cool, social smile—not for James

Elliot, but for Henri Niemeyer who might be watching them.

He most undoubtedly was watching them, for as Sally smiled, he went past them with Daphne, and could certainly have heard her say,

"You have such a lot of cousins. How do you remember them all?"

"I don't forget things," said James in a casual voice. "I'm very persevering and industrious. Would you like to take up my references?"

Sally would have stamped if she had dared. As it was, she lifted her lashes and sent him a green lightning glance. She dropped her voice to an angry breath and said as inaudibly as possible,

"If you go on talking like that, I shall either burst into tears, or have hysterics, or just do a plain swoon in the middle of the floor, and then the fat *will* be in the fire!"

"I was only making love to you," said James, aggrieved. "I thought you liked being made love to. Most girls do."

"I'm not most girls. And Henri is watching us—all the time."

"Let him watch. My manners have always been considered particularly correct. Sally, how much engaged to him are you?" That was one of the things he hadn't asked her when they were alone in the studio. It was somehow easier to say it here, in this crowd.

"I told you," said Sally. "I won't talk about it here—I can't."

"Well, it's not worth talking about," said James cheerfully. "He's not going to marry you, and I am. I expect I'd better not dance with you any more for the moment. I'll have another go at Mrs. Crane. I like her."

They all went on dancing until about one o'clock, when Daphne announced that Bonzo had a sausage-urge, and what about coming home and toasting sausages round the fire? Half a dozen people seemed to think this was a good idea—Jocko and Elspeth, Henri Niemeyer, the Cranes, Sally and James. Sally didn't share the sausage-urge, but she didn't want to go home to Messenger Square—not now, not yet, not as long as she could be with people who were laughing, and talking, and keeping thought away. As soon as she stopped laughing she would begin to think about Jocko, and about Aunt Clementa, and about James, and about what Henri really meant when he smiled and said those things which sounded, and perhaps were meant to sound, like a warning—a warning of what might happen if she did not stay very friendly indeed with Henri Niemeyer. And presently she would have to be more than friendly— and presently after that . . . A thin, cold shudder went over her, and she was glad to be going back to Daphne's, and very glad that everyone should be laughing and talking so much.

XXII

THEY TOASTED SAUSAGES ROUND THE FIRE IN THE VICTORIAN dining-room, and Bonzo produced beer, and Daphne produced champagne, which he declared was an affront to the British pig. And right in the middle of the toasting and the chatter Daphne had an urge and insisted that they should turn out the lights and tell ghost stories by the firelight.

"And Bonzo shall begin."

Bonzo refused to do anything of the kind, whereupon the pretty dark Elspeth produced a story about an uncle who went to sea, and there was Something on the ship, only they never found out what it was. At least she didn't think they ever found out, but her uncle was dreadfully secretive and shut up like a clam if he was asked about it, so perhaps he really knew and just wouldn't utter.

"I call that a rotten story," said Jocko heartily. He and Elspeth were sitting very close together, and the fire happening to blaze up, he was seen to be tempering his criticism with a kiss. Elspeth did not appear to be at all disturbed. She had a pretty, slow, drawling voice, and was understood to murmur,

"Well, what about someone else telling a better one?"

"I know a really true one," said Daphne.

"Mine was true," murmured Elspeth with her head on Jocko's shoulder.

Daphne giggled.

"Darling, there wasn't enough of it to be true *or* not. But mine is a real, authentic, first-hand story about a house I know. And it really is true, because—well, I won't tell you why till you've heard it."

"Daphne—I don't know—" This was Bonzo, just a little uneasy. Or perhaps that was Sally's fancy. His voice didn't lend itself to many shades of expression. Perhaps she had only fancied the uneasiness.

"Nonsense, darling!" said Daphne. "You're burning your sausage. I'm sure you oughtn't to take your eye off it for a moment. You look after your sausage, and I'll look after my story."

She was sitting on a low stool with her hands clasped about her knees. Her pale dress gleamed in the firelight. A diamond clip on either side made little rainbows.

"Well, it's about a place I know quite well, and it happened in the seventeenth century. And perhaps Jocko knows it, and if he does, he'd better tell it himself, because it's about the house old Lady Clementa Tolhache left him the other day—Rere Place."

"How thrilling," said Jocko. He did not sound thrilled at all, but lazy and content, with Elspeth's hand in his.

"Do you want to tell it?" said Daphne.

"Darling, I hadn't even a ghost of an idea that there was a ghost at Rere Place."

"Well, there is—isn't there, Sally?"

In her dark corner beyond Bonzo Sally was afraid, she didn't know why. She said in a jesting voice,

"But I don't believe in ghosts, so it's no use asking me."

"Perhaps Sally would like to tell the story," suggested Henri Niemeyer. "She does not say that she does not know it—she only says that she does not believe in it, which is quite another thing."

Sally looked at him, but she could see only a silhouette against the red glow of the fire—a long, thin silhouette.

"You can't tell a story unless you believe in it," she said. "Daphne's the one, because she believes in everything, even your pretty speeches, Henri. And anyhow I don't know what story she means."

"Oh, darling, the one about Giles Rere and the Queen's necklace," said Daphne.

James said nothing, but he was very much interested, and very glad that it was dark, because he didn't have to bother about whether he was giving anything away.

Lucia Crane wanted to know what queen.

"Darling, I was always so bad at history. Bonzo, what queen would it be—when they were having Cavaliers and Roundheads and things like that, and cutting the King's head off?"

Everyone obliged with Henrietta Maria.

"Yes, it must have been, mustn't it? And she went to France, but she gave this necklace to Giles Rere to take to the King because it was very valuable and she wanted him to sell it and have the money. So he came with the necklace to Rere Place, which belonged to his brother, Lord Rere, but he didn't know that his brother had turned against the King and made friends with the Roundheads. Giles told him about the necklace, and how proud he was because the Queen had trusted him, and how he had the neckplace pinned inside his coat to keep it safe. He told him when they were quite alone. And that night he wouldn't drink much, because he had the necklace to guard, but he had been a long time on the road and he slept heavily."

Daphne moved, and the diamonds flashed against her breast. She leaned forward, and the firelight caught her hair.

"Well, in the night he waked suddenly and heard the door close. He thought of the necklace and jumped out of bed, but it was gone. The lining of his coat was ripped across, and it was gone. He ran out of the room in his shirt and down the stairs, and it was dark, and there was someone in front of him all the way. He had a pistol in his hand which he had caught up, and he fired twice into the darkness at the thief, and he heard him cry out, and he heard him fall. Then he called for lights, and when they brought them, there was Lord Rere lying dead with the last two links of the necklace clutched in his hand.''

"The last two links?" said Lucia. "Do you mean only the last two links?"

Daphne nodded.

"That was all. And that was all anyone ever saw of the necklace again—just two links of it clutched in Lord Rere's hand. And he was dead, so he couldn't say what had happened. Giles Rere had the whole house searched and everyone in it, but they never found the necklace, and no one knows what happened to it. Some people say that Lord Rere was the thief, and some people say that he tried to get the necklace away from the real thief and it broke between them and the thief got away. And some say that Giles Rere pulled it out of his brother's hand in the dark before he roused the house, and kept it for himself, and cheated the King. Nobody knows the truth of it, but there's a day every year when it's better to keep away from Rere Place, because they say you can hear someone running down the stairs in the dark, and the sound of shots, and the sound of a fall. And they say it's most frightfully unlucky to hear it. They say it means you'll die a violent death quite soon, certainly within the year. And now I'll tell you the really thrilling part of it, and how I know it's true." Daphne sat up straight and her voice thrilled. "When Bonzo and I were coming back from Goldacre a day or two ago I got him to drive up to Rere Place because I wanted to look at the house. It's standing empty, you know. I got out of the car and walked about a bit, and it looked too ghostly and uninhabited for words, and I was just wishing I hadn't come, when right at my feet on the far side of the terrace I saw a bullet. Just lying there. Well, of course I picked it up, and I thought it was odd, and Bonzo thought it was odd—didn't you, Bonzo?"

"And it turned out to be a genuine seventeenth-century bullet with Giles Rere's initials on one side and the clue to the hiding-place of the lost necklace on the other," said Jocko.

"Well, it didn't!" said Daphne indignantly. "And it's all very well for you to make fun, but something very odd happened, because I put it in my bag, and when I got up to town there were letters and things, and I had to hurry and dress because we had people to dinner. And of course I told the story, and everyone was thrilled and wanted to see the bullet, so after we'd had our coffee I sent up for my bag—*and the bullet wasn't there.*"

"How could it not be there?" said Lucia.

"Darling, it wasn't. So it just shows—"

"And what does it show?" asked Henri with a laugh in his voice.

"Well, if it had been a real bullet, it wouldn't have disappeared—would it?"

"Unless someone had pinched it," said Gerald Crane. "Whom did you have dining with you?"

Daphne tilted her chin at him.

"People who dine with me don't pinch things, and anyhow it was Ambrose and Hildegarde Sylvester, and Henri, and an uncle and aunt of Bonzo's. And I know Henri didn't do it, because he didn't stay in the dining-room with the men and he was under my eye all the time. And so was Hildegarde, and of course the aunt. Bonzo's uncle is a professor of Economics. And can you see the great Ambrose tiptoeing into my room and opening my handbag to see what he could pinch?"

Elspeth in her sleepy voice enquired why anyone should pinch a bullet.

"Woman, you're being dull," said Jocko. "You're not up in modern crime literature. The obvious answer is that murder has been done, and that if you have the bullet, you can trace the murderer. The marks on the bullet will be found to correspond with the revolver which he keeps locked in his writing-table drawer. He will explain that he only keeps it there for plugging the serenading cat, but the jury will not believe him, because by that time Jocko the Boy Detective will have discovered the corpse at the spot marked with a cross on plan A. Bonzo could of course save me a lot of trouble by coming clean right away. I have him marked down as the first suspect."

Sally began to feel more and more frightened. Why were they all talking like this? Had Daphne really found the bullet which had been fired at her and James on that foggy evening which seemed about a year ago but was only the other day? And if she *had* found it, who had taken it out of her bag? And what was Jocko going to say next? His voice was fairly tingling with mischief, and in that mood he was capable of anything.

"And what does Mr. Elliot think?" said Henri Niemeyer. His voice suggested a courteous desire to include a rather neglected guest.

It was, however, Jocko who answered him.

"He doesn't think about anything except cars—do you, James? Lovely propositions, proper engineering jobs—all that sort of thing. That's what Atwells pay him a nice fat screw for. At least I hope it's a nice fat screw, because I rather fancy he's thinking of getting married on it—aren't you, James?"

It had come. Sally felt quite sick. James and Atwells had been linked, and once they had been linked there was no safety any more. She heard James say, "Not on my screw—I'm afraid it wouldn't run to it," but she heard it as you hear something in another room, and the room that she was in shook, and darkened, and filled suddenly with dancing sparks of fire. She thought she was going to faint. And then all at once a hand closed down over hers, warm, steady, and strong. It stayed there for perhaps a minute and then let go again.

Henri Niemeyer was asking, "What is Atwells?" And then Jocko was off in full cry, explaining Atwells, explaining James, rehearsing his sufferings as James's fag, and expressing the pious hope that James would be sorry for it some day.

"And do you drive for these Atwells, Mr. Elliot?" said Henri, ignoring him.

"I demonstrate cars," said James shortly.

"And have you ever been in our part of Sussex? These old stories are so much more interesting if one knows the locality."

"I'm afraid I don't follow."

"Daphne's story about Rere Place—very interesting, if one has been there. Do you know that part at all? It's between Staling and Warnley. Not more than ten miles from Goldacre—is it Bonzo?"

"About ten miles," said Bonzo.

Sally was shaken by an inward shiver. No good crying over spilt milk, because you can't pick it up again. If only somebody would talk about something else. She heard James say,

"I never heard of Rere Place. There are stories about most of these old houses. I can't say I believe them myself."

And then Jocko struck in.

"Unbelieving dog! Well, I've got a hundred-per-cent true story about Rere Place which I don't suppose any of you have ever heard before. It happened to Aunt Clementa, and she told me about it herself, and I'm prepared to swear she was telling the truth, so you can all sit up and take notice."

The hand that had closed on Sally's came down upon her shoulder for a moment and pressed it hard. Sally could not see whose hand it was, but she knew well enough. As far as position went, either Bonzo, Henri, or James could have reached across and touched her, but she knew well enough that it was James whose steady clasp had brought her back from the edge of fainting. He would have had to lean across Bonzo, but nobody ever minded Bonzo. As they sat round the fire, James was on the extreme left, then Bonzo on the fender-stool, Sally on the floor, Henri and Daphne on the stool again, Gerald Crane at Daphne's feet, Lucia with her elbow on the stool, and Jocko and Elspeth in an entwined attitude on the extreme right.

The hand left Sally's shoulder, and she sat waiting for whatever new brick Jocko was going to drop. His talent in this direction had been from childhood exceptional. Sally had never been quite sure whether he did it on purpose or not.

"Hush—not a word!" he was saying. "I never promised I wouldn't tell, so here goes. Of course, I can't ask you to promise not to repeat any of it. I can only leave it to your own discretion and—er delicate feelings and all that sort of thing."

Sally felt cold to her very spine. What on *earth* was Jocko going to say?

"I'll just tell you, and you can use your own judgment. I can only say that I'm quite sure that it's all perfectly true. I believe every word of it."

He leaned sideways and thrust suddenly at the charring log on the low fire with his balled fist. The log broke and fell, sending up a shower of sparks and a rush of brilliant flame. For a moment every face was illuminated, standing out with startling clarity against the shadowy background of the big unlit room.

"You're not getting on with it, darling," said Elspeth in a soft, complaining voice.

"I'm going to," said Jocko. "You'll hear it quite soon enough. Lucia, darling, if you'd like to hold my hand, I've got one to spare."

"Gerald's got two," said Lucia. "And you haven't made anyone's flesh creep yet, so you needn't give yourself airs."

"All right," said Jocko. "It was a perfectly good offer. You may be sorry you didn't take it. Well, as I said before, I believe this story, and here it is. My great-aunt Clementa, she was a Rere, and she married Tolhache about fifty years ago. Well, my said Aunt Clementa—by the way, this was after Tolhache died and all the other Reres, and she'd come into Rere Place and was living there—"

"Darling," said Elspeth mournfully, "you really *aren't* getting on with it."

"Yes, I am, but you keep interrupting. Well, Aunt Clementa woke up one night in the dark at Rere Place. Just at first she didn't know why she had waked, because she never did wake up till Annie came in with the tea. Then she knew it was because she had heard something. But she didn't know what she had heard. She only knew that it had frightened her awake. She said she did know that."

The broken log sent up its tongues of fire. They rose, flickered, and fell. There was no more sudden light on every face, but a glow that caught first one and then another—the nape of Daphne's neck with its fair clustering curls; Henri's hand, very long and thin, with a signet ring deeply engraved; the scarlet of Elspeth's lips.

"What was it?" said Lucia a little breathlessly.

Jocko went on.

"She waited. She began to tell herself that it was all a dream. She shook up her pillow and lay down. And then it came again. She told me it was *the* most horrible sound. It seemed to begin low down with a kind of moan and jump up into a scream.''

"Cats?" suggested Bonzo in his quiet, dry voice.

"Certainly not. Aunt Clementa said she had only once in all her life heard anything like it before."

"When?" This was Lucia again.

"Years, and years, and years before. And she said it had frightened her so much then that it had nearly made her ill, and her old nurse told her that it meant trouble, black trouble, for someone in the house. And then it came for the third time."

Behind Sally James Elliot was getting to his feet, and Sally spoke because she was afraid of what he might be going to say.

"What trouble?" she said, and in spite of all she could do her voice shook.

From behind her came James's cheerful laugh.

"The trouble of washing the kitchen floor, I should say. I've waked up myself and heard the sweep yodelling round the house because the cook's alarum hadn't gone off or she'd slept through it—only at Rere Place it would have been the kitchen-maid, I suppose."

He reached the switch by the service door and pulled it down with a click. The light in the Victorian chandelier came on, and all its many lustres twinkled as brightly as Daphne's diamonds. Daphne's eyes were nearly as bright above her flushed cheeks. Gerald Crane was laughing, and so was Henri. But had he been laughing before the light came on? James wasn't sure. Bonzo was looking at Daphne, and Lucia had been holding her husband's hand. Elspeth lifted her head from Jocko's shoulder without haste, and said with slow reproach,

"Oh, darling—what a shame! It *wasn't*—"

James laughed again.

"Come on J.J.—confess! Your bluff's called all right."

Jocko got up and stretched himself.

"I told you it was a true story," he said. "Anyone who believes in ghosts can think it was a ghost, and anyone who doesn't can say it was the sweep."

"It might have been a sweep's ghost," murmured Elspeth.

They were all getting up now. James put out a casual hand and pulled Sally to her feet, but the hard clasp was not as careless as it appeared. It said, "Buck up, Sally—it's all right."

And then Jocko perpetrated a final indiscretion.

"That's the worst of old James," he said—"he always sees through everything. You can't fox him."

XXIII

JAMES WAS OUT FOR MOST OF THE FOLLOWING MORNING. When he turned up after lunch Miss Callender beckoned him into the office.

"Oh, Mr. Elliot, what day are you delivering Colonel Pomeroy's car?"

"Well, he could have it any day. There was some talk of his fetching it himself, but he was to let us know."

"Well, that's just it," said Miss Callender. "His man came in this morning while you were out, and he asked when it would be ready, and he said Colonel Pomeroy was most particular the same driver should bring it down." She giggled and rolled her eyes. "He said the Colonel had taken ever such a fancy to you. Funny—isn't it?"

James frowned a little. Colonel Pomeroy knew him well enough—had known him when he was ten years old. There seemed to be something odd about his man's references to "the same driver." Or perhaps that was just Daisy Callender. It must be, because the chauffeur knew his name perfectly well. He said, still frowning,

"Did he say 'the same driver'?"

"Oh, yes, he did. Why, Mr. Elliot?"

"Well, he knows me quite well. Are you sure he didn't say Elliot?"

Daisy Callender shook her fluffy head.

"Oh, no. He didn't know your name till I told him."

"Oh, you told him my name?"

"Oh, yes—he asked me what it was. He said you were ever such a good driver, Mr. Elliot."

James shut the office door and went over to the telephone, where he rang up trunks and asked for Warnley 1076. A voice said, "I'll r-r-ring you," and he stood by the fixture, leaning against the wall with his hands in his pockets and thinking his own thoughts.

Miss Callender spun her office chair about and beguiled the time with conversation.

"Bert Simpson's ever such a nice boy, Mr. Elliot. I'm sure you'd like him ever so much. And he's one of six, so his mother's only too pleased for him to be friendly. I do think only children are a mistake—don't you? I mean if you've got six, you can't bother about them all the way you would if they were only one. And he's a clerk in a house-agent's office—a real good-class firm—and I always think it's a good opening. And I know they think a lot of Bert, because Mr. Ward that's one of the partners has a working housekeeper that's friendly with the woman Mrs. Rowbotham has to help her in the house, and she says Mr. Ward thinks ever such a lot of Bert."

James nodded.

"And we're going to the cinema again tonight," said Miss Callender with a beaming smile.

The telephone bell whirred, and James put the receiver to his ear and heard a man's voice very far away say "Hullo!"

James said, "Is that Fieldover? Can I speak to Colonel Pomeroy? Will you say it's about his car and the name is Elliot."

There was a pause. He caught Miss Callender's interested eye. And then Colonel Pomeroy was saying,

"Hullo, James!"

"It's about your Rolls, sir."

"I'm not coming to town. You'll have to bring her down. Stay the night if you can."

"I don't think I can, sir. Did you send Larkin here with a message about my bringing her down?"

"Larkin? Certainly not! He's here."

"Did you send anyone?"

"Of course not! Why should I? What are you driving at?"

"Someone came in this morning when I was out and left a message about my driving the Rolls to Fieldover."

Colonel Pomeroy became explosive.

"Pack of rubbish!" he said. "What are you talking about? Someone's been pulling your leg. Look out it isn't car thieves. . . . No, I shan't be coming down now, so I'd like her as soon as possible. And mind you come yourself. I don't like that smarmy fellow who kept trying to butt in when I was talking to you—what's his name—Jackson? Thinks too much of himself. Tell Atwells I won't have him! What about tomorrow?"

James said, "That'll be all right, sir," and hung up the receiver.

There was a shrewd look in Miss Callender's pretty eyes.

"What did he say, Mr. Elliot?"

"I thought you could always hear."

"Not always—not when it's long distance. But I thought he said he hadn't sent any message about the Rolls."

"Well, I should keep that to myself, Daisy," said James with his hand on the door.

Miss Callender swung round so that she faced it.

"What's it all about, Mr. Elliot? Seems funny to me. What's all this about who drove that car the day you went to Warnley? What does it matter who drove it? Seems to me there's something funny going on."

"Well, I shouldn't talk about it," said James, opening the door.

She ran after him and put a hand on his arm.

"You're taking the Rolls down to him tomorrow—I heard you say so. Oh, Mr. Elliot, you'll be careful on the road—extra careful, I mean—because—" She paused and choked a little. "I mean to say we don't want any more accidents like Mr. Jackson's, and—and—well, you'll be careful, won't you, Mr. Elliot?"

"I'm always careful," said James.

XXIV

As James walked home that evening, he thought about a number of things which he had not been allowing himself to think about all day. He had a list of them in his mind like a poster hanging in a badly lighted room. The simile flashed into his mind and out again, but it was an apt one. He had his list of happenings, but he wanted more light on them— he wanted it badly.

He contemplated the list with a dubious frown:

Two shots fired from an empty house in the dark of a foggy afternoon, and a girl who caught him by the arm and said "Run!"

Meeting with Sally, and Sally practically saying "Run!" again, and the Sylvesters talking to Daphne.

First enquiry as to the driver of the Rolls. Jackson butting in.

Jackson found dead, run over in a Surrey lane.

Sally's story about Aunt Clementa and a hidden something.

Sally's story about Aunt Clementa's letter to Jocko.

Sally's story about Jocko's accident and the disappearance of the letter.

(N.B. The Sylvesters linked with these three stories.)

Sally's ridiculous story of an engagement, or semi-engagement, to Henri Niemeyer.

Jocko's return. Jocko's intention of opening Rere Place.

Daphne's party. Daphne's story about Giles Rere and

the Queen's necklace, leading up to an assertion that Rere Place was haunted by a ghost who fired real or quasi-real bullets. Real enough, that is, to be picked up by Daphne and put into her bag, but unreal enough to have vanished an hour or two later when she wanted to convince a sceptical dinner-party. And the sceptics included Ambrose and Hildegarde Sylvester and Henri Niemeyer.

(N.B. They do keep cropping up, don't they?)

Second enquiry as to who drove the Rolls to Warnley, the enquiry purporting to come from Colonel Pomeroy's chauffeur.

A queer list of items, and the last the queerest of all. The man who impersonated Larkin ran the risk of being exposed if he, James, had been in the shop instead of out with a car. On the other hand, if the fellow had watched him off the premises, there wouldn't have been any risk at all, so that was probably what had been done. There emerged from this incident the conviction that someone was no longer certain that it was Jackson who had driven the Rolls to Warnley and subsequently blundered into Rere Place in the fog, that this someone was deeply interested in ascertaining when the Rolls was to be delivered and ensuring that the same driver would be in charge. Why?

The only answer that James could think of was a most unpleasant one. It was, of course, a ridiculous answer. It was as senseless to suppose himself in any danger as to suppose that Jackson's death had been other than accidental. You couldn't really believe that someone was trying to murder you—not in cold blood. There were murders in the newspapers, but you didn't somehow think of being murdered yourself. As far as he knew, no one in the Elliot family had ever been murdered—well, not since the fourteenth century anyway—and it seemed improbable that a quiet, steady-going chap like himself should start a new record. James regarded the possibility with extreme distaste. The idea of figuring in the headlines of the brighter press—You Want Better Murders And We Are Out To Give Them To You—

revolted him. Also he desired to score the someone off. Also he wanted to go on living, and to marry Sally.

He turned into Little Corbyn Street, walked half way down it, and turned again into Corbyn Mews.

Gertrude Lushington had chosen a good time to be away. Her flat was the fourth on the left-hand side (she always called it a flat, though it was really two converted loose-boxes and a hayloft), and extensive and messy alterations were being carried out in No. 3. Somebody was building out a bathroom at the back and knocking a series of holes in the roof with a view to letting windows in among the slates. There was a violent smell of paint, and a lot of scaffolding, and things lying about to trip you up if you weren't careful in the dark.

James stopped thinking about whether he was going to be murdered or not and picked his way warily. There seemed to be more scaffolding than usual. It seemed to run right over on to what he was convinced was Gertrude's roof. It was too dark to be sure, but he made a mental note to have a look at it in the morning and tell the foreman to stick to his own pitch. He had actually to duck under the planks before he could reach his door.

He ducked, and immediately it seemed to him that the roof fell. James had said that he was careful, but no amount of being careful could have saved him. It was something else, something much more primitive and instinctive, which saved him. He ducked under the plank, and at once and without conscious thought jerked his head and his whole body backwards. His forward movement was not only checked but vehemently reversed. There was a crash and a cloud of dust. Something struck him on the shoulder. He went on going back until he was clear of the scaffolding, then he straightened up. What had made him back he didn't know. Something had given him an order, and he had obeyed without knowing what it was. If he hadn't obeyed, or if he had hesitated, whatever it was that had sounded like a hundred of bricks and had raised such an overpowering dust would have fallen on his head, and he would almost certainly by now have been the late James Elliot. It was quite a sobering thought. He stood there and considered it.

The thing had fallen as he ducked to avoid the scaffolding. He oughtn't to have had to avoid the scaffolding. It had no business where he must duck under it in order to reach Gertrude's front door.

He looked up in a very doubting mind, and for an unconvincing instant he thought something moved where the black roof ridge cut the sky. There was so little light that he could never be sure that he had seen anything. He decided that it would be a good plan to get under cover, and that if he kept well away to the right, he could reach the door without bumping into anything else. If someone had been placing booby-traps for him, they would be laid with an eye to his arriving from the left, since the Mews entrance was on that side. It was improbable that there would be more than one booby-trap, but he felt like being careful.

Nothing more happened. He got in safely, and ate a simple meal of fried eggs and bacon, and toasted cheese. He considered himself a good cheese-toaster. And all the time that he was frying, and toasting, and eating his supper, and washing up the supper things he was grimly determined to have it out with the builder's foreman in the morning. He was a little red-haired man with a peppery temper, and there was pretty sure to be a sizable row. James warmed to the thought of it.

He rose next morning full of pleasurable anticipation but he had no sooner emerged upon the cobbled court of the Mews than he received a shock. Last night he had had to duck under the scaffolding to reach his front door, but this morning the nearest scaffold pole was three feet away. The red-headed foreman was coming down a ladder. He said good-morning to James, and James said,

"Why did you have your scaffolding right across my door last night?"

The foreman winked.

"There wasn't no scaffolding across that door," he said.

"Oh, yes, there was," said James.

The foreman grinned.

"Well, I've known what it was not to be able to find me own front door, but I didn't go advertizing it next day."

"Look here," said James—"when I came home last

night there was scaffolding out to about here, and I had to duck under it to get to the door, and something like a chimneypot or a load of bricks smashed down off the roof and only just missed laying me out."

The foreman sniggered.

"Some blind!" he said enviously. "And you don't seem to have slept it off yet. We didn't put no scaffolding across your door nor yet take any away, and if chimneypots and half tons of bricks was a-pitching of themselves off the roof, well, they've picked themselves up and walked away again— that's all I can say."

It was perfectly true. James's blood boiled with rage, and then cooled with the consciousness that he was making a fool of himself, and that the foreman genuinely believed him to have come home very drunk indeed. He gazed at the cobbled yard and found no trace of the avalanche which had just missed his head last night. If a chimneypot had fallen, where was it—if a hundred of bricks, who had picked them up? He could have enjoyed a row. He didn't at all enjoy the foreman's snigger and the foreman's wink. He went through his own door in a very bad temper and banged it after him.

XXV

James reckoned to start for Fieldover with Colonel Pomeroy's Rolls at about eleven o'clock. Colonel Pomeroy would expect him to stay to lunch, and he could catch the 4.10 at Warnley. As it was Saturday, he could have stayed the night, but he wanted to get back to town, because town meant Sally. Even if he didn't see her, even if he couldn't see her, she was within reach, and at the back of his mind there was the queer dogged feeling that he could and would if necessary walk into Ambrose Sylvester's house or any other fellow's house and walk Sally out of it. If necessary of course, not otherwise. It wasn't in James's nature to do spectacular things unless they were strictly necessary.

He was having a final look over the Rolls, when Miss Callender appeared, hovering.

"Oh, Mr. Elliot, I forgot to tell you they rang up from Colonel Pomeroy's to know when you were bringing the car."

James flicked an imaginary speck of dust from the bonnet and turned round.

"Colonel Pomeroy knows I'm coming today," he said. "I told him so when I was talking to him yesterday."

Miss Callender rolled her blue eyes.

"Oh, but he didn't seem to, Mr. Elliot. And they asked what time and all."

"Well, I didn't say what time," said James. "And what do you mean by *they*?"

Miss Callender bridled.

"Well, that's just a manner of speaking. I suppose it would be the butler or the chauffeur that was asking. It wasn't Colonel Pomeroy."

James's thick, fair eyebrows met in a frown.

"Perhaps it was the same chauffeur who came nosing round here yesterday."

Miss Callender looked blank. She was a bright girl and conscientious, but she wasn't really thinking about Colonel Pomeroy and his Rolls. She was thinking about Bert Simpson and whether he would say anything tonight when he took her to the pictures. It would be rather soon of course, but they had known each other for quite a long while, and after all what's the good of wasting time? So she looked blank.

Just at that moment the telephone bell rang and she ran back to the office.

James continued to frown. All these odd things happening, and nothing you could take hold of let alone go to the police about, and behind them the horrid concrete fact of Jackson smashed and dead. He had nearly been smashed himself last night. Jocko had nearly been smashed at Holbrunn. . . .

Miss Callender came out of the office and called to him.

"Oh, Mr. Elliot, you're wanted on the 'phone."

James took the receiver, and heard Sally's voice say,

"Who is it? Who's there?"

"James Elliot speaking," said James, a frowning eye on Miss Callender's fluffy head.

"James, it's Sally."

"Yes?" said James. "What is it?"

Daisy Callender's ear was frankly cocked. He couldn't tell her to go to blazes, and he couldn't call Sally darling on the office telephone whilst she sat there listening. His frown became positively murderous as he reflected that she could probably hear what Sally was saying too. He said,

"What is it? I'm speaking from the office."

"You mean you're not alone?"

"Yes."

"James, I must speak to you."

Daisy Callender coughed, her hand on the open door.

"Will you just let me know when you've done, Mr. Elliot?" she said. With a roll of the eye and a sympathetic smile she tiptoed out of the office and closed the door behind her.

James said fervently, "She's gone. Darling, what's the matter?"

"Jocko. I knew he was boiling up for something. He's gone to Rere Place."

"When?"

"This morning. He left a note for me."

James whistled.

"Well, you can't stop him."

"It isn't safe," said Sally with a sob in her voice. "He's gone down all by himself."

James considered. A week ago he would have said, "Why? What could happen to him?" Now it seemed to him that quite a number of things, all of them rather final, might happen at Rere Place to anyone who knew or was on the brink of knowing too much. Someone had suspected Jackson of knowing too much, and Jackson was dead. Someone— possibly—suspected James Elliot of knowing too much, and bricks fell on him in the dark, said bricks and the scaffolding from which they had fallen being carefully tidied away during the night. Rere Place was a house where people shot at you as a hint that they were not at home to callers, and they kept a most convenient ghost story to account for the row. James wondered very much who had put Daphne up to telling that story last night.

Sally said, "Are you there? Oh, don't cut us off!"

"I'm here all right," said James. "I was thinking."

Her voice was warm with relief.

"I thought they had cut us off. I'm so frightened about Jocko. He won't believe there's any danger or anything."

"Look here," said James, "I'm taking Colonel Pomeroy's car down to Fieldover this morning. It's quite near Warnley, you know, and if you like, I could blow in on Jocko and stay the night. I needn't be back here till Monday morning."

Sally gave a sort of gasp. He thought she said "*No!*" And then she caught her breath and said, "Oh, no—you mustn't! Oh, *no!*"

James's heart gave a bump, because if that meant anything at all, it meant that Sally was frightened about him— more frightened about him than she was about Jocko. He immediately felt very fierce and aggressive, and enquired,

"Why on earth not?"

"Not both of you!" said Sally a little wildly. "James, I must see you. I don't know how it's to be done, but I must."

James thought for a moment.

"Could you drive with me part of the way and come back by train?"

He heard her catch her breath.

"Yes, I could."

"Then I'll pick you up at Sloane Square—outside the tube station. Will that do? In twenty minutes. Is that all right?"

"Yes," said Sally. Then she said, "Oh, James!" Then she rang off.

XXVI

James drew up to the kerb, and Sally opened the door and jumped in beside him. The car had hardly stopped before it was off again.

"I got here," said Sally.

She was clasping a suit-case. James looked out of the corners of his eyes and said,

"What's that?"

"Just a suit-case," said Sally. She slewed round and threw it on the back seat. "I'm going on to stay with some people."

James noticed that she was rather brightly flushed. She ought to have had plenty of time to get to Sloane Square, but when girls were in a hurry they rather tended to run round in circles. This reflection merged into appreciation of the fact that the bright colour was very becoming. He took his left hand off the wheel and put it down hard on Sally's right hand for a moment. Then he gave his attention to the traffic again.

Sally sat beside him feeling happy, miserable, frightened, and adventurous in layers. The happy layer was on the top just now, like the icing on a cake, but down underneath there were horrid dark places of fear. Presently she said,

"Do you mind being talked to when you're driving?"

"Not if it's just talk. I'd rather not get down to business till we get out of this."

So they talked. James told her all about his father putting his foot down and telling the world in his best parade voice that the Elliots had always been in the army, and if any son of his didn't go into the army, he would want to know the reason why.

"There was the most frightful row. If he hadn't shouted at me so, I should probably have wanted to go into the army. But you know how it is when people shout. It makes you quite sure they must be in the wrong or they wouldn't make so much noise about it. I mean you don't have to make a noise if you're in the right."

"Are you sorry you didn't go into the army!" said Sally quickly.

"Sometimes," said James. He gave his attention to passing between a bus and a lorry full of gravel. As soon as he was through he said, "My mother was wonderful. You'll like her. She's the most comfortable person I ever met. She used to say 'Yes, darling' to my father about half the day, and then she used to come along and say 'Yes, darling' to me—whilst the row was going on, you know—and she never turned a hair. And in the end I went to Atwells."

"Oh—" said Sally. And then, "What would you really like to do now if you could choose?"

"Design engines," said James. "I've got ideas I'd like to work out. I shall too. I came in for a little money last year. I'm just waiting to make up my mind what I'm going to do with it. The worst of it is that experiments run away with an awful lot of money, and until you get down to experimenting you can't be sure whether you've really got something good or not. I've got three thousand pounds, but I don't like breaking into capital if I can help it."

Sally bit her lip. She looked straight in front of her for about five minutes. Then she said in a young, uncertain voice,

"I've got some money too."

"Yes," said James—"Jocko told me. He said you had three hundred a year."

Sally said "Oh—" Her colour was very bright indeed. She looked sideways at James out of her green eyes and murmured, "Do you mind?"

"Why should I?" said James.

Sally bit her lip again—quite hard.

"Would you mind if it was more than three hundred?"

James frowned at the King's Road.

"What has it got to do with me? I don't suppose Niemeyer will object."

"James!"

"Yes, Sally?"

"Are you being a pig on purpose?"

"Yes, Sally."

"James!" Sally's green eyes were full of tears.

He grinned at her for a moment.

"I owed you one for saying you were practically engaged to him."

"It wasn't a joke," said Sally in a miserable voice.

"What was it—blackmail?"

"Sort of."

"All right, wait till we're clear of the traffic and you can tell me all about it."

They made a quick run through Putney, and as they swung into Roehampton Lane, James looked round at her and said, "Now."

"I don't know what to tell you," said Sally. "Jocko's gone to Rere Place. I don't think it's safe for him there. I don't think it's very safe for him anywhere if he means to try and find what Aunt Clementa hid."

"What did she hide, Sally?"

Sally flashed him an odd, fleeting smile.

"You never believed it was a diamond necklace—did you? Not even after Daphne's story."

"No," said James. "Did Daphne make the story up?"

Sally shook her head.

"Oh no—it's a real story. No one knows what happened to the necklace. Aunt Clementa always said Giles pinched it. The Reres were a pretty queer lot."

"Well, what did your Aunt Clementa find," said James, "if it wasn't the necklace?"

"It was a book," said Sally slowly. "I think it was a list of names in a book—names of people who were doing something they could be run in for, and enough about what they were doing to get them run in. That's what I think it was. I think they were using Rere Place. I think Aunt Clementa made a very good screen for them. She was old, and she was ill, and she was bedridden. At least that's what they thought."

James looked around.

"I meant to go and see that maid of hers, Annie What's-her-name, but I haven't had time."

"I went first thing," said Sally. "I asked her whether Aunt Clementa could get out of bed, and she twinkled—she's a jolly, fat old thing—and said, 'Many's the time, miss, only I never let on that I knew.' So I said, 'You mean she did get out of bed?' And Annie laughed and said, 'Pretty near every night, miss, only she didn't want no one to know, and I never let on.' So I said, 'Do you mean she got out in the night and walked about in the house?' And Annie said, 'Upstairs *and* down, miss.' So then I said, 'Do you think anyone else knew—anyone except you?' And she said no, and she never told anyone, because she didn't think it was anyone's business what her ladyship did in her own house. So you see—"

James saw.

"Well then, you think she found something that compromised these people who were using the house?"

"Yes."

"And hid it?"

"Yes."

"And wrote and told Jocko where to find it?"

"Yes, I think so. They must have been most awfully afraid of what was in that letter to risk pushing him over the cliff. It was so dangerous that—"

"That the letter must have been more dangerous still?"

Sally nodded.

"And now if they think he's remembered what was in the letter—James, I'm so frightened when I think about it."

"Do you think he has remembered?"

Sally nodded again.

"Something, but I don't know how much. He won't say. He's gone there alone. And they'll never let him find whatever it is—they'll stop him somehow."

"Well," said James in his most practical voice, "if it's all that compromising, why not burn the house down and get rid of it? There's been plenty of time."

Sally shivered.

"I thought of that. But you know, James—fire—it's so

awfully uncertain. I don't believe they'd risk it. We've got a frightfully keen local fire-brigade, and if there was anything compromising hidden in the house, you bet someone would rescue that whilst everything else got burnt to ashes. I believe it would be simply bound to happen. Besides it's a big house, and the blighted thing may be anywhere. They wouldn't risk it."

James said without looking at her,

"Who are *they*, Sally? Don't you think it's about time you told me?"

XXVII

SALLY DID NOT SPEAK OR MOVE. SHE LOOKED STRAIGHT IN front of her. A queer sort of stiff silence seemed to close her in. James could feel it there like a sheet of glass between them. He stopped the car and took her by the shoulders.

"Do you want me to shake you till your eyes drop out?"

The silence broke up.

"You c-can't," said Sally with something between a sob and a laugh.

"Oh, can't I?"

She felt his grip tighten.

"James! Not on the Kingston by-pass! Oh, d-darling— don't!"

"Sally," said James, "I've run out of patience—right out. If you're going to talk, I'll listen, but if you're going to drop a few hints and then dry up, well, you'll get your shaking, and I don't suppose you'll like it a bit."

"All right," said Sally, "I will talk—I will, darling. I'd like to—really. I—oh, darling, do let go! Those people were looking at us!"

"Let them look," said James. He gave her a little shake and took his hand away. "Now we'll go on, and you can tell me all about it. And don't try to keep anything back, because if I'm to be any use to you, I've got to know everything that *you* know." He started the car. "Now you can begin. You said *they* wouldn't risk it. You just shove along and tell me who *they* are."

"Ambrose," said Sally in a little breathless voice. "At least I think so. But I don't know about Hildegarde. I don't like her, and that makes it so difficult. I mean it's so difficult to know whether you're being fair when you simply loathe someone and never want to see them again."

There was a nice clear stretch of road before them, and James put the Rolls up to sixty. He said,

"Is that how you feel about Ambrose too?"

"No," said Sally. "I wish I did. James, that's why I've been such a fool about it. You see, I used to love Ambrose—terribly."

James spoke roughly.

"How do you mean you used to love him?"

"He used to come and see me at school. He was frightfully famous—it's faded a bit now, but everyone was talking about him then—and when he came down to see me everyone thought he was too marvellous. I wasn't the only one. We all fell *passionately* in love with him."

James grinned. He couldn't help it, the relief was so great. He had been black afraid, and here was the sort of thing that Kitty, and Chloe, and Meg had broken him in to—the schoolgirl passion for an actor, a film star—or Ambrose Sylvester.

"I can't think why," said James, "but I suppose girls must have something to pash for."

"He's frightfully handsome. Nobody could possibly say he wasn't. And it was frightfully nice of him to come down and take me out, but of course he oughtn't to have made love to me."

"Sally!"

"Oh, nothing to look like that about. But I thought he meant it. In a way I think perhaps he did. I think he was wondering whether it mightn't be a good plan if he married me."

"Was he your guardian then?"

Sally nodded.

"Yes, that was just it. I was only sixteen. He'd have had to wait two years at least, and he couldn't afford to wait."

"What's all this about?" said James in a serious voice. "Why couldn't he afford to wait? Why should he want to marry you at all, if it comes to that?"

Sally's lips parted in a tremulous smile.

"Some people do," she murmured. "Some people want to very much. You said you did yourself. But Ambrose— I'm afraid it wasn't that with Ambrose—ever. You see— I've got—rather a lot of money."

"Three hundred a year? Jocko told me you had three hundred a year."

"And the rest," said Sally in a very small voice.

James said without looking round, "And what's the rest?"

"It's about three thousand a year really. Do you mind?"

"Why did J.J. lie about it?"

"I th-think he knew I was in love with you, and he didn't want to put you off."

After a minute James said, "That's a pretty big compliment. I don't know if I do mind. It's a bit of a shock. Why have you got such a lot?"

"It was my mother's money. Jocko's a half-brother, you know. Both our mothers were Reres. But his mother hadn't any money. That's why Aunt Clementa left him hers."

"I see," said James. "Get back to Ambrose Sylvester. He married Hildegarde. When?"

"Five years ago. I was seventeen. I thought my heart was broken, but if Hildegarde had been nice to me, it would have mended up again and I should probably have taken her in and worshipped them both. I—I've got quite an affectionate nature, James."

He put his hand on her shoulder.

"Wasn't she nice to you?"

"Beastly," said Sally. "Every time I was with her she made me feel as if everything about me was wrong—the way I did my hair, and the way I put on my clothes, and the things I said, and the things I didn't say. Oh, I don't suppose any man can understand, but she made me feel just wrong everywhere, and every time she called me darling she made it sound like 'See how kind I am to this awkward little schoolgirl.' And she used to look at Ambrose, and Ambrose used to look back at her, and I used to wish I was dead."

"Silly," said James with his hand still on her shoulder.

Sally rubbed her cheek against it.

"You wouldn't like to tell me I'm rather nice and all that sort of thing, would you?"

"No," said James. He patted the shoulder. "I can't do it here—not properly. And you're not getting on about Ambrose. What makes you think he's crooked?"

He felt her wince.

"Little things—stupid things—piling up one on another. Little things—about money. He'd bought Warnley Place with the money from *Links in the Chain*, and at first when he used to come down and see me at school he used to talk a lot about it. And then he started saying what a lot of money it took to keep it up. I don't think his second book sold as well as *Links*—second books hardly ever do when you've made a tremendous hit like that. And then there were some short stories, and then he never wrote anything again. I never knew him when he *was* writing, and by the time he married Hildegarde I think he was pretty desperate. And everyone thought she must have lots of money, because they began to entertain and go about a lot. But she *hadn't*, because once she was quarrelling with Henri, and I thought they knew I was in the room, but it turned out afterwards they didn't, and he said, 'It is your doing—you married him.' And she said, 'What can one do without money? One must do something. I hadn't a sou.' And then Henri saw me and hushed her up, and I thought I had better pretend I was asleep. That's one of the little things. And another time I was passing the library window at Warnley, and I heard Ambrose say with a sort of groan, 'Why did I ever begin?' And Hildegarde said, 'One must have money, my friend.' And he said it wasn't worth it, and she laughed and called him a coward."

"Where did the money come from?" said James.

"I don't know. I think Hildegarde and Henri showed him a way of getting it. I think it's something dangerous, something against the law. I *know* it is. They wouldn't go to such lengths to cover it up unless it was very dangerous indeed. But I don't know what it is—I really don't.''

James ran over the possibilities in his own mind. Spy work—sabotage—He frowned dubiously. Not likely. Not enough money in it. Crime—a great many dangerous possibilities here. Forgery—blackmail—dope—it might be any of these.

He said, ''Go on.''

Sally drew a long breath.

''I think Aunt Clementa knew. I think she found out. I think Rere Place was being—*used*. You see, Aunt Clementa was supposed to be bedridden. My father was her trustee—he looked after everything. And when he got ill he got the trusteeship transferred to Ambrose, and after that he made him my guardian. Ambrose's mother was a Rere too—rather a distant one, but they all hang together. So there was Aunt Clementa bedridden and wandery, and Ambrose could do anything he liked. Well, he got rid of all the old servants. It was quite easy. I saw it being done. Hildegarde used to go over and snoop at them till they gave notice. She put on her most foreign accent and said things like 'You do not know how to polish in England. In Belgium we would not call this a polished floor. A Belgian maid would think that you English servants do not know your work at all.' Well, you can imagine how they liked it. Annie stuck it out longer than any of them, but they got rid of her, saying that Aunt Clementa must have a proper nurse. Hildegarde got the doctor to say so.''

''Were the new servants foreign?''

Sally shook her head.

''Oh, no. Hildegarde was too clever for that. It would have made talk. But I didn't like them—any of them. Quite well trained and all that, you know, but a most horrid feeling as if they might say something outrageous at any moment. I simply hated going there. What nobody knew was that Aunt Clementa wasn't really bedridden at all. She got out of bed and walked about the house in the dark, and one night she found something. She found out that her house was being used, and I think she found out what it was

being used for. She found out, and she got away with some
very incriminating evidence—something in a book. I don't
know what it was. It might have been letters—or lists—
names and addresses—or signatures—I don't know. But it
must have been something pretty damning, because that's
where all the trouble began. They wouldn't have tried to kill
Jocko if they hadn't been pretty desperate—and your Mr.
Jackson—and—''

"Me," said James.

"What?"

"A convenient landslide of bricks last night. Nearly got
me too. And this morning it had all been tidied away.
Efficient staff work."

Sally shuddered and came closer.

"You're not hurt?"

"Of course I'm not. Go on. I'll tell you about it afterwards."

"I've told you everything—I really have. I think they
missed whatever it was that Aunt Clementa found, and then
they got the wind up. The poor old pet may have said
things—I think she rambled a lot. Anyway I'm sure they
knew she had hidden something, so when Jocko got that
letter they panicked and tried to do him in."

"How do you know they haven't found whatever it was
they were looking for?" said James.

"Because they're still looking for it. They were looking
for it that afternoon when we met in the hall and I grabbed
you and said 'Run!' They were in Aunt Clementa's room. I
could hear them whispering, and I was trying to find a good
crack to put my ear against, when the board outside the door
creaked. Someone came running, but I didn't wait. I slid the
banisters and bumped into you in the hall, and if we hadn't
run, I expect they'd have shot us dead."

"Who?" said James bluntly.

"Henri, I should think. He's a much better shot than
Ambrose."

"A pretty big risk to take."

"People who do the sort of things they are doing have to
get accustomed to risks. They'd have dug a hole in one of
the cellars, and we'd never have been heard of again. Rere
Place has the most *revolting* cellars. And if anyone had

heard the shot, there was a nice, handy ghost story to account for it. I think they've cultivated that story about Giles Rere and the Queen's necklace rather carefully. It's an old story, but it's been a lot more talked about lately. None of the village people at Warnley or Staling will go near the house after dark nowadays, and they used not to mind, so I think someone's been boiling the story up. It's a very, very handy one. They're awfully dangerous people, James.''

"Why did you go on living with them? You've got your own money. Why on earth did you stay with them?''

Sally said, "I had to,'' and caught her breath. "I can't touch my own money till I'm twenty-five—unless I marry. The money's there all right. Ambrose is only one of three trustees, but it's left to him to say what allowance I have till then. He could cut me down to fifty pounds a year if he liked. Hildegarde has threatened me with that. But that's not why I've stayed. I could have appealed to the other trustees and brought pressure to bear. It wasn't that—it was Jocko— I've been horribly frightened about Jocko ever since Aunt Clementa died. James, you don't know how horrible it's been. I loved Ambrose so much, and I always hated Hildegarde, but in the end I came to be worse frightened of him than of her. It was like kissing someone and finding out afterwards that they'd got leprosy or something frightful like that.'' She shuddered violently. "You don't know how dreadful it's been. And I couldn't prove anything. If I'd said out there at Holbrunn, 'Ambrose Sylvester and his wife have just tried to kill my brother,' who do you think would have believed me? I should have been just a neurotic female who had probably gone off the deep end about her handsome guardian and been snubbed for her pains. My name would have been mud, and if I'd had a convenient accident, everyone would have been all set to believe I'd committed suicide.''

"Sally—don't!''

"It's true. Do you think I haven't gone over it, and over it, and over it? What I arrived at was this—they'd taken a chance with Jocko and failed, but they'd got away with Aunt Clementa's letter—at least I suppose they had. I never felt quite sure about that, because if they did get it, why haven't they found what they are looking for? I think Jocko may have read the letter when he was alone and destroyed it. Anyhow they'd had their try, and it hadn't come off. And Jocko was going back to India. I thought perhaps—oh, I don't know what I thought. I did try to get away, but it wasn't any good.''

"You ought to have gone to your other trustees," said James.

"I couldn't. I used to think about it, but the more I thought, the more I knew I couldn't do it. You see, they wouldn't have believed me. One of them is General Forrester, and he doesn't believe anything unless he has seen it in print. If I was murdered, he wouldn't believe it until he saw it in the *Times*. The other one's a solicitor—*too* respectable. He belongs to a firm that's never, never had anything to do with crime. Neither of them could possibly have believed my story—I've often found it very difficult to believe it myself. So I stayed. And then Henri began to make love to me, and I got a sort of general impression that it would be much safer if I didn't turn him down. I get my money if I marry, and I suppose they'd rather get my money legally if it could be done. I mean why run the risk of murdering someone if you can marry them? Besides, I attract Henri.''

"Oh, you do, do you?" said James in an exasperated voice.

"Yes, I think so. That's one reason why Hildegarde hates me—she thinks Henri is her property. Well, you see, I stayed. I thought it would be safer for Jocko, and I thought I could manage Henri, but it's all got too difficult, and I'm frightened, and Jocko won't listen to a single word.''

The tears began to run down Sally's cheeks, and she let them fall. She leaned back and let them fall. She felt too tired to lift her hand or brush them away. She had said the things she had never been able to think of saying to anyone, and it had left her feeling as if all the strength had gone out of her.

James didn't speak, and Sally wasn't sure whether she wanted him to speak. After a bit she didn't want him to, because her own effort had spent her, and if James were to speak, she would have to make another effort. She would have to listen, and attend, and say things. She felt quite weak and empty. The things that had troubled her so much had gone past.

Presently she stopped crying, and saw a green holly bush in a bare hedge, and the leaning shapes of trees, wind-set and stripped to a delicate tracery of twig, and branch, and bough.

They had gone a long way, when James said in his usual everyday voice,

"Where do you want to be put down, Sally?"

Sally said, "I'm going to Rere Place." She said this because it was what she had meant to do when she set out, but when she heard the words they surprised her, because there was now no strength in her to want to do anything.

"I thought so!" He grinned suddenly. "What will Jocko say?"

Sally didn't care. She said so in a dragging voice!

"That's all right," said James.

They were in the neighbourhood of Wilder's Heath. Pedlar's Hill, with its long ascent, lay before them. Rising gradually at first, it has a bend about half way up, beyond which it becomes very steep. After the bend there is a long drop on one side, and on the other a ditch and broken ground.

It was as they drew clear of the bend that James looked up and saw the lorry. It came over the brow of the hill and down it at a break-neck speed, full tilt in the middle of the road. There are two places on this part of the hill where the slope is one in seven. The lorry appeared to jump the first of these and come down at them like an avalanche. And James saw that the driver's seat was empty.

The hill runs dead straight, and the lorry had the crown of the road. Sally stopped breathing, and waited for the crash. She found time to be glad that they were together, and she found time to think, "I ought to put my hands over my face—I don't want to be cut to bits." There was just time to think of that, and then, with death roaring down on them, James put the Rolls at the ditch.

They swung to take it, and Sally saw the sky and the high front of the lorry blotting it out, and the sky again, and the grass slope, all swinging too. And then they were over, with a shocking bump and a lurch which sent Sally banging up against the door, and a thud, and another lurch which flung her back against James. From behind them came a rending, splintering noise, and a crash which sounded as if someone had dropped a load of sheet-iron over a cliff.

James held the wheel with very strong hands. His shoulder stiffened against Sally. The car righted itself and plunged forward on to a comparatively level piece of ground, where he braked and brought it to a standstill.

Without a look or a word he opened the door and jumped out. Sally was perfectly safe, but what about Colonel Pomeroy's car? His whole concern was for the Rolls. To deliver a new car with so much as a single scratch upon her coachwork would be a most unpleasant humiliation.

Sally watched him stooping, bending, moving from point to point, completely absorbed, intent upon his examination. He made it a most thorough one, and long before it was ended her teeth had ceased to chatter. They had chattered at first, because being so near death had made her icy cold. She hoped James hadn't noticed, and presently decided that he had not. He hadn't been thinking about her at all. He had been much too much taken up with his precious car.

Warmth came back into Sally, and a sparkle into her eyes. The weakness and fatigue of ten minutes ago had gone. One bit of her was furiously angry with James, and another bit laughed. It was good to be angry and it was good to laugh, and oh, how good it was to be alive.

James opened the door on the driver's side and got in.

"Not a scratch," he announced in a tone of relief. "She took that ditch pretty well, didn't she? Of course, I shall have to tell old Pomeroy that he'd better let me take her back to be thoroughly gone over in case anything's been strained. But I don't think so. I think she's all right—I really do think so. It would have been the most frightful thing if I'd had to go and tell him I'd smashed her up."

"If the car had been smashed, we should have been smashed too, and you wouldn't have had to tell him," said Sally. "There's always a bright side if you look for it."

James burst out laughing and hugged her.

"You're not hurt, I'm not hurt, and the Rolls isn't hurt. It's a pretty good day!"

Sally rubbed her cheek against his.

"Darling, why put me first? I know my place. I'm not a car."

"Of course," said James, kissing her in rather an absent-minded manner—"of course she may have broken a leaf in one of the springs."

XXVIII

THEY LOST QUITE A LOT OF TIME OVER THE LORRY. JAMES climbed down and viewed the corpse. The owner's name he made out to be Curling or Gurling.

He climbed up again, and about half a mile along the road another lorry hove in sight. This one appeared to have no desire to run them down. On the contrary, the driver slowed up and shouted, "Have you seen a lorry, sir?" upon which James stopped the Rolls and got out. The name of Curling was printed large upon the lorry, which had also stopped. The driver leaned over the side and repeated his question.

"Have you passed a lorry same as this? Someone's been and pinched it."

James looked grim.

"Someone pinched it, did they? Well, it's scrap iron at the bottom of Pedlar's Hill now. Ran over the side and nearly took me with it. I went down to have a look, and the name was Curling."

"Bloke dead?" enquired the driver.

"Wasn't any bloke," said James. "She was running loose—no one at the wheel."

The driver whistled.

"That's a rum start! He must have let her get out of

control and jumped for it. And what he wanted to pinch her for passes me. They're straightening out a bend about a mile along the road here, and we're delivering ballast. Well, there's a place that sells minerals very handy, and we'd gone up there for a drink, the other man and me, and when we came back my lorry was there and his lorry was gone, and all anyone could say was that a chap had run past on a motor-bike with another chap up behind, both of them in caps and goggles so that nobody wouldn't know them from Adam. And one of the men that's working on the road says he heard the bike stop and start again, and the next thing there was one of our lorries going off down the hill, and he thought it was all right till we come back. Well, I suppose I'd better go along and look at the damage. How far down the hill did you say? And perhaps you wouldn't mind giving me your name and address."

"Just before you come to the bend," said James. He gave his name and address and went back to Sally and the Rolls.

As they drove on, he said in a meditative voice,

"They nearly got us that time."

Sally turned pale and said, "Who?"

"Ambrose & Co. I think, my dear—and a very clever show."

He told her what the driver had said.

"You see, these lorries are delivering stuff here every day. Quite easy to pinch a lorry whilst the driver's away having a drink. And now we know why someone pretended to ring up for Colonel Pomeroy. They had to make sure that I was bringing the Rolls, and when I was starting. I don't know how they managed the timing, but I expect there are places up on the downs where you can watch the flat stretch of road below the hill. If someone kept a glass on it, they'd have been able to do the trick all right. Motor-bike for two. Run past lorry and drop passenger. Passenger to lorry. Lorry to crest of hill, where passenger drops off, leaving lorry to do Juggernaut and eliminate James Elliot who isn't wanted. The only tricky bit would be the dropping off, but I expect he'd go fairly slow to the last second and then jump for it, leaving the hill to do the rest. You'd want a good nerve, but of course, as you said just now, you wouldn't be in that sort of game at all if you hadn't got a rattling good nerve.''

"I wonder who it was," said Sally.

James took no notice. He continued his own line of thought.

"Then the minute the lorry was off down the hill the chap on the motor-bike would pick the other one up and they'd be in the next county before anyone had time to think about them."

Sally clutched him with sudden violence.

"James—they went past—when I was waiting—when you were down looking at the lorry!"

"Then you saw them. That's a bit of luck. What were they like?"

"I *didn't* see them. Maddening, isn't it? I just heard a motor-bike, and I didn't take the slightest interest in it or anything. I just heard it go past, and I think there were two men, but I couldn't swear that there were. I just wasn't taking any interest.''

"Well, that's how it was done," said James in a satisfied tone. "They took a chance, and they very nearly brought it off. And now I expect they're having some light refreshment and thinking out the next stunt. Very persevering people."

"I wonder if one of them was Hildegarde," said Sally.

James said nothing for quite a long time. He was thinking of the lorry rushing down on them, and the Rolls all new and beautiful, and Sally's face—and Sally's face. He had seen her cover it with her hands, and he had known why.

Sally looked at him once or twice out of the tail of her eye and thought, "That's how he looks when he's angry," and thought, "I shouldn't like it if he looked like that at me," and thought, "He probably will—often. We shall quarrel like mad." And then something in her gave a little jig and said, "What fun!" She saw James's face relax. He looked round at her and said,

"It's a cursed nuisance when the criminals you ought to report to the police are all your nearest relations and friends—isn't it?''

Sally bit the corner of her lip.

"That's what I've been telling you all along."

James pursued the subject—earnestly.

"Because of course we really ought to go to the police, but there's next to no evidence, and it would be very awkward for you."

"*Very* awkward," said Sally, who would have jumped off Pedlar's Hill after the lorry before she would have followed James into a police-station to give evidence against Ambrose Sylvester.

"So we'll give to the police a miss," said James with sincere regret.

XXIX

JAMES DROPPED SALLY AT RERE PLACE AT ONE O'CLOCK. Seen in the daylight, the house was quite unlike what he had imagined it to be in the dark and the fog. It wasn't nearly so old for one thing. An eighteenth-century Rere had built a square Georgian front on to the old Tudor house and run a pretentious flight of stone steps up to the hall door. It was down these steps that he and Sally had plunged, and it was at the bottom that they had stumbled over Gladys's bicycle and Sally had cut her foot.

"It looks different—doesn't it?" said Sally.

"I didn't really see it at all."

"And it felt horrid—didn't it? It does, you know—or it did. Perhaps it won't now. I used to feel the horridness coming up all dank like a fog the minute I got inside the door, and that afternoon the house was full of it."

"Don't stay here," said James, frowning. "I wish you wouldn't, Sally. Old Pomeroy will be most awfully pleased if I take you along and say we're engaged."

"Oh, no, you mustn't," said Sally quickly. "You mustn't tell anyone. And we're not—not really, not yet."

"Previous engagement?" said James.

"No—no. Oh, James, that's not fair."

"Well, you can't have it both ways—not with me. We're engaged, and don't you forget it. And I'm not going away till I've seen J.J., because for all you know he's a hundred miles away doing something else. It's ten to one he was pulling your leg when he said he was coming here."

Sally shook her head and jumped out. He saw her run up the steps, but before she reached the top the hall door was thrown open and Jock West appeared. James, following Sally, received what he hadn't in the least expected, a delighted welcome.

"Hullo, 'ullo, 'ullo! Family reunion! The young squire returns! House-warming and free ale for the tenantry! Speeches, toasts, and a full-dress gala ball at which I shall lead out the cook!" He took Sally by the waist and kissed her. "And you, dear James, will dance a *pas seul*, unless you can rake up one of the family ghosts to join in the revels."

Standing a couple of steps below them, James frowned and spoke his mind.

"Look here, J.J., I don't like Sally staying here. I've told her so. I've got to deliver this car to Colonel Pomeroy at Fieldover, but as soon as I can get away I'll come back. Sally, you'd better tell him exactly what you've been telling me. I'll get away as soon as I can. I expect I'll be taking the Rolls back, because she's had a bit of a shake-up and she ought to be looked over. I mustn't stop now, because I'm late. I'll just get Sally's case."

As he drove away, Jock West's red eyebrows went up. His eyes, nearly as green as Sally's, sparkled interrogatively.

"Pretty sure of himself our James—what?"

Sally said nothing. Her colour was bright.

"Pretty sure of you?" pursued Jocko.

Sally made up her mind suddenly.

"Quite, quite sure of me."

"Oh, he is, is he? And what about you? Are you quite, quite sure of him?"

Sally permitted herself a modest smile.

"Oh, I think so."

"Are you giving it out—telling the world—telling our kind guardian, and his kind wife, and our dear Henri? *Hein*, Sally?" He mimicked Henri Niemeyer's voice and accent very successfully.

Sally lost all her bright colour.

"No, Jocko—no, no, *no*! Oh, Jocko, no—you mustn't say a word!"

Jocko whistled, looked critically at Sally for a moment, clapped her on the shoulder, and remarked that he was all for letting sleeping dogs lie.

"And what about broaching a tin of bully beef and having a spot of lunch?"

XXX

JAMES DID NOT GET BACK TILL FIVE O'CLOCK. As he turned in at the gate and drove up between the neglected overhanging trees, he remembered the first time he had come that way. There was no fog now, but it was as dark as the wrong side of the moon. Here or hereabouts he had run off on to the turf at the edge of the drive. Here or hereabouts he had turned out on to the wide sweep in front of the house and drew up by the steps against which Sally had leaned her borrowed bicycle.

He got out, and saw the whole front of the house like a black cliff with no light showing. The Georgian front ran to windows—rows of them—but there wasn't a lighted one among the lot.

As he went up the steps, his heart went down. It went as heavy as lead inside him and sank with every step he mounted. He found himself in front of the door with a horrid feeling that he might knock upon it for a twelve-month and get no answer. Which was nonsense, because, naturally, Sally and J.J. would be looking out for him. A cold, faint whisper stirred the recesses of his mind. It said, "A deep hole . . . one of the cellars . . . never heard of again. . . ."

James's nature made him justly impatient of this kind of hole-and-corner whispering. He said something short and sharp and tugged at the iron bell-pull, after which he applied himself to the knocker.

Nothing happened. He stopped knocking to listen, and a most oppressive silence came seeping out of the house like the damp out of rotting wood. James had never felt drawn to Rere Place, but he now conceived a healthy and thorough-going dislike for it and its bricks and mortar, its timbering and its stucco, its attics, stairways, desolate uninhabited rooms, dark unfriendly windows—and its cellars. Above all, and most emphatically, its cellars.

He banged on the door, and all of a sudden Jock West opened it. He held up a guttering candle.

"In a bit of a hurry, aren't you?" he said.

"Yes," said James.

"Thought the wicked guardian had spirited us away or bricked us up in one of the cellars? I believe you did. Well, well—what it is to be in love! Sally's been in the same sort of flap about you."

"I haven't!" said Sally, coming up out of the black depths of the hall with a candle of her own. Its yellow light made very little impression on the gloomy panelling and the dark stair with its huge newel-posts and heavy carved balustrades.

The eighteenth century ended as you came into the hall. It ran up two storeys high, and its panels were patterned with the Tudor rose and the Rere bats. Over the enormous fireplace a coat of arms showed black and silver in the candlelight—three bats sable on a field argent, and the motto, "I kepe the rere."

Sally held up her candle to show it better.

"The motto dates from some little battle in the French wars. Gilbert Rere kept a bridge with his sword until his men could take up the position he wanted on a hill above the river. Those medieval people did love puns.''

James put his arm round her. He couldn't help it. His imagination didn't often play tricks with him, but the moment when it had whispered about the cellar had been a bad one.

Jock West shut the hall door and came over to them.

"Council of war," he said. "As all the rooms this side are about forty feet long, I suggest the butler's pantry. It's cosier, and the candles will really light it. If you're staying, you shall have our best haunted room—the one Giles Rere slept in the night he shot his brother. There's another one with a Headless Lady, but she's a bit played out. It's about a hundred years since anyone has seen her, but Giles has been giving quite good performances lately, so I'm told. By the way, are you staying?"

"I can," said James. "But I think we had better all clear out and go to a pub. I don't quite see what good we're going to do here. I don't want to be rude, J.J., but I can't see any point in staying here without light, or food, or fires, or beds."

"Lashins of beds," said Jocko.

"Wringing wet!" said Sally.

Jock took each of them by an arm.

"Eschew the fleshpots, my children. Life is real, life is earnest. Candles were good enough for Gilbert, and Giles, and the Headless Lady, and they've got to be good enough for the likes of us. *And* in my butler's pantry you will find a nice little Beatrice stove. It's smelling to heaven because I spilt oil all over it, but it's getting up a very pleasing fug there. Just you come along and see!"

They proceeded through a swing door at the back of the hall. The smell of warm oil surged to meet them.

"I couldn't get away before," said James. "Colonel Pomeroy knows my people, and he wanted to talk. He couldn't make up his mind whether to send the car back to be gone over or not. In the end he let me take her. It took time to persuade him."

"Here we are," said Jocko, holding up his candle. "Here's my pantry."

It was a good-sized room, the walls lined with shelves and presses, the floor flagged with stone. The Beatrice stove contended valiantly with the surrounding cold. The whole place was very cold. The closing of the door set a chill draught moving.

Sally shivered.

"I don't know what you call cosy, Jocko."

"It's all comparative. You wait till Beatrice has really got going. I brought her down with me, but I think I rather overdid the oil."

"Is there anything to sit on?" said Sally.

"That chair has only three legs. You can have it, my child—you're the lightest. The Windsor chair for James, and ye olde oake table for me."

Sally rejected the three-legged chair and swung herself on to the table beside him.

"Well?" said James.

"I don't know what you mean by 'Well?'" said Jock West. "Sally's been telling me a steepish sort of yarn. If it's true, we ought to go to the police, and if it isn't, we're making fools of ourselves. We shall probably do that in any case."

"It's true," said Sally in a quiet voice. "It's true, but nothing on earth will make me go to the police, so we needn't waste time over that."

Jock patted her shoulder.

"All right, all right—I'm not keen on it myself. If we're going to play the fool, I'm all for keeping it in the family—a little decent privacy for the dirty linen."

"What has Sally told you?"

Jock put up a long, bony hand and ticked off the items finger by finger.

"One—she says you were fired at in this house a fort-night ago. Says there were at least two people here. Thinks the one who fired was Henri. Not a shred of evidence, but the female mind works that way. Sally's mind very female—Woman, don't pinch me!" He put up a second finger. "Two—says kind guardian and kind guardian's wife tried to bump me off at Holbrunn last year. Evidence very slight. I was there. They were there. I fell over the cliff. Therefore they pushed me." Another finger went up. "Three—someone asks a Mr. Jackson of Atwells whether he was the driver who had taken a nice Rolls-Royce car down into Sussex on the twenty-second of January or some such date. Mr. Jackson incautiously says he was because he is led to believe that there is a lady in the case. After which Mr. Jackson goes to swell the weekly list of casualties on the road. Again no evidence, but the female mind opines that the unfortunate Jackson was lured away and run over because it was thought that the driver of the Rolls might have seen something which he wasn't meant to see.''

"The people behind all this don't leave much evidence lying about,'' said James.

Jock nodded and put up another finger.

"Four—someone tips bricks off a roof on to our James. Five—someone runs an empty lorry down a steep hill at our James. It does look a bit as if someone was annoyed with him, doesn't it? But there ain't no evidence.''

"There never will be any evidence,'' said Sally in a desperate voice.

"Well, that's where you're wrong,'' said Jocko. "Female mind a bit mixed. *Because*, my child, according to your own story there is evidence hidden in this house, and it's such damning evidence that they're ready to go round risking their necks doing murder on the bare chance that our James got a smell of it the day he was here. Looks as if poor old Clementa had stumbled on something fairly fierce— doesn't it? The question is, 'What?' ''

"It's in the book,'' said Sally. "Aunt Clementa said 'The book' twice, and, 'I fetched it away,' and then, 'The book' again. I'm sure it's something in a book.''

"That's all very well—but what is it?''

Sally flung out her hands.

"I don't know. It's something—horrible. Something that made them risk pushing you over the cliff. They thought Aunt Clementa had told you something in that letter, and they didn't dare let you live to read it. Jocko, it makes me feel quite sick.''

Jocko patted her.

"Brace up—you can't be sick here! I told you life was earnest. We've got to find that evidence whatever it is, and we've got to look slippy about it. I don't want to tumble over any more cliffs, *or* to be picked out of the river, *or* to be a road casualty. Nor, I suppose, does James, and nor do you. My idea is to find the evidence and let them know we've found it. We let them know, and we say, 'You keep quiet, and we'll keep quiet. But if any of us, or all of us, are so unfortunate as to have any sort of accident at any sort of time, action will be taken by our solicitors, the gaff will be blown, and your numbers will be up.' This, I think, should cause them to mind their step.''

There was a pause. The smell of oil hung upon the air.

"Suppose it's something you couldn't hush up," said James.

XXXI

SALLY SAID "OH!" AND PUT UP A HAND TO HER THROAT.

Jock West flung back his head and laughed.

"Oh, my good James, there's nothing in the world you can't hush up if you give your mind to it. Sally, my child, I hope you realize what you're letting yourself in for. Fundamentally you are a Rere, and the Reres have never given a damn for the law. If you marry this serious, moral, respectable, law-abiding Scot, you'll have to keep off the grass, and within the speed-limit, and always light up at lighting-up time for the rest of your life. It's an unnerving thought."

"Well, I shan't do it, so it doesn't unnerve me."

"Then he'll lay an information against you," said Jock.

James frowned at them. There was a time for levity, and there was a time for business. He considered that they should stick to the business in hand. He said so.

"We've got away from the point. I'd like to get back to it. You say there's evidence hidden in this house. You've rather pooh-poohed it up to now—at least that's the impression I got from Sally. I want to know what has made you change your mind, and I want to know, firstly, did you ever finish reading your Aunt Clementa's letter, and secondly, how much of it do you remember?''

''Very well put,'' said Jocko. ''Now attend and listen, both of you. I don't know what I did about the letter. Sally tells me I read out a bit at breakfast, and she remembers that bit. Say your piece, child.''

Sally recited: ''Dear Jocko, I'm going to die, and I've left you this house. I want you to find what I've hidden here. I've had to hide it because of *them*—''

''That's where she stopped me, and perhaps just as well. Then I took the now famous toss, after which the mind was a complete blank on the subject of letters from Aunt Clementa. Sally reports the letter a total loss. She went through my pockets for it, but it wasn't there. Her original theory was that the enemy had it. But if they had it, why didn't they use it, find the incriminating evidence, and sit back with loud cheers of relief? Instead of which they continue what seems to me to be a futile search and go about the country murdering innocent Jacksons and trying to assassinate our blameless James.''

''You don't assassinate people with lorries,'' said Sally.

''We will now stick to the point, my child. As I was saying, the mind was a total blank. But after a good long time I began to remember things—things about the letter. They used to come and go like a flash. The minute I tried to remember, they went away altogether. I used to write them down, on my cuff, on anything handy.'' He laughed. ''I've written them in some queer places. And then I began to see pictures—when I was just falling asleep or just waking up. I used to see the cliff, and someone pushing me, but I never could see who it was. And I used to see myself reading the letter. I'd be standing by the window reading it, and when I'd read it I'd put a match to it and let it burn itself out on the window-ledge, and then I'd crush it with my hand and let the ashes blow away. The pictures were always exactly the same, so I expect that's what I did. And I think the reason I burned the letter was that I thought the poor old lady was raving, and that it wasn't the sort of stuff to leave lying about for the hotel servants to read. I don't remember, but that's the sort of feeling I've got about it in my own mind.''

"And how much do you remember of what was in the letter?" said James.

"Ah!" said Jocko. "Now we're really getting to it. That is the point. When I see myself standing by that window and reading the letter, well, I really am reading it—it's all quite clear, and I know everything that's in it. That's between sleeping and waking, but as soon as I'm wide awake I don't know anything any more. I've only got odds and ends, and bits, and they don't make sense. But yesterday—"

"What happened yesterday?" said Sally.

Jock's impudent smile flashed out.

"I went to sleep before dinner in our dear guardian's study. 'Late last night, late the night before.' " He sang the words to the tune of the *Soldiers' Chorus.* "Comfortable fire, comfortable chair. 'Snug as a bug in a rug or a pea in a pod, I was one of the little orphins of the storm.' Everything being propitious for a picture, it came along—a particularly clear one, because I was reading the letter out loud, and I'd never done that before. And all at once I woke up with a most frightful jerk, and there was dear Hildegarde bending over me and looking exactly like a human vampire bat— she's got a black dress with sleeves like wings, and I give you my word. So I grinned from ear to ear and asked if I'd got to give her a pair of gloves, and she said no, I'd waked up just in the nick, and better luck next time. There was some more light badinage, and then she went away. But when I came to think it over, what I thought was this. Suppose I was really reading that letter out loud—I was doing it in my dream, but suppose I was really talking out loud in my sleep—You bet Hildegarde wasn't trying to kiss me. Not much! She hates me like weed-killer, and if she was stooping over me, it was for something else. I've got an idea that it was to hear what I was saying. One generally mutters a bit on these occasions. And if that is so, the question is, how much did I say, and how much did she hear? I thought I'd better come along down here and do a little intelligent anticipation. If I'd given the show away, it seemed a good plan to get going before the enemy could, so I bought Beatrice and some bully beef and came along. And that is why we're not going to a pub, dear James. We stay here and we hold the fort.''

"Jocko," said Sally suddenly and earnestly, "when you dreamt you were reading that letter out loud last night, you said it was clearer than it had ever been before. Don't you remember *any* of it? You must."

"Well, as a matter of fact, I do. But it doesn't seem to get me any forrader. The whole thing was absolutely clear when I woke up, but the idea of being kissed by Hildegarde broke my nerve a bit. By the time I'd pulled myself together and got down to paper and pencil all I could do was to pick up the fragments.''

"You'd better come across with the fragments, J.J.," said James.

Jocko nodded, dived into a pocket, and produced a crumpled sheet of paper.

"The first bit is quite plain—the piece about leaving me the house, and wanting me to find what she'd hidden there, and, 'I've had to hide it because of *them*.' That came at the bottom of the page, and the next bit, at the top of the next page begins, 'It is hidden in—' and then there's a blank that I can't fill. I thought if I didn't try to force it, the blank would fill of itself, and I thought coming down here would help it, so I came. I'd been here about two and a half hours when you rolled up, and I'd spent them rummaging in all the really likely places and drawing a series of blanks. Then Sally and I spent the afternoon going over Aunt Clementa's bedroom a square inch at a time, because Sally has an idea that the thing, whatever it is, is in the old lady's room. So I didn't say anything about the letter or the bits I remembered. I thought we'd better work along the lines of her impressions first and then start on mine. Well hers are a wash-out, so we'll have to get back to what I've remembered out of the letter.''

"Oh, you do remember something then?" said Sally.

He nodded again.

"Top of the page—grey-blue paper—very black ink—

lines all running away down hill. First line, 'It is hidden in—' dash and blank. Next line two thirds blank, then, 'bats.' Third line all blank. Fourth line, 'It opens quite easily, so do not pull or try to force it.' That runs over into the fifth line, and from there to the bottom of the page is a complete blank. Then page three begins brightly, 'They will try to get it back. You must be very careful.' And lower down on the page, 'Very wicked people.' And right down at the bottom, 'Don't let anyone know, because we've always kept it a secret for the sake of the family name.' Then turn over again, and the fourth page is as clear as print—'I hope all this will not be very troublesome, but you are a Rere, though not in name. Your ever affectionate great-aunt, Clementa Tolhache.' ''

Sally made an exasperated face.

"Well, you've managed to forget everything that would be of the very slightest use."

"Not everything, my child. There remains the pregnant word 'bats.' See page two, line two. At the end of that line I could see quite clearly the word 'bats.' Let us consider these bats. This council of war, I may say, has been called for the express purpose of considering them. They may have been bats in Aunt Clementa's belfry, in which case she's got the laugh on us, or they may be heraldic bats—the reremice of the Rere coat of arms. Personally I plumped for the latter, and I began by thinking that the shield over the fireplace in the hall would be a good starting-point for the treasure-hunt. You would probably have to pull the middle bat's tail while punching the left-hand one on the nose, or something tricky of that sort."

"Bats don't have tails," said Sally. "And I suppose you realize that the hall panelling absolutely crawls with them. It's roses and reremice all the way."

"I made up my mind to pull all their tails."

"What was the next bit in the letter, J.J.?" asked James.

Jock recited in a leisurely sing-song, " 'It opens quite easily, so do not pull or try to force it.' "

"It sounds like a door," said Sally.

"Or a cupboard," said James.

Jock laughed mockingly.

"Or a box, or a basket, or a buttery, or a belfry, and there's always a B in both."

"Look here," said Sally, "it can't be the shield in the hall, because Aunt Clementa couldn't possibly have reached it. Even if she had climbed on a chair she couldn't, and I don't see how she could have got up on to a chair."

"No one thought she could get out of bed. The fact is she foxed everyone. She may have been quite capable of climbing anything."

"I don't believe it. Jocko, she *couldn't*—she was frightfully tottery."

"What other bats are there in the house?" asked James. Jock produced another piece of crumpled paper.

"I made a list of them this morning. The hall, as Sally says, is simply crawling with them. But I've about exhausted the possibilities of the hall. Short of tearing the panelling up by the roots there's nothing more I can do. There are some on the ceiling, but I refuse to believe that Aunt Clementa crawled like a fly to get at them. I couldn't do anything with the shield at all. I spent a good half hour over it, and couldn't find a join anywhere. The coat of arms is painted on a single wide panel. If it opens at all, the whole panel must open, and I don't see how the bats can have anything to do with it, because they're nothing but dabs of black paint. Well, besides the hall, there are quite a lot of bats all over the house. There's one on a piece of panelling between the windows in Aunt Clementa's bedroom, but it's all by itself, and the letter said bats with an S. Then there are three, as per coat, carved on the headboard of the four-poster in Giles Rere's room, and three more over the chimney-piece in the Headless Lady's room. These are in the oldest part of the house. That's about as far as I've got."

"It opens quite easily, so do not pull or try to force it—" said James in a meditative voice. "Let's go and have a look at those bats in the bedrooms, J.J."

The Beatrice stove had certainly raised the temperature of the pantry. Coming out into the passage was like going out of doors on a winter night. As they went up the big gloomy stair, each carrying a candle which made practically no impression upon the dark, Sally slipped a hand inside James's arm and said,

"We'll have a little, new, jerry-built house. I feel an urge for the sort where you can talk from one room to another and hear everything that's going on in the kitchen."

James squeezed the hand against his side and asked why.

"I feel as if it would be cheerful," said Sally wistfully. "I don't ever want to see an ancestral mansion again. I don't like bats, and I don't like ghosts, and I don't like cellars. I do hope we shan't have to go down into the cellars. I want electric light, and central heating, and a stainless steel sink, and lots and lots and lots of windows, so that it can't ever be dark anywhere."

James said, "Shall have." He shifted the candle into his left hand and put his right arm round Sally. "Why do you mind cellars?"

"Slugs!" said Sally with a shudder. "I once saw a most revolting yellow slug in a cellar, and if I trod on one, I should probably die." She shuddered again. "James, don't let Jocko go down into the cellars. It's not only the slugs—I used to have a perfectly dreadful dream about being buried where no one could find me, and the cellars here always bring it back. There are two layers of them, one under the other. *Don't* let him go down."

"I don't know how I'm going to stop him," said James, and with that they came to the top of the stair.

A black corridor ran away to the right and to the left. Jock turned left, and they followed him. There was a second turn almost at once. Even by candle-light it was easy to see that this was the old part of the house. Floor and walls were of stone. They passed the head of a winding stair. Jock lifted his candle to show the sloping, uneven steps.

"That's the way the Queen's necklace went, and Giles after it. It comes out on the far side of the hall. Daphne had it all wrong. This is the room where Giles was sleeping, so of course they took this way. The great stair would have been miles round. No, the thief came up this little stair, and they both hared down it in the dark."

He turned from the stair and flung open an oak door with an arched top. The room inside was small. The big four-post bed almost filled it. There was some old panelling upon the walls, but the roof was of stone. There was one small window high up in a corner. A mouldy smell hung upon the cold air. James decided that nothing on earth would persuade him to sleep in that damp, forbidding bed. The hangings might have been there since the days of Giles. They were of a dark damask which had once been red but was now all gone away to a brownish colour like rust or long-spilled blood. The mattress reeked, and pillows and bolster were clammy to the touch as he and Jock pulled them away from the bed head. In so small a space three candles gave light enough. It showed the Rere coat deeply carved with its three bats.

"Well, there they are," said Jock, "but I don't know what we're going to do about them."

They all looked at the bats. The head-board, very massive, was about two inches thick. The carving cut into an inch of it.

"There simply wouldn't be room to hide anything there," said Sally.

"Not in the head-board—at least I shouldn't think so. Let's get the mattress off."

There wasn't anything under the mattress, and after feeling and poking it all over they came to the conclusion that there wasn't anything in the mattress either. There might be a hiding-place in the panelling. If there was, they failed to find it.

"It may be simply anywhere," said Sally in a despairing voice. "A hundred people might search this place for a hundred years and never find it."

Jock laughed.

"Three very persevering people have been doing their damnedest ever since Aunt Clementa died. If they had found what they were looking for, they wouldn't still be trying to murder our James. Or would they? I dunno. The criminal mind is a very odd thing. Anyhow I believe Giles is a wash-out. Let's try the Headless Lady. Her proper name, by the way, was Eleanor Rere, and she lost her head in the reign of Edward IV—I don't remember why."

"Her husband did it," said Sally. "He was jealous, and

he had a very hasty temper. He did it with a battle-axe, and then went into a monastery to repent.''

Eleanor Rere's room was, if possible, colder and mouldier than Giles's. It was the same size and shape, but without the panelling. The stone walls stood stark, and there was no bed. There was no furniture of any kind. Across the chimney breast, three in a row, were the Rere bats carved in the solid stone. They gazed at them with a helpless feeling. What could you do to a carved stone bat—push it, poke it, bang it on the head? And when none of these things produced the slightest impression, stand helplessly back and look at it again.

''I believe this is a wash-out,'' said Jock. ''Of course you could hide almost anything up the chimney, but I don't see Aunt Clementa climbing chimneys, and it doesn't fit in with the bit about the thing opening quite easily and not to force it.

''No,'' said James.

There was a silence.

''We'd better go and have another look at the bat in Aunt Clementa's bedroom,'' said Sally. ''It's so much the most likely place—yes, Jocko, it is. And it's no good your saying it was 'bats' in the letter, because she might quite easily have written 'One of the bats—the one in my room,' or something like that.''

They went back to the stair head and along the right-hand corridor to an immense room with a Brussels carpet, a mid-Victorian wall-paper, and cumbrous mahogany furniture, but instead of the large bed which should have gone with dressing-table, wardrobe and chest of drawers, a plain iron bedstead painted white stood small and lonely against the long wall.

''They made her have it,'' said Sally, ''because of having to lift her and wash her, but she did hate it so, poor old pet. She used to go on and on about her old bed and all the Reres who had died in it.''

''Where is it?'' said James. ''And are there any bats on it, Sally?''

She shook her head.

''Oh, no. It wasn't really old, you know—just a Victorian mahogany affair like the rest of the furniture. And anyhow they'd got it away from her long before this hiding business cropped up. Now I say that this is the place where she hid the book or whatever it was. It's an obvious hiding-place, and all we've got to do is to find out how to open it.''

The room had two large windows hung with dark red curtains.

"Look!" said Sally, holding up her candle. "You see all the rest of the room is papered, but here between the windows there's a piece of panelling, and there's the bat right in the middle of it. This part of the house is early seventeenth century, and it was all panelled once. I expect the old panelling is there somewhere behind the paper still, but when they covered it up they left this bit untouched, and what I say is, they must have had a reason for not papering it over. I'm quite sure the panel opens, and that is why it was left. And the most natural place for Aunt Clementa to hide anything in *would* be her own room.''

Jock laughed mockingly.

"All right, if it opens, open it! I spent three quarters of an hour over it, broke all my nails, and completely lost my temper. By the time I gave it up I felt an inward conviction that Aunt Clementa was having us on.''

"Perhaps she was," said James.

Sally shook her head vehemently.

"Oh, no, she wasn't. You didn't see her—and hear her, like I did. She was in deadly earnest, and she only wasn't afraid because she knew she was going to die, so she didn't care. Besides, she was a Rere, and they've never been afraid of anyone. 'Rere knows no feare' is one of their jingling mottoes. If I was all Rere, I shouldn't be afraid of slugs.''

They spent half an hour over the panel without any result. Jock, declaring that he had done his bit, merely watched them with his hands in his pockets. Before the half hour was up he retired to the depths of a large easy chair and appeared to be sunk in slumber.

"It's no good," said Sally at last in a despairing voice. "What next?''

James got up from the floor and dusted the knees of his trousers.

"Well, I think I had better put the Rolls away. I suppose there's a garage?"

"Oh, yes—round the left of the house to the back and straight on. Jocko's car is there, but there's plenty of room. I'll come with you."

"Oh, no—I'll find it. You get J.J. waked up and think out what we'd better do next. I won't be any time at all."

Sally controlled a faint inward shiver. She wanted to go with him. She didn't want to stay in this horrible dark house, in this horrible dark room, where the old shaky hand had clung to hers and the old shaky voice had whispered, "They don't know that I get out of bed—and walk about the house—in the night," and then, "Wicked people—wicked, wicked people."

Without opening his eyes Jock said, "She's afraid to stay with only me to protect her—but he can't hold your hand whilst he's driving, you know."

"Better stay here," said James.

Sally stayed.

XXXII

JAMES TURNED THE ROLLS AND DROVE ROUND TWO CORNERS of the house. A brick archway at the far end of it took him into the big paved yard which went back to coaching days. He thought it was the same place to which he and Sally had come on that foggy afternoon which was, incredibly, only a fortnight ago, but they had come to it then by way of the front of the house and a flight of old steps.

An open coach-house door showed him the back of Jock's car with plenty of room beside it for the Rolls. He ran her in and got out. His mind for the moment was completely taken up with the question of whether there would be any means of locking the coach-house door. The Rolls was worth about two and a half thousand pounds, and since she was Colonel Pomeroy's property and in his charge, he had got to make quite sure of her safety. His conscience was not too happy as it was, because he ought really to have put her away before he did anything else. It wasn't to be supposed that Ambrose Sylvester was a mere car thief, but he might conceivably take the point of view that the enemy's transport was fair game. James's conscience accused him of neglect of duty. It took a nasty sermonizing tone to him as it enquired how he would have felt if he had come down to find that Colonel Pomeroy's car had been stolen.

It was, perhaps, because he was listening to this sermon that he did not hear either sound or movement in the dark coach-house. He tried to think afterwards whether he had heard anything at all, but he could remember nothing. There was neither footfall nor hurried breathing, only the sudden blow which sent him crashing into unconsciousness.

The man who had knocked him out switched on an electric torch and turned it on the slumped figure. A voice spoke from behind him.

"Take care—he mustn't see you."

The man laughed.

"*Chérie*, he will see no one—no one at all, any more." He spoke in French.

The woman's voice said coolly, "Is he dead?"

Henri Niemeyer was stooping, turning the body over. He let the beam play on James's face, on James's sightless eyes.

"I think not—not yet. I got him under the ear. You see how useful it is to be able to see in the dark. And now we will put him in the hayloft."

"Why don't you finish him?"

Henri's tone mocked her as he said,

"Dear Hildegarde, what a soft heart you have! But you shouldn't let it run away with your head. This good James will be found with a broken neck. He will have ditched his car, smashed into a telegraph-post, and been thrown through the windscreen. The injuries he receives must occur before he is dead. There must be nothing to raise a doubt in the mind of a meddlesome police surgeon. My blow under the ear will pass very nicely, and if he survives his little affair with the windscreen, it will be quite easy to finish him off. For the moment he has enough. Now if you will take his feet—''

James came to himself some time later. The process was an unpleasant one. Henri had hit very hard, so hard in fact that but for the unusual toughness of his skull there might have been no awakening. As it was, he blinked, wondered where he was, wondered what had happened to his head, and sat up. He at once became very giddy and fell over sideways upon a rough, tickling mass of hay. He found himself with straws in his mouth still wondering where he was.

His next effort was more successful. Having sat up, he remained sitting, and after some minutes his head began to clear and he began to remember. He remembered that he was at Rere Place—and he had come out to put away the car—and someone had knocked him out—

Instantly his mind was filled with a furious anxiety about the Rolls. In his present state of pain and confusion he could not get past the Rolls. If she had been stolen or damaged, his name was mud. He got up on his knees, groaned, and subsided again upon the hay. Car thieves—and he hadn't even had time to lock the doors—no, no time—the open coach-house door—another car—J.J.'s car—plenty of room— ought to have put her away before—ought to have . . . He could get as far as that, and then he couldn't get any farther, because other wasn't any farther to get. The crash came next—blackness, and pain, and this waking—troubled— *frightfully* difficult. . . .

He stayed still, and things got clearer again. It was like a space clearing in a fog. Into this clear space Sally came, looking at him with a glint of green between her lashes. And that was the first moment in which he realized Sally's danger. Sally in that enormous, dark, rambling house. Sally with only J.J. to look after her.

Quite suddenly everything became terrifyingly clear. Not car thieves—no, nothing so easy and safe as car thieves. It wasn't the Rolls that was aimed at. It was James Elliot, who knew too much, who was thought to know too much. And it was Jock and Sally West, who shared a dangerous knowledge, and who had six thousand a year between them which would go to Ambrose Sylvester—if they died. The last three words stabbed like forked lightning. James groaned aloud, and at the sound of it he made a great effort and got to his feet with a stumble which bruised his shoulder against the wall. He had to stand quite still for a minute, and at once the thought of Sally was there again. He must go to her—without any delay—because nobody knew—what might be happening—nobody—Sally—but he must know. . . .

He began to grope with his hands along the wall. He had been in a hayloft with Sally. If it was this one, there was a door in the gable end—not a real door—more like a shutter—and a ladder running up to it from the yard. But he couldn't find the shutter. It wouldn't be behind the hay, and the hay was high on two sides of him. He moved carefully and felt at the other two walls. The hay would be lowest towards the gable end, so the door would be there. And presently he found it, a rough shutter. He could feel the hinges—but there wasn't any handle. Well, that was absurd, because what's the good of a door if you can't open it?

Bright and quick out of James's mind jumped the answer to that—"There's a handle on the other side." And a lot of use that was to James Elliot or to Sally West. Well, he ought to be able to burst the blasted thing open. He had a feel of it, and found it surprisingly firm. He measured the distance, lay down on his back in the hay, and kicked at the shutter with his heel. The only thing that happened was that the impact jarred his head so much that he nearly went off again. He waited, and had another try, and another after that. When his head had settled down from the third attempt, he was reasonably sure that the shutter was held by a bar on the outside. That last kick would have sent any lock to blazes. If there was a bar, he was done. You can't break down a door with a bar across it when you've got nothing but your bare hands and no run back.

He groped about on the off chance of finding anything helpful. The place contained nothing but hay. A brickbat now—and brickbats do crop up in the most unlikely places—

or a pitchfork—there was no reason why there shouldn't be a pitchfork. It was a bitter fact that there was neither brickbat, nor pitchfork, nor anything else except hay, and dust, and the dust of hay.

James sat down, put his head in his hands, and tried to think.

It was tolerably obvious that the people who had put him here wouldn't have put him here if they had thought there was a single earthly chance of his being able to get out.

On the other hand, he was bound to get out.

Because of Sally.

If he didn't get out, anything might happen to Sally.

Also to the Rolls. They might damage the Rolls.

He thought a little more, and perceived that they would certainly damage the Rolls. Now that they had got hold of him, they would certainly do him in. The obvious way of doing him in without any risk to themselves was to engineer a car smash. He almost forgot Sally in his rage at the idea of their smashing up the Rolls.

He got up again and stood there leaning against the shutter which he hadn't been able to budge and trying to think of a way out. The loft was very dusty and stuffy. He felt as if he could have thought much more clearly if there had been some fresh air. The hay dust made him sneeze, and it hurt like blazes to sneeze. He found himself on the floor again holding his head and vaguely remembering something—something about a hayloft—long ago—he, and Daphne, and Alice Cummins who was Daphne's friend. It was Alice who sneezed. They had made a tunnel in the hay, and Alice stuck in the tunnel and sneezed. She was a bun-faced girl with freckles—very tiresome and always sucking peppermints.

James let go of his head and remembered about the tunnel. The hayloft was like this one. There was a lot of hay in it. The tunnel ran through the hay to a little flapdoor which led into the next loft. It was very convenient if you were playing hairbreadth escapes and secret passages, and that chump Alice stuck in the tunnel and sneezed. Suppose this loft had a door in the wall behind the hay. If there had been one in the loft at Cranley, why shouldn't there be one here?

He began to shift the hay from the left-hand wall, which was where it was piled highest. Suppose it was fastened and he couldn't open it. Suppose it wasn't. He heaved at the hay, and got more dust in his eyes, in his ears, in his mouth, and down the back of his neck. And presently there wasn't any more hay to shift. Just rough brick wall.

He began to feel along the wall, and all at once there wasn't any wall to feel, because his hand slipped through into a hole.

He really hadn't any idea of how hopeless he had been until his hand slipped through into that hole. With a sudden rush hope came back very bobbish and lively, and in an instant he had his head and shoulders through the hole. There wasn't any door, just a rough arch through which the hay could be pushed from one loft to another.

James went through on his hands and knees, and scrambling up, found himself in an empty place. No hay here, but an odd upward draught of cold fresh air. He leaned against the wall and drew in the air. Quite fresh, quite cold, and after a minute or two he began to wonder why. And then he guessed, and very nearly shouted for joy—a hayrack with managers below, and by the freshness of the air the stable door must be open.

It was just as well that he had played at escapes in a hayloft at eight years old, because it would have been the easiest thing in the world to break a leg or even a neck by falling over the rack into the manger.

He felt his way with extreme care and dropped safely into the tilted wooden trough. The stable door sagged from a broken hinge and creaked as he shoved it wide.

Next moment he was running across the yard.

XXXIII

As soon as the sound of James's footsteps had died away, Jock West came broad awake, sat up, and said with the bright fervour which Sally dreaded,

"I've got an idea."

Sally felt cold all the way down her spine. She had a most horrible premonition of what the idea might be. She said hastily,

"So have I. I was thinking it might be a good plan to go and cook something—for supper, you know. I suppose your Beatrice stove will cook?"

"I shouldn't fancy her myself. No—my idea was that we should search the cellars."

Sally knew it before the words came out, but her flesh crawled just the same.

"Jocko, I simply won't!"

His eyes sparkled with malicious enjoyment.

"My child, have I asked you to? No—you shall stay here, miles above ground, with a candle to help you see any family ghosts who may happen along, and if when I'm well out of earshot and it's no use calling for help, that damned panel begins—very—very—slowly to open, don't blame me."

Sally knew herself to be quite incapable of remaining alone in Aunt Clementa's bedroom or anywhere else whilst Jock went down into the cellars.

She followed him to the butler's pantry, and experienced a really strong desire to stay there. With the candle on the shelf, and Jock's candle, and James's, and her own, the place seemed quite brightly lighted, and the oily warmth diffused by Beatrice produced a most comfortably unancestral atmosphere. She had a feeling that no ghost would long survive it.

Jock crossed the room and opened a baize cupboard door on the far side. The door to the cellars lay beyond, very thick, very old, and deeply sunken in a still older wall.

"Jocko, *please* don't go down," said Sally in an imploring voice. "Or at any rate wait till James comes back, because he won't know where we are or anything, and if anything happened down there, *nobody* would know."

"Dry up!" said Jocko in an excited voice. "Sally, there's a bat under the arch of this door—at least I think it's one! Come and look!"

They peered at the arch, and Sally said that it wasn't a bat.

"Well, what is it then?"

"A broken brick and a damp-mark—that's all. Goodness knows it's damp enough to make marks come out on anything. Jocko, *don't* go down!"

But he was already half way down the worn stone steps. A horrible cold smell came up to Sally where she stood with her hand on the heavy door. What was it—petrol? How could it be? Then from behind her she heard footsteps coming down the passage. She called after her brother,

"Jocko—here's James. Do wait a second—I must just tell him where we are."

Jock called back, "All right," and Sally turned and went through the baize door into the passage. The heavy cellar door fell to behind her. The baize-covered door fell too. She ran across the pantry with her candle in her hand and out into the passage beyond. She ran straight into the arms of Henri Niemeyer.

The shock was so great that it stopped the processes of feeling. The candle tilted in her hand. She stared at Henri, who kept an arm about her and kissed her lightly on the cheek. It was his left arm which was about her. His right hand held a powerful electric torch. He passed the light across her eyes and she blinked at it. The candle guttered its boiling wax upon her wrist, and she let it fall. There was too much light already—cruel, unmerciful light in a cruel, unmerciful hand. She said in her own mind over and over,

"Don't let me scream. Don't, don't let me scream." Because this was going to be the end—for her. But it needn't be the end for Jocko—or for James—not unless she lost her nerve and screamed for help. If Henri shot this time, he would shoot to kill. The masks were off and the game played out. With every bit of her Sally was sure that this was the end.

"Well, my dear, where's Jocko?" said Henri Niemeyer in his light, pleasant voice. "And has he found what he was looking for, or hasn't he?"

Sally stared. She didn't feel anything except a certain relief, because now that it had come to the point, she wasn't afraid. She wasn't really anything. She was hardly Sally. She looked so blank that Henri shook her a little.

"My dear child, wake up! Where's Jocko?"

She heard herself say, "Not here," and from behind Henri she heard Hildegarde Sylvester's hard, impatient voice.

"He's gone down to the cellars. I told you they were arguing about it when I listened at the door. What are you waiting for? Knock her on the head and get on with it!"

Anger gave Sally a voice and words. She pulled away from Henri, and he let her go.

"If that's a joke, Hildegarde, it's a very stupid one."

Hildegarde laughed.

"Oh, it is not a joke, my dear Sally. I don't think it will amuse you—Oh, not at all."

Sally had her back to the wall. She felt the cold of it right through her clothes.

"I think it would be better for you if it *was* a joke, because it is known that I'm here, and if I don't turn up, you'll have something to explain." She was listening, listening, listening for the click of the latch, the sound of the closing door, James's step in the hall, and with all her heart she was hoping that he wouldn't come. And yet—and yet—it was so very hard to go out just now—not to see James again—never to be his wife, to have a home with him, to have their children. . . . She began to feel, and the feeling was all pure pain.

Hildegarde slipped past her into the pantry.

"Oh, my dear, if you're counting on James—I hate to disappoint you of course, but I am afraid your James is out of it. No use to count that he will come and save you. He is quite out of it. And presently the Staling policeman, that lump of a Gibbs, will find him all smashed up in a ditch, and poor Colonel Pomeroy's beautiful new Rolls all smashed up too. No, no, my dear, dead men tell no tales."

Sally stood against the wall. She looked piteously at Henri, and heard him say, "It's true, Sally." She saw him take something out of his pocket and come towards her. The ground moved under her feet. She knew she was going to faint, but through her faintness she was aware of the heavy, sickly smell of chloroform.

Henri's arm came about her hard and held her up. Something pressed against her nose, her mouth. The chloroform drowned all.

XXXIV

"It is a pity about Sally," said Henri Niemeyer. He had just straightened up after laying her down upon the cold flagstones of the butler's pantry. He spoke in a quiet, meditative tone, and if, as was possible, he wished to annoy Hildegarde Sylvester, he certainly succeeded.

She stood in front of the baize door with her hands in the pockets of a short black leather coat, a bizarre, arresting figure in the candle-light. A black beret hid her hair. Eyebrows plucked to an upward slanting line, black eyes enhanced by make-up, and lips the colour of orange-peel accentuated the irregularities of a face which, if it lacked beauty, certainly did not lack intelligence. She looked at Henri in a cold fury and said,

"You say that to me—a pity about Sally? And why?"

Henri laughed. He had a singularly charming laugh.

"Oh, my dear Hildegarde—need you ask? She has three thousand a year which will go to Ambrose. How much pleasanter to marry her and have it come to me. No risk, no trouble with the law, a charming wife, and three thousand a year. Naturally I say it is a pity."

"You will have your share," said Hildegarde.

He acquiesced lightly.

"Oh, yes—a share of Sally's three thousand, and also a share of Jocko's. It will not be too bad. But still—" he heaved a sigh—"you must allow me my regrets."

Hildegarde beat with her hand on the baize door.

"And will you indulge them until Jocko comes back? You should have got him first. I tell you there is no time to be lost. It must be all over before Ambrose comes. He is like you—there is a soft place in him for Sally. He will not have her hurt. She is not to suffer. He is not to see what must be done. He is not to know too much." She laughed harshly. "You know Ambrose—he must have her money, and he will stand by, but someone else must do the dirty work—you and I, *par exemple*." Her tone changed abruptly. "And now you will get on with your share of it!" She stood away from the baize door and flung it open. "Hurry, my friend! He is down there."

Henri smiled.

"I am to go down into the cellars and leave you here with Sally whom you love so much? Oh, no, my dear, I think not. You might—well, we will not say what you might do. You have an old score against her, but you will not settle it—here." He spoke with sudden briskness. "Oh, no, I have a much better plan, and so simple. It is you who will go down into the cellars. Our dear Jocko will search them all. He is very much bitten with this idea that he will find something, and he will search. There are three among those cellars which have a bolt on the outside of the door, as you will remember—two of them old, and one which I put on myself—in case. Well, into one of these Jocko will certainly go, and as soon as he is in, *voila*—you shoot the bolt and we have him safe. He will not break the door—I will swear to that. It will not be the first time those cellars have been useful. Oh, my dear Hildegarde, you really need not take the trouble to look at me like that. When I say that I will not leave you here with Sally, it is finished. And if you think there is need to hurry, well then, my dear, get a move on!''

Without another word she turned from him, pushed open the old oak door, and ran down the cellar steps.

Sitting on the corner of the table and swinging a careless leg, Henri looked down at Sally West. She might have been dead already. She was pale enough, and he had laid her out straight, as they lay the dead. She was bareheaded, her hair very black about the pallor of her face, her eyes half closed, the green invisible behind black lashes, one arm across her breast, the other straight beside her, her mouth relaxed and a little open like that of a sleeping child. How old was Sally—twenty? She looked much younger than that, much younger. Yes, it was a pity about Sally—a great pity.

He jumped down from the table as Ambrose Sylvester came into the room.

XXXV

SALLY CAME BACK TO THE SOUND OF VOICES. SHE HAD been dreaming a vague, confused dream in which she, and James, and Henri, and Ambrose, and Hildegarde were all running down Pedlar's Hill with a mad lorry snorting behind them. It was a very alarming dream, but for some reason it did not alarm her. About half way down the hill her feet left the road and took her gently up an invisible slope of the air. She held James's hand, and they rose together, while the lorry rushed past below. She knew just where it would swerve and go over the cliff.

She came a little way out of her dream and heard the voices—Hildegarde's voice. It said,

"We will go up now. There has been enough time lost already."

The dream came up like a wave and drew Sally back. She drowned for a moment, and saw a picture of herself a long way off lying dead on a desolate road. It was cold there. . . .

She began to come back again. There was something cold under her head. Someone was talking—Ambrose. She opened her eyes and saw him bending over her. He said,

"Sally—you're not dead—you can't be dead! Sally!"

Sally sat up. She had really had very little chloroform. She was fainting before the pad came down over her nose and mouth. She felt giddy and queer, and every now and then her mind swung back into the dream. But she would not really go off again now. She propped herself with one hand on the rough stone floor. She was in the pantry. That was why there was this smell of oil. The stove was on the other side of the table.

Ambrose was getting up from his knees as if her movement had startled him. Perhaps he had really thought that she was dead. She wondered painfully whether he would mind. His voice came again.

"Sally—are you all right?"

Sally heard her own voice say "Yes."

And then Ambrose was helping her to a chair. It was the chair in which she had sat at their council of war. She leaned her arms upon the table and rested her head upon them. The room seemed to be shaking, rocking. Ambrose was talking. She could hear his voice, but the words went by her. And then his hand was on her shoulder, shaking her.

"Sally—wake up! You are not listening—and you *must* listen. I can't bear it if you don't listen, and there's no time—there's no time."

Sally lifted her head and stared at him. She said,

"I'm giddy. What is it, Ambrose?"

"You've got to listen. I told you—that night at Daphne's— but you wouldn't listen to me then. You've got to listen to me now—before they come back. There won't be any more time after that.'' He spoke in a low, uneven voice, the words hurrying, halting, tumbling over one another.

Sally said wearily, ''What do you want to say?''

He had pulled up a chair, and sat across the corner of the table from her, leaning towards her with a hand still resting on her shoulder. His extravagant tawny hair was dishevelled, his brilliant eyes more brilliant than ever. Even to Sally's dizzy gaze there was a wildness about his look. Perhaps it steadied her. She felt fear, and the courage which controls it.

He went on speaking in the same way.

''There's so much to say, and so little time to say it, because there's got to be an accident. It's all arranged. Hildegarde has arranged it all. You see, Jocko won't leave things alone. He and that fellow Elliot, they keep interfering and butting in, and it's too dangerous. You shouldn't have got mixed up with them, and I might have got you off. But I don't know—Hildegarde doesn't like you, and then there's the money. So there will have to be an accident, but I'll make them give you some more chloroform first. I don't want you to be hurt. It will be a car accident, you see, and the car will be smashed and the three of you will be killed. It is Hildegarde's idea. She has very clever ideas, but I oughtn't to have married her—she doesn't really understand me. I ought to have married you. She always says that three thousand a year wouldn't have been enough, but it would— with you. I could have got rid of Cray's End. It has always cost too much.'' His hand dropped from her shoulder, and he repeated the last two words in a deeply tragic tone— ''*Too much.*''

Sally's mind began to work again. She thought, ''He's mad. Or is it acting? He loves acting.''

Ambrose Sylvester went on.

''I want to tell you why I married her. You thought it was because of her money, but she hasn't got any. She hadn't a penny.''

Sally sat up.

''What are you talking about?''

''Hildegarde. She hadn't any money. I didn't marry her for her money. I married her because she would have ruined me if I hadn't.''

Sally thought, "That's true. He means that." She said, "How?"

He groaned.

"Sally, I am telling you everything. You don't know what a relief it is to tell you. She knew something. She knows—a lot of things. She could have ruined me. I had to marry her. I couldn't face it."

"Was it the books?" said Sally. "You didn't write them— did you? They were Tim Merrivale's. Was that what Hildegarde knew?"

"She could have proved it," said Ambrose. "She had a letter of Tim's. It was about *Links in the Chain*. I don't know how she got hold of it. I thought I had burnt them all."

Sally was appalled. It is one thing to guess, and another to know. She said,

"A letter to you?"

"About *Links in the Chain*—about getting it published. I don't know how she got hold of it. I thought I had burnt everything."

She said, "I see—"

"So I had to marry her. You see that, don't you? The money just poured away. And then there was no more coming in, and I had to have money—I'd got into the way of it. Once you've got into the way of things you can't go back. Though mark you, Sally, I tried—you've got to believe that. You see, I'd used all Tim's stuff by then, but I didn't give up without a struggle. I wrote a book of my own, but the publishers wouldn't have it—they said it would ruin me. So what could I do? We'd got to have money."

"What *did* you do?" asked Sally.

He pushed back his chair and got up.

"How you say that—as cool as if it was all about nothing! Are you made of ice? Don't you care that I had to sell my soul because those damned publishers made a ring against me?"

Sally looked at him fixedly.

"How did you sell your soul, Ambrose?"

He began to walk up and down in the room talking all the time.

"I tell you I had to do it. We had to have money. I wasn't the only one she could have ruined. I don't know how she knew the things, but she did know them. Things like that can be bought and sold. Hildegarde knew how, and you see, we went everywhere, she, and I, and Henri, and if you go everywhere, you hear everything. But it isn't enough to know—you've got to have proof. And that's where Hildegarde was so clever—she had her spies, her jackals, and they saw to it that there was proof. And she paid well. You can afford to pay well when you rake in thousands. Rich people, powerful people, highly placed people—there's nothing they won't pay to keep themselves out of the mud."

Sally was fainting pale. She had to moisten her dry lips two or three times before she could speak, and then it was to say a single word.

"Blackmail?"

He went striding past her to the door and thrust at it with his hand and came striding back. The banged door rebounded and remained a hand's-breadth open.

"What does it matter what you call it?" said Ambrose Sylvester. "We had to have the money, I tell you."

"No, it isn't the name that matters," said Sally. "Did you make a lot of money, Ambrose?"

He flung himself back into the chair again. His hands were shaking.

"Do you think I liked it? And there was the risk. If you push people too far, they stop caring about the mud, or about anything. I know, because I've felt like that. I came very near to shooting myself the night before I was married." He groaned. "I'd better have done it."

Sally nodded.

"I don't know why you're telling me all this." But in her heart she knew. It was because she was as good as dead already, and dead men tell no tales.

He said, "I must tell someone, and it doesn't matter— now. Besides, I want you to understand. You see, Clementa found out."

Sally said, "Yes."

He looked up sharply.

"Did she tell you? Hildegarde said she did. She's always

right. I expect that's why I hate her. You see, Clementa used to get out of bed and walk about the house at night. Everyone thought she was bedridden, but she wasn't, and one night the nurse caught her. So then we knew what had happened to the book.''

Sally shivered.

''What book?''

He dropped his voice.

''It was Hildegarde's book. She wrote everything down in it—the people she got the money from, what they paid, and why they were paying it. I always said it was madness to write things down like that, but she said she couldn't keep it all in her head. There were dates, and names, and places, and the names of the people from whom the information came, and what she paid them for it. She couldn't say I didn't warn her. I always said it was too ruinous, but she swore it was all right. She kept it in a very secret place. Nobody could have found it if he didn't know the secret. But one day it was gone—Sally, I nearly shot myself that day. But we never thought about Clementa. We thought it was one of the servants. . . . And we waited, and we waited. You don't know what it's like waiting for the roof to fall in. And then we found out about Clementa, and we knew she'd got it, but she wouldn't speak. Hildegarde tried to make her, but she just laughed at her—and died. And Hildegarde swore Clementa had told you, and she wanted you put out of the way, but I wouldn't have it. And then at Holbrunn— you remember Holbrunn?''

''Yes,'' said Sally in a very low voice, ''I remember Holbrunn.''

''There was a letter for Jocko—from Clementa—and he got it at breakfast with all of us there—and you stopped him when he began to read it aloud. Well, after that I couldn't hold out any longer—against Hildegarde. She was quite right, you know. We couldn't possibly have let Jock read that letter and get away with it—it wasn't possible. But the accident didn't come off. That is to say it came off, but he wasn't killed. It would have been too dangerous to try again then, and the fall had made him forget—he didn't remember anything about the letter. So Hildegarde let him go back to

India. She always hated Jocko, and the money would have been useful, but it was safer to let him go. She saw that."

Sally's lip curled a little. She wasn't feeling afraid any longer. There didn't seem to be room for it. What she felt was a vivid horror, a vivid interest, a kind of quivering excitement.

Ambrose Sylvester pushed his chair back.

"It was Henri's idea that he might marry you."

"Kind of Henri," murmured Sally drily.

"Oh, no—he was fond of you—and there was your three thousand a year. But Hildegarde was against it from the first. She wanted you and Jocko right out of the way, because then all the money would have come to us, and with six thousand a year we could have got along. You see, the other business was too risky—I always told her so—and if we'd had your three thousand a year and Jocko's, we could have given it up and settled down, and that would have been a great relief to me, because it was getting on my nerves." He leaned forward with a sudden movement and caught her hand in his. "Sally—say you understand! You don't say anything—you sit there like a block of ice. What has happened to you? You used not to be cold like this. You used to be warm and sweet. Oh, Sally, you were so sweet when I used to kiss you!"

Sally's hand lay heavy in his—like a dead hand. She said in an even voice,

"You weren't planning to murder me then, Ambrose. It does make a difference to one's feelings, you know."

He let go of her and drew back. They looked at each other. Sally kept her head high and her eyes steady. She thought, "How wild he looks. He *is* mad. He couldn't talk like that if he was sane. Hildegarde's bad, and he's mad, and we've all come to the end. I suppose Jocko's dead. I should like to see James again. . . ."

The silence went on between them. The dreadful word murder seemed to have stopped all the other words which might have been said.

In the silence Sally began to hear something—something so faint and far away that she would never have heard it at all if every other sound had not been stopped. It was in itself hardly a sound, but it went on endlessly, steadily, regularly, like the throb of an engine or the ticking of a clock, only it wasn't either of these things. And all at once Sally knew what it was. "Jocko's shut into one of the cellars, and he's kicking at the door." Something rushed in upon her with an intoxicating force—joy—hope. With the road broken off before her and her own foot touching the brink, this half-heard sound had brought her back. If Jocko was alive, life was worth fighting for. If Jocko was alive and she could get to him, they might have a fighting chance together.

Ambrose Sylvester's voice broke in. He said her name, "Sally!" and then again, "Sally!" in a hurt, pleading voice.

She understood that she was being accused, reproached. Ambrose had been enjoying his confession—wallowing in it. He had been bang in the middle of the stage with the limelight full upon him, and instead of taking her cue and playing out her appointed part she had imported a note of cruel satire and quite ruined his big scene. She understood all this very well, and in a remote corner of her mind something wept. She said quite briskly,

"Well, what about it?"

He looked at her with a tragic, wounded expression.

"You wouldn't marry Henri. I didn't want you to, but it would have been safer—for you."

"You don't marry people just to be safe," said Sally.

"Henri tried to save you, but you wouldn't be saved. You've made it very difficult for anyone to save you. Why couldn't you leave Rere Place alone? I could have saved you if you had kept quiet. But you didn't keep quiet. You came over here the day of the fog, and you brought James Elliot with you. It was a mad thing to do. It was just as if you were asking to be put out of the way, because you see, we were here, all three of us, up in Clementa's room looking for the book. We knew she'd hidden it somewhere, but we could never find it—we couldn't ever find it." He was speaking in a low, excited voice, very fast indeed. "But this time Hildegarde had an idea. It didn't come to anything, but she thought it was going to." He ran his hand through his hair. "There have been so many ideas, but they never come to anything. And then just as we were in the middle of it—all of us up there in Clementa's room, and Hildegarde talking, talking, talking about all the things in the book that would ruin us if they came out—just then—just then, Sally, there was a sound outside the door. A very little sound, but we all heard it—someone sneezed—''

"It was the dust," said Sally in self-defence. "Everything's inches deep."

"You were very lucky not to be caught. Henri got out his pistol and ran. We heard him shoot—twice. You are very lucky to be alive. He doesn't often miss."

"I said it was Henri," said Sally.

"But we didn't know it was you—not then, or you wouldn't be alive. We thought it was the man with the car, but we found out afterwards."

"How?"

"Hildegarde guessed, and one of the housemaids said you had taken her bicycle. And that was the end. I couldn't save you after that."

"You've got it all wrong," said Sally. "I didn't bring James—we blinded into each other in the dark. And I don't know what you think we heard or saw, but first of all there wasn't anything, and after that if there had been anything to see, we shouldn't have been able to see it, and anyhow I don't know what you're talking about. You know, if Henri had hit somebody, you'd all have been in a bit of a mess—wouldn't you?"

He waved that away with a kind of gloomy scorn. The problem of the unwanted corpse did not concern him. Hildegarde would have seen to it.

"You know, Ambrose," said Sally with sudden earnestness, "you really have made a most awful mess of things—haven't you? Why not stop all this rubbish and start fresh? We'll hold our tongues, and you can cut loose from the Niemeyers and begin again."

Ambrose caught her hands in his hand held them hard—cruelly hard.

"Don't be a fool, Sally! How can I cut loose? They'd ruin me wherever I was. No, no, I've got to go on, but I want you to understand—''

"What have they done to James?" said Sally quickly.

He stared at her, offended. She ought to have said "Oh, but I *do*," but that was Sally all over.

"Where's James? What have they done to him?"

"You keep on interrupting!" he said peevishly. "I told you there was going to be an accident. Hildegarde is quite right—it's the only way out. I wanted them to let you go, but they're perfectly right, it's too dangerous. But I won't have you hurt, Sally—I've made them promise me that."

"How kind of you," Sally murmured with stiff lips. She tried to pull her hands away, but he held them fast.

"Yes, I was firm with them. I wouldn't give way. I insisted. I said, 'She mustn't be hurt, or I won't consent. She must have chloroform and not know anything about it. You can do what you like about the others, but I won't have Sally hurt.'"

Of course he was mad. Only a madman would talk like this. But it was horrible, and horrible to be touched by him, horrible to feel the hot clasp of his hands. She leaned back as far back as she could, and said in an exhausted voice,

"Please let me go. I want my handkerchief."

Impossible to persist in a romantic pose in the face of so homely a necessity. He released her hands with a deepening of his air of offence.

She said rather faintly, "Will you get me—a little water?"

The question was, could she get through the two doors, the baize door and the oak door, and down the cellar steps? She thought she could—Ambrose had a terribly long reach— if he went to the sink he would have to turn his back—he would have to go to the sink to get the water she had asked for—he couldn't refuse. And all the time with a regular, persistent rhythm she could hear Jock kicking.

Ambrose went past her to the sink at the end of the room. The baize door was perhaps six feet from him, and at least eight from her. She would have to get out of her chair and turn the corner of the table before she dare make a rush for it, and until she got clear of the table he would be nearer the door than she. Like the nastiest sort of nightmare came the thought of being run down in that dark underground place which she had always feared.

And Ambrose was mad.

There was no time to think, or to plan, or to be afraid. The moment he was past her she got to her feet and moved behind him as he moved, only instead of going towards the sink she was skirting the table. She heard the tap turn and the water run. She was nearer the door than he was now, but at the next step, or the next after that, he must see her—he couldn't fail to see her. She took that step, and the next, and then ran for the door. She heard the glass smash against the sink, and then she heard nothing but the pounding of her own heart. The baize was rough under her hand as the door swung in to let her through—rough baize, hard oak, and the dark stone flight down which she half ran, half fell. She was on her hands and knees at the bottom, and then up again. A torch flashed after her, showing a confused litter of straw and paper rising almost roof high, the accumulation of years, and ahead of her the long, dark passage which led to Jocko. She could hear him much more plainly now—kick, kick, kick—kick, kick, kick.

She caught at her courage and ran towards the sound. From behind her came a shouting, and a scream, and the sound of a crash.

Sally ran on.

XXXVI

THE NIGHT AIR HAD AN EDGE ON IT LIKE ICE. JAMES WAS gratefully aware of this as he ran. He came to the corner of the house and round it, and there checked. His head was clear again. It behooved him to go warily. He must get into the house, but he must get in unheard. No going up to the front door and ringing the bell.

He went back to the wing which faced the stables, and there broke a window with his elbow and got in. He did not know what part of the house he had come to, but it must at any rate be some way from the hall. It was the hall that he had to make for. He wished ardently for a torch, but it was no good wishing. He must just go slowly and take care not to stumble over anything or make any noise.

The place he had entered was quite small. He found the door, and came into a narrow passage. It began by going towards the front of the house, but soon turned and took him in the direction he desired. He felt his way along it, going softly. He kept thinking, "Sally's all right. Why shouldn't Sally be all right? Why should anyone want to hurt her?" It did not occur to him till afterwards that he had quite forgotten about the Rolls.

He began to think that it was time he got somewhere, and for a moment he had the horrid nightmare feeling that he might be going round and round in a maze of passages, returning upon his own tracks, and never getting any nearer to Sally.

His groping fingers reached and touched a door. The nightmare went, and he came thankfully into what felt like a large room—large and very cold, with a most horrible unlived-in smell. He wondered when the windows had been opened last, and whether the smell was plain frowst, or frowst-cum-damp, or frowst-cum-damp-cum mice—, or, appropriately, bats.

His hand touched the edge of a table, and after following the said edge for about fifteen feet he concluded that it was the edge of the dining-table, and that he was therefore in the dining-room of Rere Place—or perhaps they called it a banquetting-hall; it was large enough. Anyhow it probably opened into the real hall, and once there, he thought he could find his way back to where he had left Sally and Jocko.

It took him a little time to find the door. He kept bumping into large, solemn chairs set back against the wall. But presently there was a door, and he came through into what he believed to be the hall from the sense of open space above him and the strong downward draught.

He was lucky here, because he walked straight into the right-hand newel-post of the stair. With his hand on the balustrade he went up, and when he came to the place where the stair divided he took the left-hand turn. As he remembered it, Lady Clementa's room was no distance from the stair head.

With a hand on the panelling which the hands of many generations had polished and worn smooth, he moved forward, and before he had taken a dozen steps the sound of voices broke the strained silence in which he was listening for some sound or sign of Sally.

But this wasn't Sally's voice or Jocko's. It was a voice which he had heard only once before, but he recognized it with perfect certainty as Hildegarde Sylvester's—a voice with a convention of sweetness, a convention of breeding and culture. Through the half open door of Lady Clementa's room he heard her say,

"They must all be dead before midnight."

It was a startling thing to hear, and James was certainly startled. He also found himself getting bitingly, coldly angry. He continued a slow, careful progress, and heard Hildegarde speak again.

"Hold the torch up—I can't see like that! We've got to be quick! Now where's that paper?"

James reached the doorway and looked cautiously round the jamb. There were two people at the far end of the room, Hildegarde Sylvester and Henri Niemeyer. An electric lamp stood on the heavy mahogany chest of drawers a couple of yards away, and its light was directed upon them and upon the single panel between the windows. In the hand of Henri Niemeyer was a pocket torch whose powerful beam picked out the carved device of the bat upon the panel.

Undoubtedly something very odd was happening. James wondered what the paper might be, and decided to stay where he was and observe the course of events.

"Read it out!" said Hildegarde Sylvester impatiently, and Henri read aloud:

"It is hidden in my room behind the
panel with one of our bats on it.

The spring is
It opens quite easily, so do not try
to force it. The middle board
between the windows moves when the
spring is pushed down, and the panel
will then open. The book is there,
with our family secret. We have
always kept it secret for the
sake of the name—''

He broke off and said smoothly,

''It is a pity that you had to forget the one piece that mattered.''

Hildegarde swung round upon him blazing.

''How many times am I to tell you that I did *not* forget? What I have heard, that I remember! It is infallible with me! I have told you so a thousand times! But I cannot remember what I do not hear, and I tell you when that stupid Jocko was talking all his secrets in his dream I heard everything he said except just this one bit. He spoke quite clearly, as if he was reading the old woman's letter out to me, but when he came to 'The spring is—' he stopped and said it again, 'The spring is—' just like that. And he moved his head as if he was going to wake and muttered something to himself, and then went on about the panel opening quite easily.''

''Oh, well, we can always force it,'' said Henri.

James had drawn back when Hildegarde turned. He could hear, but he could no longer see the windows. If they forced the panel and found whatever it was they were looking for, he thought he would have a try at getting it away from them. He would have to make a plan, and a good one. They were two to one. Henri at least would be armed, and James was prepared to bet on Hildegarde being able to give a good account of herself in a scrap. She might, he thought, favour a knife. On the other hand, he would have the advantage of a surprise. He thought he would let them open the panel, and launch his attack when they were getting away with the swag. He rather fancied the idea of a charge from behind. He thought he would probably run a very good chance with a surprise rush on the stair.

He stood on one leg at a time and took off his shoes. On the feet they would merely give his movements away, but in the hand they would prove quite useful missiles. He heard Henri say with half a laugh, "I borrowed this. It ought to do the trick. Stand back and take the torch." And then he heard the sound of wood splintering. "This" was probably a jemmy, and the panel was being forced. They would both be looking that way and have no eyes for anything else.

He took a step or two on his stocking feet and looked into the room. Henri had both hands on the panel, wrenching at it, whilst Hildegarde held the torch with a steady hand. The wood cracked and gave. A gap appeared all down one side of it. The gap widened, showing a black space beyond. Henri let go and stood back panting and rubbing his hands, but Hildegarde Sylvester ran forward and thrust in the torch.

"Ah—it is there! Henri, it is there! Oh, *mon ami*—what a relief—what a relief! You do not know what bad dreams I have had ever since it was lost! Embrace me!"

James drew back just in time. If Hildegarde was about to fling herself upon Henri's neck, she would inevitably be in a position to observe the half open door. She might be too much overcome with emotion to notice him, or she might not. He had no desire to take the risk. He thought he heard a kiss, and then he certainly did hear Henri say in a voice of gentle sarcasm,

"There are more comfortable places than this, I think. Perhaps the old lady's ghost walks—it is cold enough. Let us go down and make sure that our good Ambrose is not allowing his feelings to run away with him in the pantry. I do not like to trust him too long with Sally. I do not trust him too far in any case."

Hildegarde's voice had a muffled sound as she said,

"There is something else in here—something done up in paper—heavy."

"Bring it then—but come!"

James sympathised with Henri's impatience, because he was sharing it. He wanted to get a move on and find Sally. He heard Hildegarde say, "What can it be? The letter spoke about a secret." And then he didn't wait to hear any more. There was a door on the other side of the passage a little nearer the stair. He slipped across and into the dark room beyond. The footsteps and voices in Lady Clementa's room came nearer. He stood well back with the door ajar and heard them go past.

This was a matter for very careful timing. The stair came from the hall to a half-landing, where it divided and so ran up to a corridor on either side. He decided to make his rush the moment they got past the stair head, because the farther there was for them to fall the better, and if there was going to be any sort of mix-up on the landing, there might be a chance of heaving Henri over the balustrade, or at any rate chucking him down the rest of the stair.

With his shoes in his left hand, he padded noiselessly along the passage, Hildegarde and the torch about four yards in front of him, Henri a shadow at her side. They were talking, arguing, perhaps quarrelling. At the stair head they checked for a moment, and he heard Hildegarde say in a low, angry voice,

"You can weep afterwards! For me, I tell you I shall laugh to see Sally die."

James felt the raging fury which comes upon sane men once or twice in a lifetime. It gave him the strength of the man who is not sane. He came leaping out of the dark with an extraordinary velocity, and before either of them knew what was happening they were off their balance. James's right hand, open and flat, caught Hildegarde between the shoulders and sent her flying. Henri got the shoes in his face as he turned at the sound of the padding feet. He cried out in pain. The shoes went after Hildegarde, and he was taken by the shoulders, spun round, and kicked over the edge of the stair. There was a confusion of sound from below. The torch had gone out.

James ran down the dark stair and barged in to Henri, who was getting painfully to his feet on the half-landing. He had a hand at his hip pocket, but no time to draw before James hove him clear over the balustrade into the hall below.

In the dark behind him Hildegarde screamed, and James remembered that she had the book. Now that he had dealt with Henri, he could remember that. He made towards the scream, and a shot fired from not more than a yard away went by his temple. So it was a pistol after all and not a knife. He lunged out and caught a wrist. Twisting it, he had the satisfaction of hearing the weapon drop.

With her free hand Hildegarde clawed at him like a furious cat till he got hold of her other wrist, when she went suddenly limp and he had to hold her up. He spoke as one speaks to a deaf person, loudly and slowly, "Where is Sally? What have you done with her?" and got no answer. He was wasting time. Sally was in the pantry. He had heard them say so.

He felt about with his foot and found the pistol, got both Hildegarde's wrists into the grip of his right hand, picked it up, and put it in his pocket. He did not think she could do much harm without it, which goes to show that you never can tell. She gave a sudden wrench as he was putting the pistol away, and nearly got free.

By the time he had got her under control they were hard up against the bottom step of the stair down which he had pushed her, and there, where it had fallen, his foot encountered the missing book. As he stooped for it, his fingers touched something else, a small package done up in paper—the other thing which Hildegarde had taken out of the secret place. He pushed it down on top of the pistol, picked up the book, crammed it into a trouser pocket, and considered what he should do with Hildegarde. He knew what he would have liked to do with her, but civilization tells.

He could hear Henri groaning and cursing below. He really had no time to bother with Hildegarde. He pushed her down hard upon the bottom step, let go, and ran down the rest of the stair. He wanted to get to Sally. He ran past the cursing Henri and through the baize door into the corridor beyond it.

Sally was in the pantry, and he wanted to get to Sally. He felt quite capable of getting to her wherever she was. He felt that he could have gone through a stone wall. He raced into the pantry, and found it empty with the door at the far side standing wide. He did not hear the footsteps which raced behind him or Hildegarde's angry sobbing breath. He caught the lighted candle from the mantelshelf and went through the door, to see the old cellar door hanging open too, and, in the narrow space, Ambrose Sylvester looking down the dark, uneven steps and muttering to himself. James flung him aside, held him a moment, and said in a murderous voice, "Where's Sally? What have you done with Sally?" and getting no answer, let go of him and ran on down the steps and into the cellar.

He had the candle still, and at the foot of the steps held it up and looked about him. He saw the rubbish piled high—old tins, old papers, old boxes, and a mass of mouldy straw. A reek of petrol came up from it. He saw the long, dark passage down which Sally had run only a moment ago. He actually saw the movement of her dress as she ran. And he too ran, the candle flickering and guttering in his hand.

And then someone screamed behind him, and he looked back and saw Hildegarde Sylvester standing there at the top of the steps, a shrieking fury, with the Beatrice stove held high between her hands. Even as James looked, she flung it crashing into the pile of rubbish, and screamed again, and stood there screaming to watch the fire break out and go up in a roaring sheet of flame.

XXXVII

JAMES DID NOT WAIT TO SEE WHAT WOULD HAPPEN NEXT. He took to his heels and ran as fast as he had ever run in his life. Sally was in front of him, running away from him. No, not from him, because she didn't know he was there, but just running away, wild with fright, down a horrible dark passage which might end in a flight of steps, or a well, or any one of half a dozen other dangers. The fire roared and flared behind him and threw his own shadow in fantastic length upon the black, uneven flags, but it didn't show him

Sally. He called her name, and his voice came back echoing from the roof and walls.

His shadow appeared before him, suddenly upright. He had very nearly run full tilt into a wall. It stood across his way, and the passage went off to the right. He swerved just in time, lost the fiery glow, and was glad that he still held on to the candle. It had gone out, but it did not take him a moment to light it again. The passage stretched before him with doors opening upon it. He called again, "Sally—Sally—Sally!" and a horrid pack of echoes took the name, and mouthed it, and sent it back to him distorted and torn.

He went on, not running now because of the candle—a very good thing for him, because suddenly the flags ended and the steps went steeply down into a blacker dark. He stood still above it, and for the space of nearly half a minute his heart stood still too. Sally so afraid of the dark, Sally who hated cellars, Sally running wild—how easy for Sally to pitch headlong down these steps in the dark and be lost to him without so much as a cry. He made a strong effort, thrust out the thought, and called again. And again there was no answer except from those detestable echoes.

There was no time to be lost, because if the fire took hold, the house would probably fall in upon the cellars and bury them. He thought of this quite dispassionately, his mind being too much taken up with Sally to give it more than a very surface attention. He decided to go down the steps. They were very steep indeed, and some of them seemed to be broken away. About half way down he stopped, unable to believe that Sally had come this way. He remembered her saying that there were cellars under the cellars at Rere Place, and the bare thought of them had set her shuddering in broad daylight. From where he stood the candle-light showed him the bottom of the steps. If Sally had fallen, she would be there and he would see her. But there was no one—most blessedly there was no one there.

He drew a long breath, turned round, and came up again, and as he came up, the air of the passage met him, full of smoke and the smell of burning. He had a momentary sensation of horror—the old fear of the trap, the common fear which man must share with the creatures of the wild.

The fear of the trap and the fear of fire are the two oldest fears of all. They came on James for a horrid moment, and then he beat them off. Panic meant death, and it meant death to Sally too. He beat it off.

He called her again, and this time amongst the echoes there was another sound, the sound of a key grating hard as it turned in a rusty lock.

And upon that, Jock West's voice saying, "Who is it?"

James ran towards the voice. He called out "James" as he ran, and kept the light up so that Jock might see him. But it was Sally who came running out of the third door on the left and flung her arms round him, and it was Sally whom he kissed. She put her face up to him and he couldn't help kissing it, but next moment he was talking over her shoulder to Jock.

"I think the place is on fire. Hildegarde pitched your stove in amongst the rubbish at the foot of the cellar steps, and the whole thing went with a bang."

Jocko snuffed the smoky air.

Smells like it. But I shouldn't have thought it would take hold—everything's so damp. If it's only that rubbish heap, it'll burn itself out."

Sally swung round in the circle of James's arm.

"They were meaning to burn the house. I'm sure they were. I'm sure that pile of stuff wasn't just accidental. I'm sure I smelt petrol. I wasn't *quite* sure because of the chloroform, but—yes, I smelt it when Jock went down."

"Yes, I smelt it," said James.

"And if they left those two doors open, it would draw like a chimney and the wood in the passage would catch. There are shelves, and a cupboard or two—old ramshackly things— and a wooden stair going up to the servants' quarters. It would burn all right."

"Well, we've got to get out," said James. "What's our best way?"

There was a pause. The smoke made Sally cough. It was blowing towards them steadily on a warm draught.

"There is only the one way out," said Jock in an odd, casual voice.

"Well, what is it?"

"The way we came," said Sally.

Nobody said anything for about half a minute. If the fire held, the way they had come would be its chimney—a chimney full of smoke and upward rushing flame. There was no way out there. But to stay where they were till the roof fell in—

James said, "Are you sure?"

"I've never heard of any other way," said Jock. "I don't believe the place will burn—it's too damp."

James thought this would depend on how much petrol had been used—he thought a goodish bit. He thought Henri Niemeyer had his head screwed on pretty tight. If he wanted Rere Place to burn, he would take good care not to make a boss shot at it. It wasn't any good saying these things, so he didn't say them.

"I expect they were going to have one more shot at finding whatever it was Aunt Clementa hid, and then if they didn't find it, burn the place about our ears."

"They found it all right," said James.

"Where?"

"In Lady Clementa's bedroom, behind the panel with the bat on it. You were quite right about the letter—you read it aloud in your sleep, and Hildegarde had it pat. The line that ended in 'bats' was, 'the panel with one of our bats on it.' And there was something about a family secret and not giving it away. The only part she hadn't got was the bit about the spring. So Henri forced it with a jemmy. I chucked him over the stairs and came down here after you, and Hildegarde lost her temper and pitched the stove after me. Sally, why on earth did you go into the cellars? You said you hated them."

Sally rubbed her cheek against his shoulder.

"Jocko went down, and I thought I heard you in the passage and I ran back. But it was Henri." She shuddered violently. "I think I began to faint, and he put a thing soaked with chloroform over my face. I can smell it still. And when I came round I was on the pantry floor and Ambrose telling me the story of his life. James, he's mad—he really is—quite, quite mad. He said they were going to kill us in a car accident, but he'd see I had some chloroform first, because he didn't want me to be hurt. And all the time I could hear Jocko kicking at the door of the cellar where Hildegarde had locked him in, so as soon as I got a chance I asked for some water, and whilst his back was turned I made a dash for it and unbolted Jocko's door. I was telling him what had happened when we heard you calling. At first we thought it was Ambrose, so we didn't answer. We just locked ourselves in and waited for him to go away. And then it wasn't Ambrose, it was you. James, what are we going to do?"

The smell of fire was all about them now. The candlelight showed how the smoke drove, and eddied, and swirled towards them from the corner where the passage turned. A terrible roaring sound came with it. James reckoned that the rubbish must have burned itself out by now or nearly so, unless there was wood in it. Paper and straw burn fiercely and give off a great heat, but they burn quickly and die back upon their own light ash. He let go of Sally, put the candle into Jock's hand, and ran towards the corner holding his breath and half closing his eyes against the heat. At the turn it met him full. The roar was prodigious. There was a fierce crackling and an orange glow.

He ran back, his chest labouring and his eyes streaming.

"It's got hold all right. All that old panelling will burn like tinder. Look here—what's down those steps?"

"More cellars," said Jock briefly.

"Then we'd better go down there. You say there's no other way out. How do you know there isn't?"

"I've never heard of one."

"Well, you go first and take the candle. I'll bring Sally. Have you ever been down here before?"

"Once. Sally dared me. I didn't like it very much."

They went down the damp, uneven steps, and as they went, James said,

"We'll be away from the worst of the heat. I think we can probably stick it out here."

XXXVIII

THE LAST FEW STEPS WERE BADLY BROKEN. JAMES REflected that it was as well that they had the candle. If you were to take a toss here and break your leg, well, here you might lie, with Rere Place a heap of ruins over your head and the world going merrily on without you. Oddly enough, it came to him quite sharp and clear that it was his father who would take the knock if something of the sort really happened. His mother would weep her placid tears, and dry them again, and talk about poor darling James, but it was his father who would go on missing him. It took him just the moment he was lifting Sally down the last two steps to be quite sure of this.

They looked about them by the candle-light. Walls, floor, and roof were all of stone, very solid, very old, the roof vaulted and the stone roughly grooved to simulate pillars on either side of a low arch. Beyond the arch a passage ran away into the dark.

James stood frowning at Jock West.

"What is this place? Why did they have two lots of cellars? These look much older than the others."

Jock said, "Yes," and, "I don't know much about it. They've been disused for donkey's years. I believe they belonged to a much older house. There's a bit of it built into Rere Place—that stone part where Giles's room is, and Eleanor Rere's."

"Why are they so deep down?"

Jock said, "I don't know."

And with that came a shock. It stopped the words upon

his tongue. There was a noise and a shaking, the noise not loud but with a horrible effect of impact, and the shaking one which seemed to come from everywhere at once. James thought something had fallen in. "Not the roof—there's not been time. The pantry floor, and the stair above it, and perhaps the kitchen too. No, not yet—that'll be for later. We must get out first if we're ever going to." He said out loud.

"We'd better try the passage. It's no good staying here."

The air blew down the cellar steps behind them. It blew harder than before, it blew hotter, and it reeked of smoke. Whatever the passage held for them, they must chance it, for with one floor gone there was no hope that the fire would burn itself out.

Jock went first. He had to bend his head to pass the arch. No one said anything. They all watched the candle, and it burned bright. There was at least breathable air and enough room to walk two abreast, though the men had to keep their heads down. Floor and walls were dark and clammy with moisture, but the air was dead and dry.

Sally felt as if she were in a dream—the sort you can only just bear because you know you must be going to wake up soon. Her head was still muzzy with the chloroform. It couldn't really be true that they were deep in a deserted cellar with Rere Place blazing to ruin overhead. The dream sense was heavy upon her, and she was glad not to be alone in a dream like this. She was glad to be with James, and to feel his arm about her shoulders. It didn't much matter what happened in a dream.

They had gone about eight or nine yards, when Jock stopped.

"There's a door," he said, and held the candle for them to look.

It was a very old door, very old and very strong. It had been made to be very strong. There were three great bolts, one at the top, and one at the bottom, and one in the middle.

James began to wonder why. He was very far from being in a dream like Sally. He was conscious of a tension, a speeding up of thought and observation. He was noticing things which he had never noticed before. If what he could see by the light of their one candle was limited, at least each smallest detail of what he saw was imprinted on his mind. The strength of the door, the strength of the bolts—these things impressed themselves deeply. The bolts though rusty could be moved. They must have been moved within some recent time. There were signs of their having been oiled.

The last of them creaked clear, and the door opened. Yes, it was very strong—very thick, and old, and strong. It let them into a small octagonal chamber with a vaulted roof. It was perhaps ten feet across, and in the middle of it, flush with the floor, was the open, black mouth of a well.

Sally's mouth formed itself into an O. If she hadn't been in a dream, she might have screamed. If one had come in here walking alone, walking barefoot, walking in the night without a candle, how suddenly that black mouth would have swallowed one up. She shuddered and pressed against James.

"I thought it was a prison," said Jock—"all those bolts—and then nothing but a well. It seems a crazy sort of thing to me, but we ought to be safe enough here. The door will keep the smoke out." He spoke in his usual careless tone.

James thought, "He knows as well as I do that we haven't a dog's chance of getting out if the house falls in." He said aloud,

"Where's the nearest fire-station?"

Jock laughed.

"Warnley! One-man show. Keen parson and half-hearted farmers' lads. They won't make much impression on Rere Place, I'm afraid. There's no water nearer than the Warne, and I don't suppose there's much in it. It went dry last year. How about it, Sally?"

"A trickle," said Sally in an odd detached voice. "James, I don't like that well. Why did they have it there, right in the middle of the floor?"

"I don't know," said James.

He wasn't really thinking what he said. His mind was registering the well, occupying itself with its own picture of the well. It had two pictures to be busy with now, the picture of the door and the picture of the well. He became completely engrossed with these two pictures. Sally and

Jock were talking, but the sense of what they said went by.

And then Jock was shouting at him.

"Oi—you, James! Wake up, can't you! If we've got to do time down here, we might just as well be chatty. Let's have all about it. You said they found what they were looking for. You did say so, didn't you—Hildegarde and Henri?"

"Oh, yes, they found it. Here it is."

He let go of Sally to get the book out of his trouser pocket. It was a thick cheap account-book with a shabby cover which had once been shiny black. Jock West took it, set his candle on the floor, sat down beside it, and began to turn the leaves with an expression of lively curiosity upon his face. After a minute or two he looked up.

"Read any of this?"

James shook his head.

"No time."

"You should have made time. It's a liberal education. Hildegarde's a sweet creature. It's all in her writing. I should say she had a really first-class blackmailing connection, all among the nice rich, virtuous middle class who would die—or pay—before they would allow their peccadilloes to come before the public eye. There's a fair sprinkling of nobs, but the backbone of the business seems to be the great middle class. I always said Hildegarde had her head screwed on pretty tight. . . . So that's how Ambrose raised the wind—he took the cash and let the credit go. Well, well!"

"Jocko—don't!" said Sally.

The dream had broken round her, and she was awake. She put out her hand, moving round the well towards Jock, who appeared to be immense entertained.

"I say—here's something about Lydia! How amusing!"

"Jocko!"

"All right, see for yourself. But you must let me have it back."

He put the book into her hand, and with one movement, and before anyone could stop her, Sally had dropped it into the well. There was Jock's laugh, and the darting movement of her hand, and then nothing for so long that it seemed as if the silence had gone on time out of mind. And then at the end of it an odd, faint sound. With that sound the stagnant water at the bottom of the well had received all those secret sins, and follies, and mistakes. The people who had sinned and been foolish had sinned and been foolish to their own hurt, and they must make their own account, but the record of what they had done lay drowning in the well. Even now the water was blotting it out, name by name, and word by shameful word. Soon there would be no words, no names at all, only a little sodden paper. And after a while not even that.

Sally thought her own thoughts whilst Jock grabbed at her wrist—too late, and demanded in a furious voice what she thought she was doing. Perhaps that withdrawn look of hers disarmed him. Perhaps it came over him that their time might be too short to quarrel in, for he burst into sudden laughter and let her go.

"Quick work, Sally! I suppose you're out to save Ambrose. I can't think why. He's always bored me stiff, but you had a fancy for him, didn't you?"

"I loved him—long ago," said Sally in an exhausted voice.

James felt in his pocket and produced the other thing which Hildegarde had taken from behind the panel. He didn't want Sally to think about Ambrose. He wanted her to wake up, to come back, to be the Sally who would be all there if it came to the pinch. He thought the mysterious packet would at least distract her mind from Ambrose Sylvester.

She had drawn back and was leaning against the wall, as far from the well as possible, in a half sitting, half kneeling position. James put the parcel in her lap and sat down beside her. From her other side Jock West leaned forward.

Sally picked up what looked like a roll of brown paper clumsily fastened with string. The string had some old sealing-wax clinging to the knots, but it was so loose that it was quite easy to slip it off. There was tissue paper inside, very much creased and lumped together round something which weighed heavy and loose in her hand.

Jock gave a sudden curious laugh.

"It was in the letter—Aunt Clementa's letter! She put

Hildegarde's book behind the panel with one of our bats, in the place with the family secret. And what's the betting this is the family secret? Off with the paper, Sally, and let's see if it's what I think it is!'' He held up the candle.

Sally pulled away the paper, and there came out, long and flexible, link falling from link, a necklace. The links were dusty, but the diamonds dazzled in the candle-light. There was a row of them, one to each link, very large and shining, and then a tracery of smaller stones set in festoons, and from the three middle festoons three swinging tassels with a very great diamond at the head of each.

''It's the Queen's necklace!'' said Sally in a frightened voice.

Jock laughed.

''So Giles pinched it. I always thought so—the dirty dog! What are you going to do about it Sally—throw it down the well?''

She looked at him with a sort of shocked reproach.

''Of course not! It isn't ours. It belongs to the King.''

Jock burst out laughing.

''Oh, Sally—you treasure! Henrietta Maria started it off to the King getting on for three hundred years ago, and you propose to deliver it just as if nothing had happened in between. Is that the great idea?''

Sally said, ''Of course.'' She looked at the big diamonds, and thought about Giles Rere who had betrayed his trust, and about Ambrose Sylvester who had betrayed his. She felt James's hand on her shoulder, and knew that he would never betray anyone. They would have their quarrels, and they would have their troubles, but it wasn't in James to betray. The knowledge was warm at her heart, and the necklace cold in her hand. She was glad when James took it away from her and wrapped it up again.

''It's as safe in my pocket as anywhere,'' he said, and put it back there.

XXXIX

SOME TIME LATER.

"We ought to be sitting in the dark, you know," said James. "That candle won't last for ever, and we may want it badly."

Jock laughed cheerfully.

"Lots of candles," he said, patting a pocket. "About half a pound of 'em, I should think. I don't come down into cellars without the wherewithal to see 'em by."

"How are we going to get out?" said Sally suddenly.

She hadn't thought about it at all until this moment, because first she had been feeling all queer and detached, and then she had had her mind quite taken up with other things—with Giles Rere, and Ambrose, and the Queen's necklace. But now, all at once, she really did wonder how they were going to get out, because she wanted passionately to get out, and go right away from Rere Place and never see it again. So she asked her question.

"We'll have to wait for the fire to burn itself out," said Jock on one side of her.

And then James on the other:

"Unless there's another way out. Is there another way, Sally?"

Sally said "No" in a hesitating voice.

James's hand pressed her shoulder.

"Think—think hard, Sally."

She turned her troubled eyes upon him.

"I don't know any."

He shook her a little.

"Think! How did the coals come in? We had a house with cellars once, and there was a shoot for the coal, and steps that went up to a door at the side of the house. Isn't there anything like that?"

Sally shook her head.

"Not any steps, and Aunt Clementa was always grumbling about the coal. There's a shoot outside in the back court, but it takes two men to move the flagstone, so that's no use."

James got up.

"I think I'll go and prospect. If you're full of candles, J.J., you can give me one. . . . No, I don't want you to come—I want you to look after Sally. I shan't be long."

When he was gone, Sally said, "How bad is it, Jocko?" And Jocko said, "A question of how much will go when the roof falls in, I fancy." After which Sally said, "I see—" and they both sat listening and watching the dark passage.

Sound was deadened so far below the surface, but they could hear the dull roar of the fire. It was like the roar of traffic a long way off, the roar of breakers on a rocky coast heard through a fog. No, it was like the roar of fire and nothing else. It was Rere Place going up in a pillar of flame into the night, a blazing beacon over their heads—perhaps a blazing pyre. She thought the roar was louder than it had been when James opened the door, and she thought, "Suppose he doesn't come back. Oh, why did I let him go?"

But James came back running, with his candle out. He came back running, and shut the door behind him with a heavy thud.

"I couldn't get up the steps. The whole place is red-hot. We'll have to stick it out here," he said.

And each one of the three had the same thought—"How long will the air last?"

James came back to his place by Sally and put his arm round her. The well gaped at him. The door was shut. How long could they stick it out? How long would they have to stick it out? And even as the thought formed in his mind, the second shock came. Its violence was beyond expression, and the noise prodigious. Sally's faint cry was lost in it. Everything rocked, and rocked again, and overhead the vaulting bulged and cracked.

"It's coming down," said James in an odd, light voice—"the whole damned house. That's about the size of it."

James pulled Sally to her feet.

"The bolts on the door!" he cried. "They were there to keep the back way in—they must have been! They don't make sense any other way. The air's quite fresh in here, and it's coming up from the well. The well is the back way in, and it's our way out. Hold up, Sally, while I have a look!"

Sally shut her eyes, because she heard the stone crack again above her, and she thought that was the end. Then James was speaking, his words hurrying and stumbling.

"There's a ring—*there*! Look J.J.! And steps—notches—good enough for foothold anyhow. Rings, and notches! There's our way, and we'd better get going!"

Sally stood against the wall, and thought she felt it move. She said,

"I can't go down the well. It's no use—I just can't."

And then she opened her eyes and saw only Jocko, there on the brink of the well—only Jocko, not James—whilst her heart nearly stopped with fear. She heard his voice coming up with a strange echoing sound.

"It's all right, J.J. There's a cross passage about ten feet down—quite dry. You'll have to let the candle down to me."

Jocko said, "All right—I've got some string."

The rock above them cracked again, but Sally watched him set two lighted candle ends on the edge of the well some way apart and then quickly and deftly make a noose for the candle and candlestick and lower them down and out of sight.

James's voice came back in a moment.

"Good work! Now for Sally!"

Sally turned faint. Her heart knocked against her side, and the blood drummed in her ears. She heard voices, but they were just a noise without words or sense. And then Jocko had her by the arm. He shook her a little, and his grip hurt. He said with harsh authority,

"You're not to faint! Do you hear? Stop it at once! I'm ashamed of you!"

Sally gazed at him blankly. She couldn't see the well, only his face—in a mist—coming and going. He shook her roughly.

"Pull yourself together! Oh, yes, you can! Now listen! I'm going to hold you and let you down to James. There's plenty of foothold. He'll guide your feet. It's perfectly easy—you've only got to do what you're told." He put his lips against her ear and said in a hard whisper, "If you faint, you'll fall, and if you fall you'll kill James, and if you stay here you'll be crushed to death, because the roof's going to fall in. *Now* will you behave?"

Sally said "Yes" on a faint, piteous sob. She would much rather have been crushed to death than go down the well, but she couldn't kill James. She bit deep into the corner of her lip as Jock took her by the arms and made her kneel on the brink.

James's voice came up to her.

"It's all right—you can't possibly fall."

And then Jock was swinging her over.

"Feel with your foot—a little more to the left—no, lower down. That's it. Now catch that ring on your right. I'm going to shift you sideways so that you can reach it. It's all right—I won't let go."

Above them the roof cracked again, ominously, heavily, and from somewhere far away there came a low, distant rumbling sound. The air was very hot.

Sally got hold of the ring. The rust on it made it rough and easy to hold.

Jock said, "Take your weight for a moment—I've got to lie down." He let go.

It was the most dreadful moment in Sally's whole life, but it was only a moment. Then he had her left wrist. He was lying face downwards now, leaning over the well.

"Now, Sally—one more step down and James will be able to help you. I won't let go again. Put down your other foot and feel for the next hold."

Sally thought, "I *can't*—I *must*—"

She reached down with her foot. Jock's arm was now at full stretch as he leaned over the well. Her right hand gripped the ring a yard below the brink. Her left foot clung to a small, slippery ledge. With her right foot she sought vainly for the next step. A hand closed round her ankle— James's hand. Her foot was guided to its hold. James spoke.

"It's all right—I won't let you fall. Jock's got to let go of you now. All you've got to do is to hold on with your right hand and bring your left down to the next ring."

Jock let go of her. Her arm felt numb from the upward strain. Her mind felt numb. Her hand went groping down the wall until it found and clutched the second ring. James said,

"Only one more step. Bring your left foot down and I'll guide it."

The numbness was increasing. And then, blessed relief, there was an arm about her waist.

"Bring your right foot down now. There's quite a wide ledge. *There!* Now shuffle along a bit."

Her feet were planted side by side, and she had let go of the ring. She was at the mouth of a dark passage which broke the side of the well, and James was pulling her in. The candle burned on the floor a yard away. Sally sat down beside it, and heard James call.

"All clear J.J. Hurry up!"

Sally crouched down and shut her eyes. The passage rocked—everything rocked. There was a grinding noise, and she was jerked to her feet and raced along, she didn't know where, and hardly knew how. Her feet slipped and stumbled, but James's arm kept her up. She thought, "Jocko must be safe because he's got the candle." And then she thought, "That's nonsense." And then thought went out in noise as roof and walls crashed in behind them.

XL

SALLY HEARD VOICES. ONE OF THEM SAID,

"She's all right. I expect it's partly the chloroform."

She thought, "That's years and years ago. I wonder if

I'm dead." She didn't mind whether she was or not. She said this out loud.

"I don't mind about it at all—I only just want to know."

James put his cheek against hers and said, "Sally!"

She said in a vexed voice, "I do think someone might tell me."

"What, darling?"

"Whether we're dead," said Sally. And the minute she had said it she began to laugh, because it sounded so silly.

She opened her eyes, and saw James's face, and candle-light, and a dark roof, and a heap of straw. She was lying on the heap of straw. At least she was partly lying on it, but James had his arms round her and her head was on his shoulder. She thought he had been kissing her.

"Oh, we're very much alive," he said.

She held on to him and pulled herself up.

"Where are we? I thought everything crashed."

"The passage caved in—behind us. We're in the stables. Did you know that there was an old well in one of them?"

Sally nodded.

"Yes—I did. Aunt Clementa said it was as old as the oldest part of the house."

"Well, she was quite right. That was the back way into Rere Place—down the stable well to the cross passage, and then up the other well to the place that we were in. That's why there were all those bolts on the door—they didn't want people sneaking in unbeknownst."

Sally put her head down again.

"How did we get here?"

"We brought you up the stable well. J.J. went up first and got a rope. I expect it was a good thing you didn't know anything about it. The top rings were gone this side."

Sally shuddered.

"*Don't,* darling!"

"Sorry," said James. "You know, I couldn't make out why they had those two lots of cellars one under the other. I mean I couldn't see the point of the lower one, but of course they had to have it to get their connection between the wells—the stables are so much lower than the house. I remember your bringing me down a lot of steps the day we met in the fog, and the car had to come down quite a slope when I put it away just before they laid me out. So of course they had to keep that bottom cellar."

Sally sat up. She wasn't feeling any interest in secret passages, or cellars, or wells. James was here, but where was Jocko? She said this aloud very insistently,

"Where's Jocko?"

"Gone to have a look at the house. There won't be much left of it. The crash that nearly got us was the old part falling in. Jock went and had a look as soon as we got you up. He says he wouldn't have believed that anything could burn so fast."

"Old houses do," said Sally. "There was a lot of old wood in it."

She had a sudden picture of Rere Place burning, burning, burning, and Ambrose burning with it—Ambrose, and Hildegarde, and Henri. But it was the thought of Ambrose that knocked at her heart, and because of that she couldn't get his name across her lips. She drew away from James. The thing was dreadfully, pressingly on her mind. She said what came to her to say.

"Where are they? They're not in the house. Oh, James, they're not in the house! Henri was hurt! You hurt him!"

James did feel justly annoyed. All Sally's solicitude seemed to be for the people who had done their best to murder her. This concern for Henri seemed particularly uncalled for.

"And there was nothing to prevent any of them from walking out of the front door. I can't see what you're worrying about. Henri was cursing very heartily when I went past him in the hall, and if he couldn't walk without help, there were two of them to help him. Anyhow there's no sign of their car, so I suppose they've made off. Hullo— that sounds like J.J. in a hurry."

Jock West it was, and he was out of breath with running.

"Hullo, Sally—all right?"

Sally scrambled up.

"Oh, yes. What is it? What's happened?"

"Fire Brigade just arriving. There isn't much left for

them to save. The question is, do we stay and chat with them, or do we do a bunk?''

"If we do a bunk," said James, "and anyone sees us, you'll be suspected of burning the house to get the insurance money.''

Jock laughed.

"Thank you, James, it's not insured. But perhaps we'd better stay—only we must all tell the same story, and it's got to be water-tight.''

"The truth is the only really water-tight story.''

"Good boy! Go to the top of the class! But how much truth do we tell? Are we going to prosecute our dear guardian and his wife, and her boy friend?''

"Oh, no!" said Sally. "Oh, no, no, *no!*''

"Quite immoral, but I agree. Very well then, we leave them out. We tell the truth, but we don't tell too much of it. We came down to have a look at Rere Place—a nice piece about that, with a special mention of Beatrice. Then, to account for the fire, precipitous cellar stair with pile of rubbish below—Beatrice unfortunately capsized. If anyone wants to know why she was down there at all, I shall produce the simple fact that cellars are cold. I don't think anyone will really bother very much. Come along and meet the parson. He's a very good fellow, but fires are meat and drink to him, and as long as he's got a good one he won't care a hoot who started it.''

Half an hour later when Rere Place no longer blazed but merely smoked, a shapeless, blackened ruin, James took the Rolls down the drive and between the tall gate-posts into the road. He had Sally and Jock to direct him, so he took the right turning this time. Easy enough to take the wrong one at night.

They passed through Staling and found it asleep, and ran on by way of a steepish hill to the blind corner where the road forks for Letherington, and there, just on the bend, was a ditched lorry and the remains of a car. Another car was standing by, and a group of people—an A.A. scout, a policeman, and others.

James drew up.

"Looks like a bad smash. I'll just see if they want any help," he said.

He and Jock got out.

But Sally was looking at the car. She looked once, and then she looked away. When James came back she said,

"He's dead, isn't he?"

James said, "Yes. They're all dead." And then, "How did you know?"

"The car," said Sally in an odd, stiff voice—"Hildegarde's new car."

"She was driving. She ran full tilt into the lorry. It's what they planned for us, you know."

"He was mad," said Sally. "Ambrose was mad. Oh, James, he *was*!"

James got into the car and put his arms round her.

"Sally, do you mind so much—about him?"

"I think I'm glad," said Sally.

XLI

SALLY LOOKED AT HERSELF IN THE GLASS, BECAUSE SHE wanted to see what Sally Elliot looked like. She thought she looked rather nice, veil thrown back, eyes soft and happy, mouth red and smiling. And a little bunch of orange-blossom on either side amongst the dark curls. She was *very* glad that she had dug in her toes and refused to have a halo.

She turned round with a sigh, but it was a deep breath of contentment. She was married to James. They had been married for just three-quarters of an hour. Bonzo and Daphne had lent their house, and Jocko had given her away. She had cut the cake and been kissed by all her friends. James had not kissed her—yet, but he had looked at her as she came up the aisle. "Oh, James, don't ever stop loving me that way!" Deep in her own heart Sally knew that he never would. When you know a thing like that, it makes you feel quite, quite happy. Sally was quite, quite happy.

Daphne and three bridesmaids helped her out of her wedding-dress, all talking at once. Two of them were Daphne's sisters, and the third was Elspeth Reid. Sally hadn't the slightest idea what they were talking about. They all said "Darling" a great many times, and told her she was marvellous. The wedding was marvellous. The weather was marvellous—and April could be too icy. James was marvellous. Everything was marvellous.

Sally was going away in green, to match her eyes. Violet and Lilian said she looked marvellous and slipped out of the room.

"I've forbidden rice, but I'm sure they'll get hold of some," said Daphne in a distracted voice. "Elspeth, catch them! Tell them I definitely forbid it! But it won't be the slightest use—they're as wild as hawks."

"Darling, I *must* have some too," said Elspeth in her drawling voice. "Don't say I didn't warn you, Sally." She went out, leaving the door open.

"Oh, Sally!" said Daphne. "I do hope you're going to be very happy. I always thought I should hate anyone who married James, because he used to be in love with me, you know. You don't mind, do you?"

Sally kissed her.

"I don't mind in the least. We'll both love you."

"Yes," said Daphne. "Of course it's not quite the same thing. But if he'd got to marry anyone, I'd rather it was you—I would really. Darling, you were marvellous!" Then, as James looked round the open door, "James, *doesn't* she look marvellous?"

James didn't say anything. He looked at Sally, and Sally looked at him. Then she laughed and said,

"Those horrible cousins of yours are loading up with rice. We shall get it down our necks and in our shoes, and it will fall out of our pockets and give us away for weeks and weeks. We must be as quick as lightning. Is everything ready?"

James nodded. He kissed Daphne.

"Thank you for our wedding, Daph. Thank Bonzo, will you?"

Sally kissed her too.

"I've loved every minute of it."

Then she took James by the arm.

"Run!" she said.

THE END